Richard Temple, Elizabeth Rosetta Glover

Life of Sir John Hawley Glover

Richard Temple, Elizabeth Rosetta Glover

Life of Sir John Hawley Glover

ISBN/EAN: 9783337332792

Printed in Europe, USA, Canada, Australia, Japan

Cover: Foto ©Andreas Hilbeck / pixelio.de

More available books at **www.hansebooks.com**

SIR JOHN HAWLEY GLOVER

SIR JOHN HAWLEY GLOVER

LIFE

OF

SIR JOHN HAWLEY GLOVER

R.N., G.C.M.G.

BY LADY GLOVER

EDITED BY THE

RIGHT HON. SIR RICHARD TEMPLE, BART.

G.C.S.I., D.C.L., LL.D., F.R.S.

WITH PORTRAITS AND MAPS

PREFACE

This Memoir cannot be given to the public without a word of explanation from me as to the circumstances in which it was written. After the Ashanti War in 1874, there were various books written by people who took a part in the expedition: by Mr. H. M. Stanley, then War Correspondent of the 'New York Herald'; by Mr. Henty, Correspondent of the 'Standard'; by Sir William Butler; and, more particularly, by Major (now Sir Henry) Brackenbury.

There was a strong feeling at the Colonial Office, which was also entertained by a number of Sir John Glover's personal friends, that he should write a history of his share in the Ashanti campaign of 1874, and the Colonial Office intimated to him that they wished him to undertake it. He proceeded to collect his papers and despatches with the view of writing the book. He had got some way towards arranging them, and had finished writing the introductory chapter, when an appointment to a new Governorship prevented him from continuing the history of his share in the war. This appointment was again followed by others, when the work of the colony in itself was more than enough employment for his time. Thus the book never was written.

During his last illness, and shortly before the end, seeing by his face that he was pondering very deeply about something that seemed to be weighing on his mind, I asked what he was thinking of, and he answered: 'Work that I have left undone ; that book will never be written now.'

Since that day I have looked upon the writing of a book containing some account of the Ashanti War as a last wish, which it was my duty, if it were possible for me, to carry out. I knew that his intention had been to write a very full and detailed account of the war, and I saw the innumerable difficulties of writing the book as he would have done it, or wished it written had he given any directions or expressed any desires in the matter. But I thought that the memories of the life of a man who had worked so long in the service of his country would always be acceptable, and might help others in following in the footsteps of one, who, by his own hard work, energy, courage and endurance, had placed himself in the ranks of the foremost men of his day.

An author was selected to write the book, but, from one cause or another, he, as well as others who subsequently undertook the work, was unable to carry it out, and thus his literary project remained in abeyance. At the earnest request of friends, and with the kind assistance of Sir Richard Temple as Editor, I at last consented to put together the materials in my possession for the purpose of this Life or Biographical Memoir. Chapter VIII., 'Native Expedition against the Ashantis,' was written by Sir John Glover, and is printed from MS. in his own handwriting. The Introduction to this book and Chapter IX., 'The Ashanti War,' is written by the Right Hon. Sir Richard Temple, G.C.S.I., C.I.E., F.R.S., from papers and despatches in my possession, and I am also indebted for much valuable assistance to Sir Andrew Clarke, R.E., G.C.M.G.; Sir Gilbert Carter, K.C.M.G., late Governor of Lagos, Captain Eardley Wilmot, R.N., and Captain Robb, D.A.A.G., of the Intelligence Division of the War Office, who has kindly prepared the map on page 40.

The map, which appears on p. 1, and has the signature of Sir John Glover and General R. W. Sartorius, V.C., was left in the keeping of the Haussas. It was subsequently stolen from them, and afterwards found, by Captain Davison Houston, in an old box forming part of the loot taken at

Kumasi in 1896, where it had probably been for several years.

I have long been accustomed to keep journals in considerable detail, but I have never written a book before. I have never been in Africa, nor was I with Sir John Glover during the earlier scenes described in his life, which took place long before I knew him. But I am well acquainted with all he thought and said and did since our marriage, and was with him in Europe, North America, and the West Indies. Therefore, what I state is either from my own knowledge or from my husband's graphic descriptions of events in his earlier life, and of things he knew and remembered of men and affairs in those earlier times. Indeed, I claim a knowledge which could hardly be possible to any-one else, even with the fullest access to papers and despatches which verify all that I state. What I write, therefore, may have a living force of its own, which no other hand could give. I have depicted the man, not as some might have supposed him to be from a study of papers, but as he really was in private as well as in public life, and I have searched out and selected papers and documents for this purpose. Not having the literary experience needed for writing an account of the Ashanti War, I have been assisted by those who have had practice in such matters.

My description, however authentic and life-like, may be very imperfect; still it does show something of the character of those who work in the Imperial interests of our country, and it may thus assist others who are striving for the good of the Empire. If this be so, I shall feel that I have not written in vain.

In conclusion, I am the less inclined to regret the delay which has unavoidably occurred in the publication of this volume, because I feel that its appearance at this moment may be the more useful, as it synchronises with the re-emergence of the West African question into the sphere of practical politics.

E. R. G.

CONTENTS

CHAPTER III

CHAPTER IV

CHAPTER V

1861-1863

CHAPTER VI

1863–1872

CHAPTER VII

MR. POPE HENNESSEY IN WESTERN AFRICA

CHAPTER VIII

NATIVE EXPEDITION AGAINST THE ASHANTIS BY SIR JOHN HAWLEY GLOVER

CHAPTER IX

CHAPTER X

1874–1875

CHAPTER XI

1876–1881

CHAPTER XII

CHAPTER XIII

1883–1884

CHAPTER XIV

IN MEMORIAM

PORTRAITS

MAPS

INTRODUCTION

By SIR RICHARD TEMPLE

JOHN HAWLEY GLOVER was born in 1829, and died in 1885, aged fifty-six years, his powerful constitution having been prematurely broken by fatigue, exposure, and climatic suffering, undergone in the Imperial service of Britain. He belonged to the Royal Navy, and served afloat for twenty years. On land he showed the resourcefulness and adaptability, the enterprise, the aptitude for exploration, and the tact in dealing with various nationalities from coast to coast, for which British naval officers have ever been conspicuous.

His African service began, in 1857, with the survey of the Niger, which then loomed large before the national eye. This gave rise to his West African career, which lasted for seventeen years. It comprised his greatest successes, founding his permanent fame, and establishing his claim to public gratitude. But it was spent in one of the worst

a 2

climates in the world. It was attended by malarial fever, which no precaution could avert. The cheerful excitement of action did, indeed, help him for many years in battling with this malady, and a brave front was preserved to the very last.

For this African crisis of his life, some seventeen years of instructive preparation had been allowed him. He had passed through the grades of midshipman and lieutenant in several ships and in various parts of the world. Primarily he was employed in surveying the eastern coasts of the Mediterranean, thus training his naturally fine eyesight, noting mentally all objects seen, learning how to delineate and portray, loving the beauties of nature, and through them becoming interested in the lands where he was to labour. Here, too, he first came into touch with races, wholly differing from himself, with whom he must cultivate friendship in order to obtain their co-operation in his work. Next he voyaged round the Cape of Good Hope to Rangoon at the mouth of the Irawadi, to bear a part in the second Burmese War, which added the Pegu province to the British Empire. In that region he disembarked with his brave sailors to join the soldiers on an inland expedition. Thus he practised that art of fighting ashore, in which our naval officers have ever shown themselves readily proficient. Severely wounded, he returned to England, but soon he resumed active employ, and saw some operations of the allied forces in the Baltic during the war with Russia. Then he was engaged in a delicate and difficult service off Heligoland, for the purpose of receiving on board ship the recruits for the North German Legion, who were being enlisted by the British Government. In this work he dealt successfully with authorities whose susceptibilities might either be soothed into co-operation or roused into opposition.

When the British Foreign Office under Lord Clarendon chose him for the survey of the Niger, he was an officer of varied experience, though still young; a man of dash and daring, strong in frame, so fond of riding and driving that he might almost be called a tamer of horses, a superb marksman, a competent draughtsman, a graphic word-painter, and a negotiator gifted with the power of ingratiating himself with strangers. This choice proved to be the turning point in his career.

This career of his in West Africa, from 1857 to 1874, has a bearing upon British interests at that time and in that quarter, with a significance respecting Imperial concerns generally. But these points cannot be understood without recalling the geographical features of the country where these services were rendered.

The West Coast of Africa, though somewhat

rounded in shape, runs generally north to south, from Morocco down to Liberia. Then it turns with a bend or corner eastwards for some two hundred miles, till it approaches the mouth of the Niger, where it forms another bend or corner and resumes its course southward to near the Cape of Good Hope. The portion of the African coast, then, between Liberia and the Niger mouth, used to be called the Coast of Guinea; in later times it has been known as the Gold Coast, to which has sometimes been added the name of the Slave Coast ending in the Bight of Benin. This shore is dotted from point to point with British settlements. The commercial capabilities of these settlements were for some generations undeveloped. But within this generation their development has advanced with great strides. Above the coast, on the north, lay the Ashanti kingdom—a scene of victorious strategy, under Sir Garnet Wolseley, to which John Glover materially contributed. The region now forms virtually a part of the British Empire.

In this region, then, for John Glover, the scene of his life's drama is partly to be laid.

Apart from the teachings of experience, and the familiar allusions to the ' white man's grave,' any observer of atmospheric and terrestrial influences would surmise that the climate of the Gold Coast must be unhealthy. For those who come later, such a climate may be improved by civilised arrangements ; but on those who, like the hero of this story, came early, the climate acted with all its baleful potency. It is equatorial, being a little more than four degrees north of the equator. Consequently, though not without excessive heat in summer, it affords no bracing or invigorating air in winter. The coast lies, so to speak, in a corner, in an angle formed by the southerly and easterly trends of the shore, where they meet. In consequence, it has not the full benefit of the west oceanic winds, and none at all from the cooling north winds. Indeed, it fully feels only those which blow from the south-western main. This fact is, indeed, indicated by the local nomenclature, the western end of the coast, towards Liberia, bearing the cheerful name of the Windward. On the other hand, in so far as land winds may be objectionable, the coast has a double measure of them—from the north and from the east, from the mountains behind Ashanti, and from the hilly region that dominates the lower course of the Niger. On the whole of the enormous coast-line of Africa there is probably no point so largely affected by land winds as this.

The vegetable kingdom here displays barbaric magnificence. Thus, it attracts the moisture-bearing clouds from the Atlantic, and the rainfall ou the coast is heavy. Inland hill-ranges and mountain chains rise to arrest the vapours in their course. Hence the streams and rivers are charged with floods, which may flow rapidly to within a short distance of the sea; but that fatal interval, consisting of alluvial deposit, will be flat. Therein has lain, and still lies, the danger to our settlers, pioneers, and administrators. The level surfaces, at the mouths of the streams and rivers, will be pestilential morasses, breeding malarial effluvia, not subtle but palpable to the senses. It suffices not for the visitor to avoid approaching them, inasmuch as the noxious gases may be wafted for some distance by the breeze. He may thus casually inhale them, and so take in poison with every breath. The germs may incubate in the human system for a while till malarial fever appears. Many evils may be, and are, mitigated or removed in the British settlements—by clearance, by drainage, by sanitation generally; but this plague of the river-mouths, if not incurable must be very hard to cure. It dogged the steps and hampered the proceedings of the strenuous career which is now to be described. Its effects probably closed that bright existence before the sands of the hour-glass had properly run out.

It is well to recollect these phenomena, so that we may comprehend what our countrymen—and many of our countrywomen, too—have dared and braved, have faced and suffered. Despite it all, there is commerce to be extended, there are careers to be followed, and fortunes to be carved out. In consequence, there is patriotic duty to be done, and the protection of humanity to be vindicated. For the sake of all this, many of our people have succumbed while yet in their prime, never to return home; administrators have laboured and striven; the British Government has expended both blood and treasure.

Such, then, in brief, was the region for which Lieutenant John Glover set out in 1857, buoyed up with hope and vigour.

He started from Liverpool in a little vessel, the 'Dayspring,' which had been constructed for river service, but had only one hundred horse power, not nearly strong enough to withstand the Niger's current. This error proved fatal to the vessel afterwards, and might have spoiled the expedition, had it not been for his energetic perseverance. As a surveyor and observer he was in a scientific rather than in a naval capacity, and he had scientific colleagues. Arrived at the mouth of the Niger, he, together with his companions, advanced up the mighty river. With them he passed up stream for five hundred miles, as far as Rabba, a place of some note in African story, surveying,

studying the physical features, and holding interviews with the chiefs on either bank. Near this point
he was suddenly roused by finding the ' Dayspring '
unequal to stemming the rapid current of the
Niger, and driven backwards on a sunken rock to
be wrecked. Then he showed that mastery of situations, that inborn command over men, which distinguished all the rest of his career. His party
was encamped on the left bank of the Niger in
comfort and safety, in the hope of obtaining the
means for their return to the coast. But he undertook to ride on alone at least to Boussa (another
place of note), a hundred miles further, and beyond
that, as far as he might be able to reach, in the
direction of Kibbi. He had by this time felt his
way with the native chiefs, enough to feel sure
that he could, by good humour and conciliatory
manners, obtain their kind offices.

A carefully kept journal of his proceedings at this
time has been preserved. It is full of picturesque
scenes of his interviews and dealings with the
natives. It throws light on the social life in Africa
at the end of the generation preceding our own.
It is indeed worthy of separate treatment, as being
the only record extant of one among the earliest, if
not the very earliest, official explorations of the
Niger by the British Government.

Thus, having penetrated, with surveys and

observations, for nearly seven hundred miles up the Niger, he returned to his party in camp at Rabba, and found them as they were, still unable to move, and without prospect of obtaining the means for moving.

He thereupon conceived a plan of characteristic boldness, which proved a turning point in his career. From a consideration of the geography which has been outlined, it will be evident that, owing to the bend of the West African coast, there was a short cut across the country to the lagoons of the Gold Coast, near the rising British station at Lagos. He resolved to pursue this route alone, and so procure the means for extricating his party from their situation. This adventurous march, over unknown uplands for about two hundred miles, carried him through the country of a Moslem tribe of Africans, the Yorubas—a good and brave tribe, whose name ought to be borne in mind by those who care for the just interests of Britain in this quarter of Africa. He thus formed with them an acquaintance which enabled him thereafter to use their services on critical occasions of war and politics. Then and there, also, he fell in with the Haussas, members of a most remarkable though scattered tribe. He had previously studied their history, which was shrouded in some uncertainty, but was probably romantic, and sprang from the far-off interior of the Dark Continent. He perceived that they had a physique and a morale which, under British leadership, might render them of real value as auxiliaries. Arrived at Lagos, he made a survey of its lagoons, little thinking that hereabouts the foundation of his fame was to be laid. Having collected the needful supplies and transport, he again crossed the Yoruba country to rejoin his party at Rabba on the Niger, and so ensured their return to the coast. He returned to England, and received the official thanks of Lord Clarendon for what he had done.

In 1861 he was appointed to the command of the 'Handy,' which, among her other duties, was to be employed in surveying the Gold Coast ; and this proved one of the long list of instances wherein the employment of war-vessels in the survey of distant coasts has promoted British interests generally. Thus he returned to the neighbourhood of Lagos and its lagoons. This was the last ship in which he served; for, being appointed first Administrator, and then Governor, of Lagos in 1863 he resigned active employment in the Navy, and served under the Colonial Department of the British Government, with but short interruption, for the rest of his days.

He found Lagos a humble and miserable place. Though destitute of fame, it had, locally, he knew, a lurid notoriety as being the worst slave-market on the Gold Coast. This was the place he set himself to make, and actually made, until it came to be called the little Liverpool of the Gold Coast. There was, indeed, no warding off the malaria which the land breezes wafted from the lagoons and from the mouths of streams; but throughout the island itself he introduced order with sanitation, and houses sprang up as trade grew. His Haussa friends were organised and disciplined as armed police, while, in fact, they became soldiers fit for any service. Remembering the Yorubas inland, their martial characteristics, their productive and comparatively healthy uplands, he opened communication with them. His policy was to establish trade routes to their inland country from the coast opposite Lagos, and their co-operation was assured. But such lines had to pass through the territories of coast tribes, who, as owners of and traders in slaves, were hostile to the extension of British influence into the interior; and with these tribes he had many troublesome negotiations. At length he overcame their resistance for the most part and for a time; under his care the island of Lagos was converted from a mart for the captive, to a home of refuge for the free.

One of the most independent and impartial narrators (Mr. H. M. Stanley, who collected information near the spot in 1873) wrote thus regarding John Glover's administration of Lagos :—

'His career, while in charge of this African Colony in the Benin bight, has established his fame as one of the wisest administrators the British Government ever sent to Africa; he has endeared himself to the whole native population of Lagos and its dependencies; his name is as universally known among the tribes of the interior bordering the West Coast, as Livingstone's is known in Central Africa. He has enriched the country beyond belief, until, from a miserable settlement with an unenviable notoriety for fevers, its annual imports and exports amounted in 1872 to 5,432,310 dollars, and the port of Lagos is as healthy a place to live in as any town in West Africa. Its wharves, piers, drains, houses, public buildings, order, systematic government, its local police, and its volunteers, mark the port of Lagos as having been under the fostering care of a man who took an interest in his work, and was possessed of the requisite energy and will to carry out his projects of reform and improvement.'

In 1873 he obtained leave to proceed to England, attended by the affectionate regrets of his countrymen at Lagos, and the reverence of several tribes, among whom his name, translated into African as 'Golobar,' had become a household word.

Besides the natural need of health and rest, he had another reason for leaving Lagos at that time. Mr. Pope Hennessey had arrived as Governor-in-Chief of the British settlements in West Africa, including Lagos. That gentleman did not remain long at Lagos, or on the coast generally; but his proceedings in respect of Lagos form an episode pregnant with instruction for all who desire the preservation of our Imperial interests in Africa, or in regions similarly situated. It is no exaggeration to say that Mr. Pope Hennessey not only reversed some of the most important parts of Captain Glover's policy, but did so straightway and summarily. The views of the slave-owning and slave-dealing tribes on the coast were to be adopted; the communication with the Yorubas inland was to be suspended; slavery in Lagos itself was no longer to be prohibited; the titular king, pensioned by the British, was to be restored to his throne—in short, the British position outside Lagos was to shrink almost to nothingness. All this may have been arranged by the Governor-in-Chief with the best intentions; but it certainly was done without any inquiries from the British Governor on the spot, or his officers; and, so far as can be seen, without the previous sanction of Her Majesty's Government in London. As trade was checked for the moment, and imperilled for the future, protests were raised in Manchester and Liverpool. Mr. Pope Hennessey's stay was not prolonged ; and soon the affairs of Lagos resumed their former course, in which they have happily continued. But such a change as that—which was attempted offhand, without inquiry, warning, or preparation—must have, for the moment, endangered British interests, and lowered the confidence of friendly or allied tribes in the steadfastness and continuity of British policy.

Of the signal and memorable services rendered by Sir John Glover in the Ashanti War of 1873, a detailed account will be found in Chapter IX. For the moment, however, it may suffice to say that on a comparison of his recorded achievements with the commission entrusted to him by Her Majesty's Government, and with the orders given to him in consequence by the Major-General, it was found that he had done all, and more than all, he had undertaken, or had been expected to do. This, too, he had accomplished, despite troubles with the Africans, and physical obstacles—all greater even than had been anticipated.

The generous and hearty recognition of his services by Sir Garnet Wolseley, on the spot immediately after the occurrences ; the further appreciation by Her Majesty's Government ; the thanks of Parliament ; the honour graciously conferred by the Sovereign—stand recorded in history.

Among the many public recognitions from his countrymen after his return to England, the testimony of Colonel, afterwards Sir Evelyn, Wood, may be cited, as given in the course of a lecture before the Royal United Service Institution in 1874 :—

' It would be a mistake to value Captain Glover's gallant and successful advance according only to the number of Ashantis detached to watch the threatened roads. The Ashanti monarch was supported by powerful feudatories, and the war being unpopular with those chiefs who had fought with white men south of the Prah, they gladly seized the excuse of their territories being invaded to diminish their contingents ordered up to defend the capital. . . . I wish to express the high admiration felt for him (Captain Glover) by those officers who, having led comparatively small bodies of natives with several Europeans, can appreciate his difficulties when the proportions of officers and men were reversed. It is improbable that the present generation will see on the Gold Coast any equal to Sir John Glover, whether we consider his determined courage, his abilities, his long experience of, and immense influence over, the natives, or the iron constitution which, with an indomitable will, has enabled him to withstand the evil influences of a detestable climate.'

Sir John Glover had now quitted the African

Gold Coast for ever, of which he might have truly said that it was *regio nostri plena laboris*. The rest of his active life—alas! too short—was to be spent in another hemisphere.

After seventeen years of exposure to the climate of the Gold Coast, with but slight intermissions, and with more than a full share of the sickness incidental to that region, he spent two years in the British Isles. This respite must have braced up his shaken health. But in the midst of it he met with a railway accident, which so injured him that he lay for some time between life and death; very probably this mishap caused some shock to his already overtaxed nervous system. However, in due course he recovered sufficiently to be able to accept an offer from Lord Carnarvon of the Governorship of Newfoundland. He proceeded thither, assumed the government, and shortly afterwards came home again, in order to be married. Then he took the young bride to his Colony amidst the delighted acclamations of the colonists.

As Governor of Newfoundland, with his powerful frame and nervous force re-invigorated, he set himself to work in his old way, conversing with the colonists of all sorts and conditions, consulting all interests alike, and striving, with much success, indeed, to please everybody. From the first he was a peripatetic ruler. He still acted on his old belief in the advantages of locomotion, in seeing every requirement with his own eye, in hearing what people had to say while on their own ground. He rode, drove, boated, sailed, and employed many picturesque methods of moving about among his fisher-folk. Soon he had penetrated to every creek and station of fishermen, to every rock-bound shore where, for some months in the year, men risked their lives for a precarious subsistence. Though their ills were but too often such as governors cannot cure, yet his outspoken sympathy, and his pains in searching out their rough abodes, did warm their hearts. The disputes regarding the rights of fishing reserved to the French were then becoming acute, and he mastered the controversy. Having had some dealings with the French in other lands, he knew how to adopt a conciliatory method with them here. Though, as governor of a colony possessing responsible government, he only reigned, and no longer had the power once wielded by him on the other side of the Atlantic, still he soon exercised moral authority in many directions, and was able to give an impulse to many public improvements.

During the spring, summer, and autumn he delighted in the life out of doors. But there followed the long winters, with deep snow and much confinement indoors; and once more his health suffered. Indeed, some such consequence was but too surely to be predicted from the change to a northern extremity of America after a long equatorial residence; there was already some doubt whether he would be able to withstand the effect of several winters in Newfoundland.

At this juncture he was appointed Governor of the Leeward Islands in the West Indies. With his eye long practised in observing nature, he could not but be struck by the loveliness, the grace, the charm of the scenery which, in spite of its bounteous display, was unlike the rank luxuriance and overpowering abundance seen by him on the opposite shore of the ocean. The queen of his isles was Dominica, a veritable paradise, a gem set in the sea. His work here, though he performed it manfully, was not to his liking. He had been commissioned by Her Majesty's Government to carry out several invidious and troublesome changes. Consequently, he did not expect to find the loyal true-hearted service he had been wont to receive in regions where his agents were with him in spirit and sympathy. Though he procured the execution of various improvements, he still met with more impediments than of yore. Yet with his unfailing tact he had made some way—for manliness in a ruler soon attracts friends everywhere in the British dominions—when once more he was stricken down by his old enemy. He pathetically declared that this attack was worse than anything known in Africa. He lay desperately sick in his Government House while a ball (which he would not allow to be put off) was going on there. When the last hope had been abandoned by the physician, his wife, with happy presence of mind, applied ice in a manner which brought back the life that was on the point of extinction.

Shortly afterwards he repaired to England on leave, and it is asserted that a high medical authority warned him to be very careful, but that he smilingly said he must go on working.

At that time a mixed commission of English and French gentlemen was sitting in Paris to consider the questions relating to the fisheries in Newfoundland ; and advantage was taken of his presence in England to depute him thither, in order that he might afford them the benefit of his local knowledge.

In those days, his successor in the governorship of Newfoundland died suddenly. So he was directed to return to his former post there, to receive the Fishery Commissioners on their arrival from Europe, and, ultimately, to settle the pending questions. So he returned to Newfoundland, with all his old alacrity in obeying orders, but, inwardly, with some foreboding. At first, however, the heartiness of his reception by the colonists, on his return among them, the recognition of old friends and admirers, and the glorious weather, sustained his spirits. But the long, snow-bound winter, and the confinement indoors, came round again; and his health, shaken by the West Indian fever, once more declined. No positive apprehension, perhaps, was felt till one day in the next spring when, after a long protracted sitting at desk-work, he felt very faint in the evening. The physician pronounced him to be suffering from a strained heart—whatever that might mean. At all events, the symptoms were ominous, and he soon sailed for England, growing daily weaker. He proceeded to a German health resort, but in vain; and returned home to die. He had the ministrations of his devoted wife in London. Motionless, helpless, restless, he suffered without complaining. His mind remained clear as crystal to the last; but its working could seldom be followed, because breathlessness rendered him almost inarticulate. One morning, his wife and child were struck by a strange brightness in his large open eyes. It was the last flash of vanishing life; in a few moments they closed for ever, and the weary was at rest.

The first words of condolence came from the Sovereign herself, and then from comrades in peace and brethren in arms scattered over the British Isles, and across the sea from Western

Africa, from North America, from the West Indies. These were followed by many tributes to the rectitude of his conduct, the charm of his conversation, and the unfailing courtesy of his manner. For his walk through life had been such, that around it bright-coloured recollections had ever clustered—just as flowers spring from the earth under the West Indian sunlight, or splendid creepers cling to the giant stems of the African woodland. Soon there was a movement among troops of friends to set up a permanent memorial. A bust was placed in the crypt of St. Paul's Cathedral, and the ceremony of unveiling was performed by Sir Garnet Wolseley, a most competent witness of the career which was being thus commemorated.

This career—alas! closed too soon for his friends and for his country—was devoted to the promotion of British interests across the seas, in the highest sense of the term. He strove ever for the extension of British trade; he thought of his toiling countrymen at home, and searched afar to find markets for their industries. But he anticipated more than equal benefits to the natives from such intercourse. He not only thought, but knew—with a knowledge which only travellers and explorers can have—that such relations can rarely, if ever, prosper, without the influence of that flag which must be displayed in the right place, and at the decisive moment. He would not always insist on that being accompanied by arms; but there must be a certainty in the minds of men, that such force, though out of immediate sight, exists somewhere irresistibly. He preferred to venture among strange nationalities, almost or quite alone, either with the slightest protection, or altogether unprotected. Before them he would bear himself in a mild yet masterful manner, indicating the unspoken belief that if he were struck down hundreds, or even thousands, of his armed countrymen would come to demand the reason why. His ambition was untainted by the lust of conquest or of domination; it was the aspiration to rule over races for their protection against cruel tyranny and vile abuses, and to work for their welfare just as if they had been people of his own race. He held that European civilisation had, in these respects, a mission, which Britain alone among the nations had the will and the means to fulfil. For the sake of this mission, which was not only his day-dream but his fixed ideal, he shed his blood on necessary occasion, and unremittingly spent his nervous force. He was a type of the men who have built up what is now known as the Empire of the British Sovereign. They have always been found when wanted; they have never failed when brought into action. Their conduct, too, has been exhibited in infinitely various forms, and in all sorts or conditions of climate or circumstance. So long, and only so long, as she can rear and call out such sons, will Britannia rule the seas, the shores, the isles, the continents. Therefore, is she bound to note the deeds they have done for her sake, to honour them in life, and after death to keep alive their memory as an ensample to those who shall succeed them.

His education was mainly in practical science; but in literature he had to educate himself. He read the English classics with that affectionate attention which often affords to self-imparted instruction an effectiveness which could not otherwise be attained. In a dreamy and imaginative, almost a poetic way, he loved Nature in all her moods. He had been carefully and wisely brought up, and so, while wondering at the phenomena of creation he looked up from them to the Creator. He saw God in the storms of the Mediterranean— in the tropical tornados—in the cyclones of eastern seas—in the mountainous billows of the North Atlantic. He planned churches in Western Africa. He saw the efficacy of Christian teaching upon those among the tribes whom it reached, arousing their conscience for the performance of duty in danger as well as in peace, and for evincing fidelity of conduct amidst temptation. He exerted himself in England to support the Protestant Mission whose efficiency he had witnessed.

His genius, however, lay in dealing with men. This quality happened to be chiefly, though not entirely, exercised in contact with strange and wild nationalities. Still he was to some extent tried with other classes. Had his career been prolonged, and had he been engaged in matters of grave and urgent diplomacy, he might have rendered national service therein. As it was, he had argued, treated and negotiated with fishermen in Labrador, Frenchmen on the Newfoundland Coast, Germans on the Elbe, Greeks and Turks on the Levant, Creoles in the West Indies, Burmese on the Irawadi, chiefs on the Niger who had never seen a white man before, tribes warlike and unwarlike on the Gold Coast. His persuasive and commanding personality—made up of eye, countenance, voice, diction, manner, stature—was ever a factor potent on the British side.

He was a humane man, feeling a manly grief for the manifold sufferings that came under his gaze. At first he was animated by a benevolent enthusiasm for remedy and reform. Ascending the Niger, he brooded over the blood-feuds, the human sacrifices, the fetish superstitions. He aspired to stop these things of darkness before many years should pass.

To him the horror of slavery was ineffable, as he saw the canoes on the mighty river freighted with sorrowful humanity. He hoped that within his lifetime they might bear other loads, the products of European industry. Years of hard and chequered experience taught him that the full realisation of these hopes might yet be distant. Still he pertinaciously contended with slavery in the interior to the last day of his African service. As Governor, he asserted his jurisdiction in the Coast settlements as the guarantee of human freedom. In his epitaph it might be truly inscribed that he was one of those who struck off the fetters from the slave.

In moments of danger he was quick in succouring others; from his own pains he turned instantly to the relief of those around him. He escorted the sick wife of a Christian missionary through a horde of menacing Africans; with signal presence of mind he saved the life of a French child near Paris; though blinded with his own blood he carried off one of his wounded sailors from the Burmese ambuscade; in Ireland, when himself stricken sorely in a railway accident, his first thought was to help his injured fellow-passengers.

His friends described him as a man among men, and a born leader of others; indeed, the sum total of his character could not be better expressed. He was naturally endowed with, and had by practice cultivated, the faculty of inducing men, whether of his own race or of divers nationalities, to follow him for better, for worse; to cleave to him as a brother, even in extreme hardship and peril; to work for his policy as if it had been for their own nearest interest; to vindicate him loyally ever afterwards. He bore his honours and wielded his authority with unassuming quietness and sailor-like simplicity. And to crown his thoughts on national affairs, he had faith in England, and in her absolutely—in her pride and power—in her virtue, benevolence and philanthropy—in her expansiveness and tenacity—in her imperial destiny. In fine, of him it may be written—he was a true Englishman!

LIFE

OF

SIR JOHN HAWLEY GLOVER

CHAPTER I

Early life of John Hawley Glover, 1829–1849—Descent—His father, the Rev. Frederick Glover—Important inventions—Literary works—Incidents of the New Zealand War—Mrs. Glover's personality—Early education of John Hawley Glover—Appointment as first-class volunteer to H.M.S. ' Queen '—Mrs. Glover's death—Mr. Glover's re-marriage—Difficulties begin with respect to John Glover—Reason for sending him to learn surveying—Effect on his character of early influences—Appointed midshipman—Return to the Mediterranean—Beginning of active career, 1847–1851—Mr John Glover, midshipman—Return to Mediterranean—Life at Malta—Constantinople—Survey of coast round Athens—Self-education—First command—Sport in the Archipelago—Leave granted by Admiral Sir William Parker—Stay at Bonn—Reappointed to command of ' Auxiliaire '—Survey round Crete and Cyprus—Transfer to ' Victory '—Appointment to ' Penelope '—Return to Bonn—Sojourn on banks of Rhine.

JOHN HAWLEY GLOVER, born on February 24, 1829, at Yately in Hampshire, was the son of the Rev. Frederick Glover. He came of an old family distinguished in arms, who for many generations had given their blood and services to their country. Their descent is traced to Egbert, and through the Plantagenets to Charlemagne and Hildegarde

B

of Swabia. In the reign of Henry VI., Thomas Glover was warden of Rochester Bridge. His grandson Thomas bore the canopy at the coronation of Henry VIII. as a baron of the Cinque Ports. His grandson in turn, Robert Glover, was the well-known Somerset Herald who died in 1588. In the ensuing century Thomas Glover was Ambassador at Constantinople, where he spent a hundred thousand dollars in redeeming three hundred Christian slaves. On October 13, 1614, a grant was made to him for life of the office of collector of fines in ecclesiastical causes. In 1617 Robert Glover was clerk to the Farriers' Company.

Mr. Frederick Glover's grandfather, Colonel Glover, was an officer in the Royal regiment which served in the Peninsular War. A story is told of him that when he was with his regiment at Gibraltar he considered it his duty to remonstrate with the Duke of Kent about what he looked upon as an unfair interference with his regiment. At first the Duke was angry, but on reflection perceived that the remonstrance was fair, and from that day onward showed special kindness to him and his sons. Many years afterwards, when George III. was at Weymouth, the Duke introduced Colonel Glover to him as an officer to whom 'he owed much.'

The subject of this memoir was the eldest

son of Mr., afterwards the Rev. Frederick Glover, a very remarkable man in many respects. · He was destined for the Army, and in due time passed through Sandhurst, joined the 1st Royals, and exchanged into the 69th Regiment, proceeding to Cape Coast to take part in the Ashanti War, which was concluded in 1826. Shortly afterwards he married Mary, the second daughter of Admiral Broughton. She was a lineal descendant of Queen Catherine Parr, the founder of the King's School at Canterbury, where two of her sons were educated. As founder's kin, her family have enjoyed the right of this privilege for more than two hundred years.[1]

Three or four years after his marriage, Mr. Frederick Glover retired from the Army, to the regret of his brother officers, and entered Peterhouse, Cambridge, with the view of taking Holy Orders. In due time he was ordained, during 1833 obtaining a curacy in Hampshire, which he shortly afterwards exchanged for a cure in Dorsetshire, and finally settled down at Charlton, near Dover. Here, in 1841, he lost his wife, who had borne him four sons and one daughter, who died young.

---

[1] Catherine Parr, after the king's death, married Lord Thomas Seymour, elder brother of the Protector Somerset. Their daughter, who is stated in most English histories to have died an infant, actually grew up and married Sir Edward Birchall. This fact is alluded to by Miss Strickland in her *Lives of the Queens of England.*

Soon after his wife's death he resigned his living, re-married, and went abroad, having accepted the chaplaincy of Cologne, where he remained till 1861, when he resigned on the death of his second wife. Then he gave up clerical work, and turned his attention to that of mechanical invention. He had a creative mind, and, possessing acute powers of observation, was able in this new phase to render much service to the cause of science and to humanity. Among the earliest of his inventions, which claims special notice, was an ambulance-car for conveying the wounded with greater comfort and despatch from the field of battle. The invention, though offered to the British War Department, received no recognition until Napoleon III. had accepted it, and proved its utility. Another important invention was the 'anchor fall.' This ensured the immediate holding of the anchor, while it greatly facilitated the operation of weighing and securing it after it had been hauled up. To prove the value of this invention, Mr. Glover chartered a steam yacht and went round the English ports in it. Though it was universally approved, the Admiralty long refused to make use of it, and it was not until the mercantile marine had very generally adopted it that the Government gave way. 'He was always ready at a glance,' wrote one who knew him well, ' to offer a suggestion to improve or simplify the working of any machine.' Even during his last moments he was engaged in giving final touches to his invention for the raising and moving of invalids.

It is impossible to pass from this remarkable man without noticing another aspect of his many-sided mind. He was an ardent supporter of the Anglican Church, and wrote several works relating to sacred subjects, and he laboured for the development of the Episcopal system abroad, having himself held a cure on the Continent, and being interested in his nephew's work, who was then a Church dignitary at the Cape of Good Hope.[1] Further, he was a firm believer in the English people being 'the remnant of Judah.' For the purpose of investigating this, he accompanied Mr. Piazzi Smyth to Egypt, and wrote several elaborate books on the 'Great Pyramid,' and made valuable discoveries in regard to it. When upwards of seventy he went to India to communicate the result of his researches, not only to the English but to the Brahmin students, and returned to England full of zeal and energy, which was only equalled by his faith and piety, till the close of his life in August 1881, in the eighty-second year

---

[1] Mr. Glover's four nephews were all Wranglers of their time at Cambridge, and some of them received College livings. One of them was Archdeacon at the Cape of Good Hope.

of his age. His genial manners, remarkable activity, and ready sympathy made him many friends, who still revere his memory. Besides the subject of this memoir he had three other sons : Frederick, who held a staff appointment, and died at Ottawa in Canada in 1867, and Robert and Guy, fine young officers in the 43rd Regiment, both shot the same day during the Maori War in New Zealand. They had already been mentioned in despatches, and their value was fully appreciated at headquarters, for on the first opportunity the Duke of Cambridge had of seeing their father after this sad event, he deplored their having been 'thus sacrificed.' The Duke added that he 'might well be proud of two such sons.'

John Hawley Glover, like most eminent men, inherited the characteristics and qualities of his mother, a woman of great force and charm of character, in whose veins ran the blood of a long line of sailor ancestors. Her father, Admiral Broughton, had fought at Aboukir, when the English troops under General Abercrombie took that town from the French in 1801, and received the commemoration medal struck by Sultan Selim, bearing his imperial cypher. When leaving H.M.S. 'Cornwall,' in 1813, Captain Broughton received a service of plate and a gold snuff-box in token of the esteem he was held in by the officers under his command. Doubtless this great love of the sea and strong sense of discipline was transmitted through his daughter, Mrs. Glover, to her infant son, who at the early age of three was nearly lost to her by a singular adventure, while staying at Bath with his grandfather, Colonel Glover, then commanding the Volunteers. Walking with his nurse one day in that town the boy lagged behind, while the nurse's attention was occupied with his baby brother. Two gipsies approached and asked him if he would like a ride on a pony. This proposal was irresistible, so he went with them to the corner of the street, when one of them hoisted him on his shoulder and carried him off to their encampment. The nurse reported that her charge was missing. After fruitless attempts had been made to find him, and his mother had begun to despair of ever seeing her son again, a lady remembered having noticed a well-dressed child in company with some rough-looking men. This directed suspicion to the, gipsies, and after some further search he was found in their camp, eating sausages, and perfectly happy with his new friends.

From his earliest years the boy showed a strong inclination to enter the Navy and be with his grandfather Admiral Broughton, whose stories of sea life appealed powerfully to his young imagi- nation. His father, however, always intended him for the Royal Engineers, and opposed his wish to become a sailor, seeing that he gave evidence of more than ordinary ability. He personally directed the boy's education, even during his hours of recreation, his object being to give an engineering turn to his mind. In after years, when the boy had grown to be a man of practical ability, he described how he obtained his first knowledge of surveying from the conversation and practical illustrations given by his father as they took their afternoon walks at Dover by the sea-shore. The father would draw maps on the beach with his walking-stick, making plans of outworks, lines of communication, and elements of fortification, by raising entrenchments in the sand. All this helped the son afterwards in the special line he adopted in the Navy. But though the father was determined, the son was still more so, and at last made up his mind to run away to sea. This project his mother discovered, and spoke to Vice-Admiral Sir Edmund Owen, who gave him a nomination, and took him on board his ship the 'Queen' as a first-class volunteer on December 4, 1841, his grandmother, Mrs. Broughton, giving him his outfit, which his father refused to do, declining, indeed, to assist him in any way. The boy was then under twelve, and short for his years. An amusing story is told of his first meeting with a tall marine appointed to

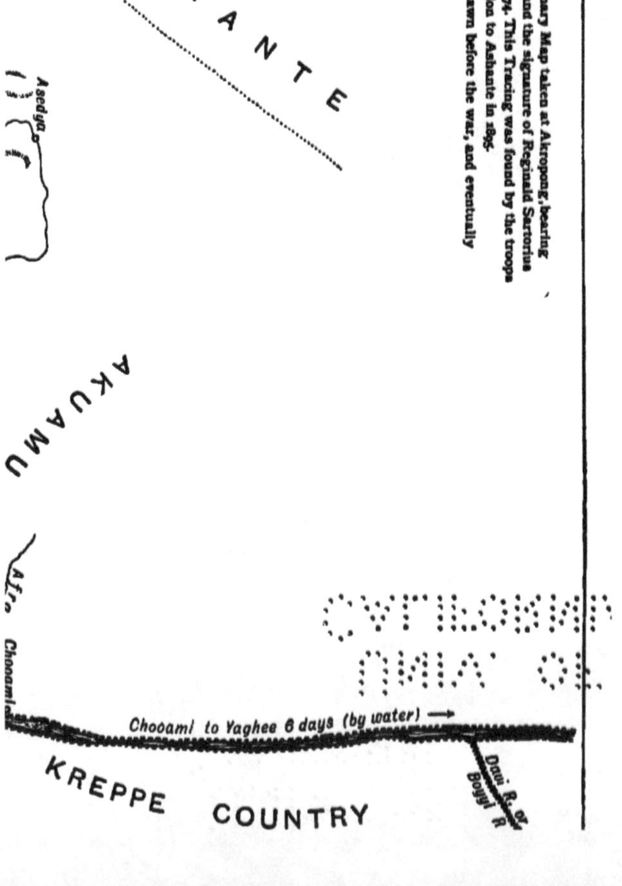

Reduced from a Tracing from a Missionary Map taken at Akropong, bearing
the initials of J.H.G. 4th October 1873, and the signature of Reginald Sartorius
6th. Bengal Cavalry September 23rd. 1874. This Tracing was found by the troops
under Sir Francis Scott in his Expedition to Ashante in 1895.
The route marked on this map was drawn before the war, and eventually
was not followed.

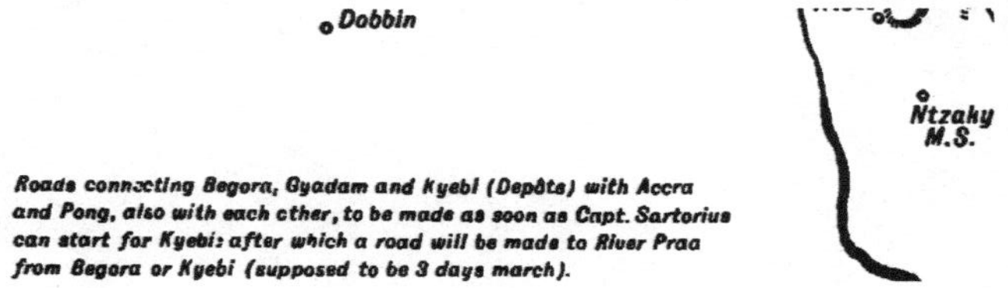

Dobbin

Ntzaky
M.S.

Roads connecting Begora, Gyadam and Kyebi (Depôts) with Accra
and Pong, also with each other, to be made as soon as Capt. Sartorius
can start for Kyebi: after which a road will be made to River Praa
from Begora or Kyebi (supposed to be 3 days march).

act as his servant. In looking through his outfit, articles of clothing were discovered which had been made by his grandmother, who had an anxious fear lest he should catch cold from the draughts on board ship, as he had at one time suffered from croup. Among these garments was a flannel dressing-gown, which the tall marine immediately appropriated to himself, with the remark that 'such an article is quite unnecessary for a young officer.' He also volunteered to take care of his money.

Soon after young Glover had left home his mother died, and during the following year his father married again. In announcing this event to his son, he desired that the boy should address the lady by that endearing name which is due from a son to but one being in the world. The boy declined to obey, having been passionately devoted to his mother, whose early influence caused him to cherish a life-long affection for her memory. His father, who had never forgotten nor forgiven the defeat of his intention with regard to his son's career, wrote to him saying that he would discontinue the small allowance he had hitherto made him. This announcement was enough to stagger the bravest heart, for the yearly stipend of a lad in the position of young Glover amounted to 9*l.* a year, and of this modest sum 5*l.* went to pay the naval instructor. But yet he was not daunted, for on this occasion, as on all others of importance in his eventful life, the directness of purpose which was his great characteristic asserted itself. In his dilemma he went straight to the captain, with whom he was a favourite, and told his story, saying he must leave and join the merchant service. The admiral, upon hearing this, sent for the boy and told him that he was too good to lose, and that they would manage to keep him in the service, that he was no longer to pay the naval instructor, but to work at surveying, which would bring him extra pay. With this and occasional presents from his grandmother he was enabled to continue his career. There must have been something winning in the boy's nature to have thus enlisted on his behalf the influence of his superiors. He was at the same time a great favourite with his comrades, their leader in the most daring pranks and practical jokes, which were ever the delight of his adventurous spirit, though these traits were combined with an unusually strong sense of duty and a scrupulous exactness in his work. On one occasion he took a header off the yard-arm of the ‘Queen,’ striking the water at a distance of seventy-four feet. He was brought on board bleeding from the ears and nose, but not otherwise injured. At this time he felt very much cut off from all his family and relations, which probably was the cause of the great reserve in his nature. Having to rely upon his own resources from such an early age, he acquired independence of character, and the very fact of his being obliged to take up this surveying branch of his profession was the means of getting his foot on the first rung of the ladder of his after success in life.

Shortly after this he was transferred to the 'Beacon,' then surveying in the Mediterranean, where he learned his work. This ship being paid off in 1846, he joined the surveying ship 'Mastiff,' but did not remain long in her, for on the 'Volage' (also a surveying vessel) being commissioned, he was appointed midshipman, and returned in her to the Mediterranean in 1847. His life had been in many respects hard and toilsome. It admitted of few holidays and fewer recreations, but he still dearly loved the sea and the profession he had chosen, and he now hailed with delight his return to the blue skies and waters of the Mediterranean. Like many sailors of a thoughtful turn of mind, his impressions were deepened by a constant observation of nature. There was time for reflection during long dark midnight watches, while he listened to the wind tearing through the cordage on wild stormy nights, or when watching the angry sea and the sudden changefulness of the elements.

All this impressed him with a deep reverence for the Divine Being who 'holds our destinies in the hollow of His hand.' Thus began to arise in his mind a longing to do some work in His service. When his day's work on board ship—spent in making charts and maps—was over, he would often go on shore for a long walk. Tired by the dust and heat and glare in some Eastern city, he would turn into one of the churches for a few moments' quiet and contemplation. Here, the solemn evening service in these cool dark buildings produced a calm and restful feeling which made a lasting impression on the thoughtful side of his nature. The opera house at Malta was his chief delight, for here, for a very small sum of money, he could indulge his love of music to the full. From Malta the ship moved to various ports that were then being surveyed. Cyprus and Crete were places of considerable interest, where he spent a great deal of his time as soon as he got an independent command. In the 'Volage' he also surveyed the coast round Athens; the Acropolis with its historic ruins formed an education in itself, and became the subject of many of his sketches.

Here he obtained his first command as mate of the tender to the 'Volage' named the 'Auxiliaire.' His work, indeed, caused him to visit all the most interesting and historic portions of the Eastern

Mediterranean and the Levant. His cabin in this little vessel was well stored with books, and amongst these the English poets held an honoured place. In the midst of some of the loveliest scenery in the world and under the blue sky of the Mediterranean, lying lazily on deck, he would commit to memory long pages of Scott and Byron, while watching the compass and listening for the soundings being called out by the midshipman, his sole fellow officer on this little craft.

The most profitable result of this life of comparative solitude, arduous as it must have been in many respects, was the opportunity it afforded him of storing his mind with the knowledge which the circumstances of his previous life had combined to withhold from him. Up to the time of his departure from his father's roof, he had little opportunity of acquainting himself with the great authors of English literature. His after life was largely influenced by this mental training. Not only did it impart to his mind a poetic turn, but it softened his nature by awakening his sympathies. It aided him in another way to deal successfully in after life with the native tribes of Africa. For, little resembling the matter-of-fact sons of Europe, these races are remarkably susceptible to the influence of imagination. With them, where argument fails, allegory succeeds. So when the time came for him to deal with them, this vital difference between the two organisations became at once apparent to his practical mind. It was then that his intimate acquaintance with the best poets of his native land enabled him to meet the natives with the one charmed weapon which always constrained them.

He had taken with him a brace of pointers and a double-barrelled gun ; and when the cutter lay in port, it was his habit after the work of the day had been completed, to shoulder his gun, and taking his dogs to wander in quest of quail, which abound in the Archipelago. By constant practice he acquired a skill so rare, and an aim so unerring, that he was at last able not only to make certain of killing, but of killing in such a manner as to spare the plumage. The skill thus acquired was in later years employed with lasting effect in the service of his country; for the birds which were brought to England as one of the results of his first survey of the Niger, and are now in the South Kensington Museum, fell to his unerring aim. His rifle practice was attended with equal success.

In bad weather, and during the winter months, the little cutter would lie up in Malta harbour, and the day was spent in drawing charts—the result of the summer's work in the Archipelago—the evenings at the opera, where he was a constant attendant. After a year spent in this manner he was transferred to the ' Volcano,' another surveying ship, but only remained in her a short time, when he obtained leave in December 1848 from Admiral Sir William Parker to return to England at his own expense, for the purpose of passing his examination for lieutenant.

On his way home he went to Bonn, where his father then lived, and for the first time met his stepmother.

On his return to the Mediterranean, he was again given command of the ' Auxiliaire ' for another year's surveying, in which he visited Crete and Cyprus. It was here he experienced his first attack of malarial fever. In after years he used to say that, ' bad as was the fever of Cyprus, that of Africa was worse, but that the West Indian fever was the most terrible of the three ; ' and as each of the fevers was more severe than the preceding one, they expelled the traces of the former. Possibly his constitution being so. severely tried by such frequent attacks was less able to resist the strain on its resources, and doubtless was at last completely undermined by the malarial poison.

When he finished his work in the ' Auxiliaire ' as mate in command, she was paid off in December 1850, and he again came home, being borne on

the books of H.M.S. 'Victory' until transferred to
the 'Penelope.' About this time, when staying
with his father at Bonn, he made the acquaintance
of a lady to whom he became sincerely attached,
and this attachment continued to be a very powerful influence in his life for many years. He had
always a great respect and admiration for women,
though, unlike most sailors, he was rather shy in
their company, probably from the fact of not
having sisters of his own, and also because his work
on board ship prevented him from having much
time for their society. This lady was older than
he was, beautiful as well as clever and refined, also
well read and versatile. No doubt the books they
studied together and her softening influence at this
period did much to brighten his life, and give a
deeper and warmer tone of colour to his thoughts.
The recollections of this visit were pleasant for him
to look back upon during all the lonely years in
Africa that were to follow. Thus the result of his
time spent on the banks of the Rhine was that later
on, when he was ordered out for his first expedition to Africa, he went, considering himself engaged.
His journals sent home to this lady are all the
records we have of the great object of his life, viz.,
the opening up of Africa to civilisation. Doubtless
the attachment now formed was a good influence in
his life, as well as a protection against the many

temptations which beset young men, and materially affected his moral character throughout his life.

Such was Mr. Glover's early life and training. His future was now before him, and that future depended mainly on the use he had made of the opportunities already afforded him.

CHAPTER II

Service in Burmah, 1851–1853—Steam-ship ' Penelope '—Command of ' Teazer ' on the African Coast— Promotion to rank of Lieutenant— China Station—Appointment to ' Sphinx ' at Rangoon—Second Burmese War—Command of paddle-box boats on the Irawadi— Cholera—Death of Admiral Austin—Fighting at Pegu—Landing at Donabew—Fighting with the Burmese—Severe losses—Captain Loch killed—Lieutenant Glover severely wounded—Bringing ship back to England—Receives public thanks from Sir George Lambert—Recommended for promotion—Baltic and Heligoland, 1854–1855—Russian War—Appointment as Senior Lieutenant to the ' Rosamond '—Sighting Russian Cruiser—Court-martial—Sir Michael Seymour's opinion—Promotion stopped—Service off Scot- land—Command of the ' Otter '—On special service—Heligoland— Despatch to Lord Clarendon—Naval Review.

In December 1850, as already mentioned, Mr. Glover's command of the cutter ' Auxiliaire ' came to an end. When she was paid off he was appointed to the ' Victory,' but almost immediately transferred to the steam frigate ' Penelope,' bearing the pennant of Commodore Bruce, on the South Coast of Africa, and served in command of her tender ' Teazer.' He was at this time expecting his lieutenant's commission. Here we find him on the threshold of his African career, having learnt the various duties of his profession—seamanship, navigation, and surveying—and having already assumed the responsibility of independent commands. During his first visit to Africa he was still employed in surveying, and acquired some knowledge of the estuaries of the great African rivers. He visited St. Helena and the Cape, but did not remain long in South Africa.

In October 1851, he was promoted lieutenant, and was then employed in surveying on the China Station until appointed to the 'Sphinx,' on the East Indian Station, the following May. This occurred on the outbreak of the second war with Burmah, for the cause of which the following brief account will suffice.

The war itself proved to be of great political significance, for it ended in the annexation of the province of Pegu, which led subsequently to the establishment of British Burmah, and at last to the incorporation of the Burmese as a kingdom in the British Empire up to the frontier of China.

At the beginning of the century the King of Burmah, viewing the increase of our power in India with uneasiness, had made repeated inroads upon our Eastern frontier, so that in the spring of 1824 operations against him were undertaken. These resulted in the surrender of Rangoon and the capture of other important towns. Peace was made in 1826, and not disturbed for many years. By 1851, however, the lesson the Burmese received twenty-five years previously was forgotten, and our traders in those parts complained bitterly of the treatment to which they were subjected by the Governor of Rangoon.

Lord Dalhousie, who was then Governor-General of India, did not enter into protracted negotiations for redress; but finding no peaceful means would suffice to procure satisfaction, declared war against Burmah on April 2, 1852. He sent a force of 6,000 men, under General Godwin, from India, while Rear-Admiral Austin, then Commander-in-Chief on that Station, furnished a squadron under Commodore Lambart of the ' Fox ' (40 guns). The towns of Martaban and Rangoon were attacked and fell. Bassein was also occupied. Our line of operations was marked out by the course of the Irawadi, and having been so successful in the former war they were repeated on this occasion. Consequently Commander Tarleton was sent up the river to attack Prome.

In the meantime the ' Winchester ' (50 guns), commanded by Captain Loch, had arrived from China, and Lieutenant Glover joined the ' Sphinx ' (Commander Shadwell). At the end of August this vessel went up the Irawadi to relieve Captain Tarleton, and later on Lieutenant Glover took part in the successful expedition against Pegu which resulted in its capture. Prome had been taken previously, and our flotilla was constantly engaged in destroying defences which would harass our vessels approaching to or returning from Prome.

Thus Mr. Glover joined the ' Sphinx ' as first lieutenant on September 15, 1852. Cholera had broken out in India, and the suddenness of the deaths from its ravages caused the greatest depression. He often went out for a stroll in the morning with a friend, over whose grave he stood before sundown. The Irawadi is a broad river, with many shallows, which flows with great rapidity. The flotilla of river steamers had been the means of keeping off projected attacks from various quarters on Rangoon. Mr. Glover went up the river to survey and ascertain the proceedings of the enemy, in short, to feel the way and see what fortifications the Burmese were erecting, to get the depth of the water, and ascertain the disposition of the people towards us. He was in command of the boats of the ' Sphinx.'

Towards the end of the month the weather became hot and sultry; the mosquitos were abundant, while large black-beetles and other abominations did not add to the pleasures of Rangoon life. Steamers were constantly coming down the river to convey troops to Prome, the steam flotilla being engaged in destroying the defences which the Burmese had attempted to erect within range of their guns. The King of Ava was still determined to consider all who dared to seek our protection in the light of enemies, when some of the steamers got aground through ignorance of the navigation of the river. Villagers hastened down to assist in getting them afloat, and seemed very eager for annexation, which would prevent them from ever again suffering by the cruelties of their oppressors. The river had risen to a greater height than it had been known to rise for many years, and they attributed it to the signal inter-position of a higher Power in our favour, in order to enable our steamers to navigate the creeks without obstruction. It was held that by the Irawadi we could have a direct route to China, which could only be rendered available by keeping the King of Ava under our influence, and nothing short of the possession of the province below Prome could effect this. Every day an attack on the village of Puyendon was expected, the object being that the Burmese wished to carry off the ex-Governor of Pegu. A sufficient number of sailors and marines had to be sent to ensure the security of the place. Just at that time, to the great sorrow of all who served under him, their commander, Admiral Austin, died in harness, in the service of his country, with his flag flying—'Thus the pride of British sailors and soldiers to die.' He had shortly before suffered from an attack of cholera in Rangoon.

Mr. Glover was then sent to protect Shank Shag Keence, and the sailors were indefatigable in defending him against the Burmese. On the evening of November 19, the 'Sphinx' boats were anchored a little below Pegu. The force landed at daybreak, in a dense fog, by noon sighting the first armed Burmese, with whom they exchanged many shots during the day. In the evening the Burmese came boldly down and fired on the steamers.

Years afterwards, when describing the incidents of the day's fighting, Mr. Glover used to mention a little 'Middy' he noticed on board the 'Sphinx,' a frail, delicate-looking child, apparently little over twelve years of age, who ought to have been at his mother's side. This boy was working hard carrying powder for the guns that were keeping up a heavy firing, crying bitterly all the time, his face blackened and besmirched by powder, but never flinching for an instant as he ran along the quivering deck with the ammunition, not heeding the enemy's shots, nor the deafening roar of the guns.

The river was found to be staked. It had steep banks where the landing took place the next morning. A hard day's fighting was expected. By the time General Godwin and the attacking force had arrived at the walls of Pegu the men were suffering a great deal from fatigue and heat, but nevertheless the sailors were some of the foremost, and were conspicuous that day in the storming of Pegu. There were three hearty cheers given when the first breach in the wall was made, and they rushed in over the crumbling *débris*. Mr. Glover was specially mentioned in despatches for his coolness and bravery.

On February 3, 1853, there happened one of the darkest events which marked this war, viz., the expedition undertaken against a notorious robber chieftain called 'Mya-Myati-toon,' who had won for himself an all-powerful name in Donabew and its vicinity. He had captured our boats in their progress up and down the river, and had proved himself a Dacoit so bold and resolute, that it was deemed necessary for the safety of the transports to send a considerable force against him. This consisted of 150 seamen, 60 marines and 25 officers. Mr. Glover was in command of two paddle-box boats which were sent up the Irawadi. The river was overhung by trees and bamboos growing to the water's edge, affording cover to numbers of the enemy, who kept up a heavy fire. Consequently orders were given that before dawn the boats should be manned and move silently up the river. Lieutenant Glover was in the leading boat, and passed as close to the high banks as possible in order that the brushwood and long grass might assist in concealing him and his men from the enemy. The force was landed at six in the morning, and formed on the plains of Donabew. It consisted of 142 officers and men of the 'Winchester,' 20 from the 'Fox,' 20 of the 'Sphinx,' and about 300 men of the 60th Bengal Native Infantry, with three field pieces dragged by Burmese, and two Europeans to each gun. After about two hours' preparation they moved off towards the forest. When they had advanced about a mile through a thick jungle, composed of high trees and underwood, two musket shots were fired by the enemy, evidently as a signal; and a few shots were interchanged with them by the advance guard. They continued to march comparatively unmolested until three o'clock, when they arrived at an open space with a few deserted huts, and encamped there for the night. Some shots were fired during the night, but they were not aroused until five o'clock the following morning, when, after a hearty breakfast, the march was resumed through the jungle, the ground on each side showing evident signs of recent occupation. The guns were moved with great difficulty owing to huge trunks of trees having fallen across the path. On arriving at a creek the advance guard, led by Captain Loch, were received by a tremendous fire on both flanks and in front. The guns were dragged forward, but the Burmese attached to them dropped everything and ran off into the bush. The force instantly opened fire, guided only by the flashes of the guns of the invisible enemy, many of whom were hidden in the branches of trees above their heads. The seamen and marines pushed on to the front, led by Captain Loch, but while he was rushing on, a ball struck him in the abdomen, carrying the broken fragments of his watch, which was dangling loose, into his body. The officers fell in numbers, fifty of the Europeans were killed and wounded; and there being no prospect of crossing the creek, owing to its width and depth, a retreat was ordered. Lieutenant Glover, struck by a bullet, which entered close to the corner of the right eye, splitting the bone and coming out just above the ear, fell insensible behind some timber. Commander Lambert of the 'Fox,' upon whom the command then devolved, endeavoured to save the guns, but found that if he did so it would be impossible to carry off the wounded, and in consequence, after dismounting and spiking them and blowing up the ammunition, they retired.

Lieutenant Glover had been lying behind the fallen timber of a stockade over which numbers of Burmese had passed, apparently not noticing him, thinking he was dead. When recovering consciousness he was aroused by the doctor turning him over, saying, 'Poor Glover's gone too, there is no one left to command,' and on hearing this he staggered to his feet. In spite of his severe wound and great loss of blood, he exerted himself in encouraging the men, who were greatly exhausted, in assisting the wounded and conveying them away from under fire. The enemy continued to press heavily on the rear-guard. Lieutenant Glover was supported by two of his 'Sphinx' men, his arms round their necks, the mortally wounded Captain Loch being carried by his side. About a mile from the scene of the disaster, as they were crossing the dry bed of a stream, the enemy again opened a heavy fire on both sides, which struck down two of the men who were carrying Captain Loch; and the men of the 'Fox,' being exhausted and unable to carry their captain, Lieutenant Glover ordered his bearers to raise Captain Loch, while he himself was obliged to stagger on without further assistance. After many halts to enable the rear-guard to keep up, the force came to a stream three miles from Donabew just before dark, having been harassed by the enemy the whole day. An indescribable scene of confusion here ensued. Every man rushed into the muddy water to quench his raging thirst. The wounded were dropped by the Burmese bearers, and there was great difficulty in getting them to convey the sufferers further; indeed, it was only by pointing muskets at their heads that they could be induced to move at all.

Equal difficulty was experienced in getting the Sepoys to form a rear-guard, they having to be driven back by the flat of the officers' swords. An eye-witness says, ' I specially noticed Glover of the " Sphinx," who, after lying on the ground insensible from a severe wound in the head, got up again, and was foremost in encouraging the men all the way. Carrying off the wounded was a most harassing duty, as the retreat to the boats had to be made for several miles through a thick jungle, the enemy following close. Though never showing, they kept up a galling fire, which had a very demoralising effect on the men already in retreat. The heat was also great, but in spite of it, and the weak state he was in, Glover never flagged for a moment in his efforts to save his comrades, whom to abandon, all knew was to leave to certain death and mutilation. At length, about half-past eight, they reached Donabew and embarked the wounded.' Thus ended this fateful day, in which there were eighty-one killed and wounded, the greater part of the loss falling on the officers, who were picked out by the Burmese sharpshooters. On Mr. Glover's return to the ship the doctor pronounced his wound even worse than was supposed. Fortunately, the sight of the eye was uninjured, but he suffered pain in it till the end of his life. He was also in a very exhausted condition from loss of

blood, which had trickled down and filled his boots.
But there was no time now to rest, as the ' Sphinx '
was ordered to England and was short of officers,
therefore, with head bound up, he was obliged to
take command and navigate her home. A shipmate
writes : ' I remember him perfectly as he was in
those days, youthful looking for his age, but with a
frame of iron, which he never spared at the call of
duty, and which enabled him to get through more
work than any ordinary man, and led him sometimes
to expect rather more from others, not so gifted,
than they were well able to perform. His zeal and
energy were untiring, and had a most inspiriting
effect on all who served with him. . . . I can
recollect how we midshipmen were roused by his
example, and also how hard and cheerfully the
men worked for him at a time when their endurance and temper were severely tried by the strain
put upon them through the extra work and exposure entailed by the war. . . . He was always a
favourite with them, for though strict and exacting
where duty was concerned, he had a pleasant,
cheery manner, and they willingly shared hard
work with an officer who showed a capacity for it
himself. . . . During his passage home, on more
than one occasion the doctor had to exercise his
authority and insist on Mr. Glover taking more
care of himself, for I remember his wound broke

out once or twice, owing to his over-exerting himself on the voyage.' On arriving in England he saw the ' Sphinx ' paid off at Portsmouth on July 22, 1853. He was specially mentioned in despatches, and received the public thanks of Rear-Admiral Sir George Lambert for his services while in Burmah, and for his gallantry at Pegu and Donabew. Indeed, he was specially recommended for promotion for his signally good conduct, but for this he was considered too young by the Admiralty, being then in his twenty-third year.

While these events were occurring in the East, a storm was brewing in Europe, which, the following year, involved us in what is now known as the ' Crimean War.' In the beginning of 1853 there were indications that the Czar of Russia considered the time had arrived when certain matters in which Turkey was directly concerned should be remedied, and our ambassador at St. Petersburg was sounded as to the view this country would take of any proposed action. One matter was that of the Christian subjects in Turkey, and the holy places in Palestine; while the other was that of the Danubian Principalities—Moldavia and Wallachia. In June 1853, the Czar invaded the Danubian Principalities, and Turkey declared war against Russia.

Events now proceeded rapidly, though negotiations were still maintained between the British and Russian Governments. England and France were acting in concert, and in October their fleets passed through the Dardanelles and anchored off Constantinople.

This was a direct menace to Russia, against which her ambassador in London vigorously protested.

Then occurred an event which caused great indignation in England, as well as other countries, though it was an incident of war justifiable under such conditions as prevailed between the two countries.

A squadron of Turkish frigates were lying at Sinope in the Black Sea during November 1853. The commander was aware of, and had pointed out to the authorities at Constantinople, his dangerous position within a short distance of Sebastopol, where a powerful Russian fleet was collected. No heed was taken of his warning, and the opportunity was not lost by the enemy. On November 30, a Russian squadron under Admiral Nachimoff stood into the Bay of Sinope. Having anchored, they poured in a tremendous fire upon the Turkish frigates. In a little over an hour all were destroyed except one small steamer, which carried the news to Constantinople. To prevent a repetition of such acts the allied fleets entered the Black Sea in

January 1854, and war became inevitable. For a short time longer the diplomatists on both sides kept up negotiations in the hope of preserving peace, but this had become impossible, and, on March 23, Queen Victoria declared war against Russia.

It is unnecessary here to dwell further upon what took place in the Black Sea, for it was in the Baltic the subject of this memoir was destined next to see service. After returning home in the ' Sphinx,' and being a short time on shore, Lieutenant Glover was appointed to the ' Royal George,' in which ship he served in home waters till barely a month before the declaration of war with Russia. He was still suffering from the effects of his wound, and the doctors did not consider it advisable for him to seek active service in a hot climate. It was not, however, likely that he would remain inactive while such stirring measures were in contemplation. For the navy, the chief expectation of glory in the coming war was in the Baltic. There lay the principal forts and arsenals of Russia and her most powerful fleet. The Government exerted all its energies to despatch thither a squadron which could not be surpassed, and which would be able to deal some severe blow to the enemy, either in the destruction of its fleet, should it venture to face ours, or in the capture of some important stronghold.   To equip such a squadron was no easy task, for the navy had been suffered to decline for many years, both in ships and men.   Admiral Sir Charles Napier was selected to command the Baltic fleet. Sir Charles Napier's flagship was the screw line of battleship ' Duke of Wellington ' (130 guns), and, placed under his command, were eighteen other ships of the line, eleven frigates, and a similar number of smaller vessels, the majority being screw steamers.   Portsmouth, Plymouth and Sheerness had to furnish this force.   At the last-named port the 6-gun paddle sloop ' Rosamond ' was commissioned for the Baltic by Commander George Wodehouse, and Lieutenant Glover was appointed to her as senior lieutenant on March 3, 1854.   It was three weeks before she sailed and proceeded to Dover, where she remained—doubtless completing her crew—until April 16.

The ' Rosamond ' then proceeded to the North Sea and joined the Admiral, who had gone out in the middle of March with a portion of his fleet, leaving the rest to follow as they were ready.   The ' Rosamond ' met the fleet off Gottska Sandö, a small island between Faro Sound and the Gulf of Finland, and she continued in that neighbourhood for some time to intercept any vessel that might pass down the Baltic.   Little, however, of interest appears to have occurred as far as this ship is concerned, with

the exception of two incidents, which are described
in a letter from a friend of Lieutenant Glover, who
was well acquainted with the circumstances :—

'The "Rosamond" was steaming on her course
when a smart-looking vessel was observed proceeding leisurely close in shore. Mr. Glover said they
"might cut her off and capture her," but the captain thought it would not be prudent to attempt it
as the enemy was in force in the neighbourhood.
Lieutenant Glover rejoined, "You don't know, you
might be losing the chance of a lifetime by neglect-
ing it." They watched the strange vessel, which
presently passed out of gunshot distance, when the
Russian standard was run up and a royal salute
was fired. It turned out that the Emperor was on
board ! ! ! Mr. Glover said he thought they might
have effected the capture, and if so the war would
doubtless have been brought to an early close.'
Soon after this incident happened, some newspapers
were brought on board containing an account of
'The wonderful escape of the Emperor from an
English cruiser.' Mr. Glover's despair was even
greater than when the captain refused to follow his
advice, on which occasion he shut himself up in his
cabin, and it was not safe to speak to him till he
had got over his disappointment.

'The medical officer on board the "Rosamond"
at this time was a very irascible man, who quar-

relled constantly with every shipmate. This officer one day spoke very disrespectfully of Her Majesty, when Mr. Glover said, " Wearing the uniform you do, you ought to be ashamed of yourself for so speaking of the Queen," upon which the doctor repeated the offence. Whereupon the lieutenant said, " If it were not for your uniform I would pull your nose." The doctor made a service matter of it, reported it to the Admiral, and called for a court-martial on Mr. Glover for using language calculated to lead to a breach of the naval regulations. But while he was under arrest the ship ran aground, and the only man to get her off again was the captive lieutenant, who was sent for from below. When the court was held Mr. Glover was formally acquitted. The president of the court was Admiral Sir Michael Seymour, G.C.B., who was a personal friend of mine, and upon the return to England of the expedition at the termination of the season in the Baltic, I took occasion to express my hope that my young friend Glover had not suffered in his estimation through the court-martial, and he replied, " No, I think all the better of him for it, both for his outspoken loyalty and his manly resentment of an insult to the Queen." Nevertheless, it was in consequence of this that his promotion was stopped, and he went out to Africa.'

On November 19, 1854, Lieutenant Glover, by

order of the Commander-in-Chief, took active command of the 'Rosamond,' on the promotion of Commander Wodehouse. She was then at Kiel, and winter approaching, it was necessary for the fleet to leave the Baltic before the ice set in. Acting-Commander Glover therefore brought the 'Rosamond' home, and on arrival, at the beginning of December, she was employed on the Scotch coast. This was not very congenial service to one of Mr. Glover's temperament.

But early in the following year he was offered an appointment for a duty which, besides being of an exciting nature, required great discretion and ability. The particulars of this service cannot be given in their fullest detail. Indeed, he was unaware of them when receiving his orders from the Admiralty at Woolwich, in March 1855, to fit out the 'Otter' for 'particular service,' the nature of which did not then transpire. In May he was despatched with 'sealed orders,' and found in them that he was to proceed to the Elbe for the purpose of conveying to Heligoland recruits for the British German Legion assembling at that island. In reference to the war with Russia some general understanding or agreement had been formed between England and Germany, to the effect that Germans might of their own free will enlist in the British military service. Heligoland was a station

where recruits would be assembled.   On his arrival
at this island Mr. Glover found about fifty men in
garrison.   There was anxious vigilance on the part
of the several lesser states bordering on the Elbe
and Weser to prevent any exit from their territory
to persons travelling to Heligoland, except in the
strictest accordance with law.   Consequently Lieutenant Glover's endeavours to take the recruits
from the mainland to Heligoland were for a time
checked.   But after an interview with the German
agent, finding he was jealously watched, Mr. Glover
thought it advisable to act entirely on his own
resources and effect the object for which he was
sent by the aid of his own knowledge of the
German language and such information as he
could procure.   It was an anxious time, by reason
of the espionage continually exercised over his
movements, and the difficulty of avoiding infringe-
ment of the laws.   That he succeeded in all this
will be seen from the following letter from the
agent at Hamburg to the Earl of Clarendon :—

'I hope that I am not overstepping the
bounds that I ought to observe in my official
communication, if I venture to lay before you the
testimony that I conceive is but justly due to the
services of Lieutenant Glover, commanding H.M.S.
steam-ship " Otter," who was employed during last
summer, and until very lately, in conveying persons

who wished to take service in the Foreign Legion from the coasts in this neighbourhood to Heligoland. Knowing as I did the anxious vigilance of the neighbouring Governments to obtain even the slightest ground for complaint, I was not without apprehension, when a vessel under H.M.S. flag first entered the Elbe, lest the officer in command might in his zeal for the performance of his duty be led to do anything that could be construed into a violation of the law, and thus cause misunderstanding between Her Majesty's Government and the Government of the States bordering on the Elbe and Weser. But I have great satisfaction in stating to your lordship that, throughout, Lieutenant Glover acted, as far as came under my observation, with the greatest zeal and success in carrying out his instructions; nevertheless, he, in no instance, committed any act which could possibly be deemed a breach of their laws; while the services that he was engaged in were of an arduous and difficult nature, requiring much tact and discrimination. I therefore beg to submit this statement on behalf of Mr. Glover, with whom I was quite unacquainted before he arrived in the Elbe, trusting that if my doing so may not be strictly in accordance with my duties, yet, under the circumstances, I shall stand excused.'

The island of Heligoland is a plateau with steep

sea-washed cliffs. The 'Otter' would lie under the cliffs during the day and her commander could exercise his discretion in taking her into the waters of Germany at such hours as might best suit the purpose for which she had been sent by the British Government. In September 1855 she was withdrawn from this service. During a period of four months she had conveyed upwards of eight hundred recruits to Heligoland from the surrounding country. After the withdrawal she took part in the great naval review when the Queen inspected the ships on their return from the Baltic and Black Sea.

CHAPTER III

A CRITICAL point had now been reached in Mr. Glover's life. It may indeed be called a turning point in his career, for it really led to several steps in his subsequent advancement. He was now about to enter that region of the Niger which abounded in capabilities and possibilities, some of which have been and are still being realised for the benefit of the British Empire. He was to follow illustrious explorers of his own nation and of other nations in that quarter. But he was to be the first person to make official surveys for England on the Niger; and his work was to be the foundation for the charts and maps of the British Government in that extensive valley.

At this time the attention of the scientific world in England was directed to the Niger; and the Royal Geographical Society in particular, under the presidentship of Sir Roderick Murchison, urged

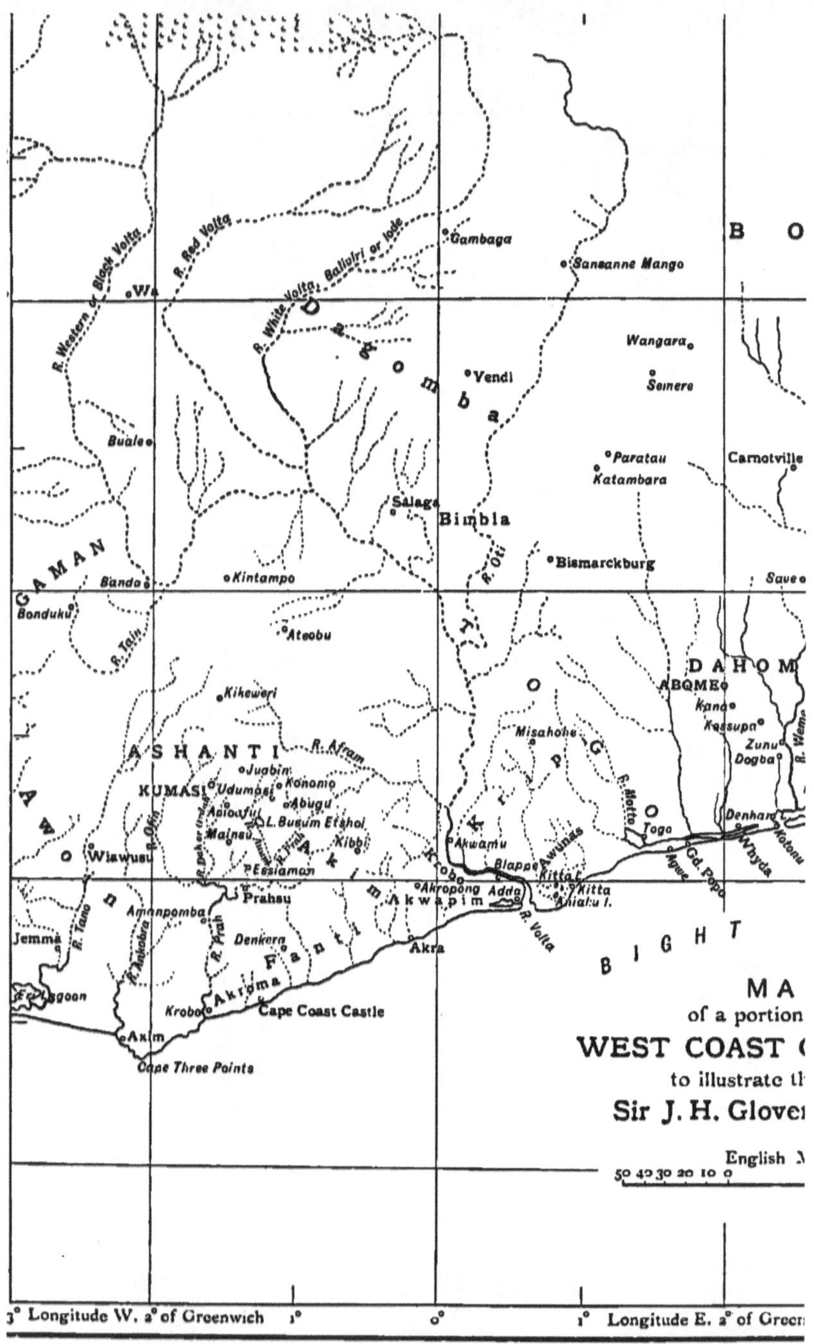

B O
Gambaga
Sansanne Mango
Wa
R. Western or Black Volta
R. Red Volta
R. White Volta
Baliuiri or Iode
D A H O M b a
Wangara
Vendi
Semere
Buale
Paratau
Katambara
Carnotville
Salage
Bimbla
Bando
Kintampo
Bismarckburg
Save
Bonduku
R. Tain
Ateobu
D A H O M
ABQME
Kano
Kikeweri
Kassupa
Misahohe
Zunu
Dogba
R. Weme
A S H A N T I
R. Afram
Juabin
KUMASI
Udumasi
Konomo
Abugu
Ajoufu
L. Busum Etshoi
Denhar
R. Ofin
Mainsu
L. Prah
Kibbi
Togo
Wiawusi
Essiaman
Akwamu
Awunas
Whyda
Motonu
Krobo
Blappe
Kittat
G.d. Popo
Akropong
Adda
Kitta
Akwapim
Ahiaku I.
Jemma
Amanpomba
Prahsu
B I G H T
R. Tano
R. Ankobra
R. Prah
Denkera
R. Volta
Akra
Fa Lagoon
Krobo
Cape Coast Castle
Axim
Cape Three Points
M A
of a portion
WEST COAST (
to illustrate th
Sir J. H. Glover
English
50 40 30 20 10 0
3° Longitude W. 2° of Greenwich   1°   0°   1° Longitude E. 2° of Green
London: Smith,

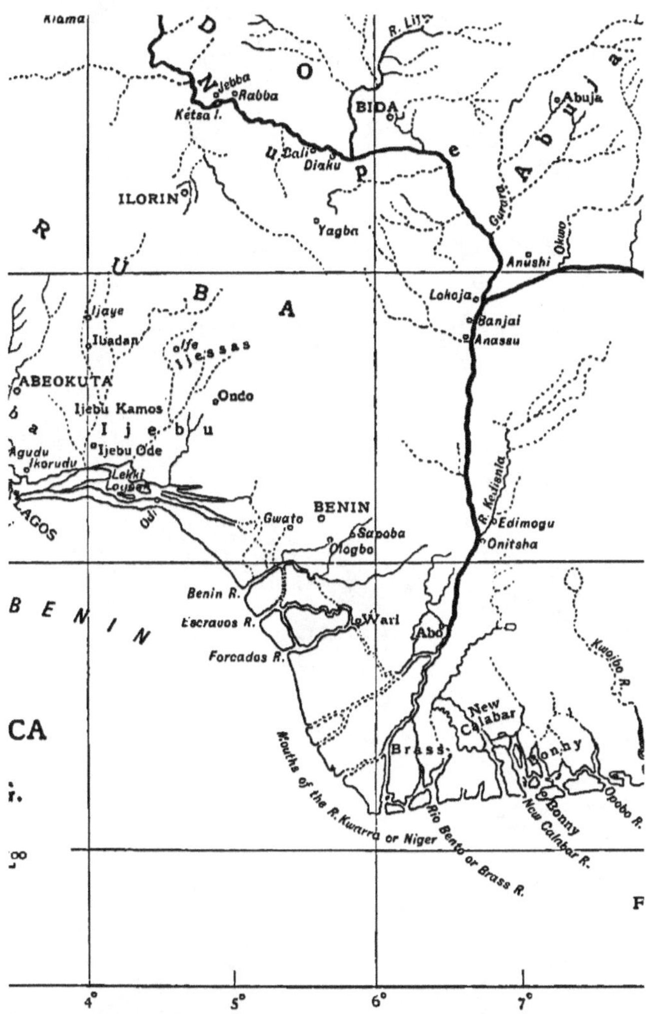

; Waterloo Place.

the British Government to undertake surveys and other scientific operations there. These representations had such weight with the Foreign Department, of which the Earl of Clarendon was then the head, that his lordship decided to despatch an expedition, of which the scientific head was Dr. Baikie, while the surveying work was entrusted to Mr. Glover, whose previous experience, as already described, gave him special qualifications.

Mr. Glover left the 'Otter' March 3, 1857, and the next day was appointed by the Foreign Office to join the River Niger expedition.[1] He was employed in this service until 1861, during which he surveyed the lagoons at Lagos, and that portion of the River Niger comprised between Boussa and the sea. After receiving his orders in England for this service, he was during the next few weeks busily employed in gathering his outfit, guns, rifles, surveying instruments, and all requirements for a protracted stay in Africa. The yawl screw steamer 'Dayspring,' specially built and fitted out for the expedition by Laird Bros., Birkenhead, was an iron vessel of 77 gross register tonnage, with engines of about 100 indicated horse-power, driving a screw propeller. The dimensions of the vessel were :— Length, 76 ft. 3 in.; beam, 22 ft.; depth in hold,

---

[1] For the geographical features and climate in this and succeeding chapters, reference may be made to the Introduction to this Memoir.

5 ft. 8 in., while her figure-head was a dove bearing an olive branch. She carried, with Captain Grant, her commander, and the officers of the ship, in all sixteen Englishmen, who trusted to engaging a crew of natives to make up her complement at Fernando Po, where Lieutenant Glover was to meet Dr. Baikie, naturalist and chief of the expedition, and Mr. Davis, afterwards deputy surgeon-general. In a letter from the latter he says: 'Glover and I were warm friends from the first, and never had a difference or misunderstanding; though nominally second, he was really chief of that Niger Expedition.' A few extracts from Mr. Davis's journal will describe the objects of this expedition and the meeting at Fernando Po of those who took part in it. The 'Dayspring' sailed from Liverpool on Thursday, May 7, 1857 :—

'I have been asked to give some information regarding my late friend Sir John Glover, and I write with a deep sense of regret that he is no more. An Irish peasant once said of a departed friend, "The Lord be good to his soul, he was a whole man." This could be said of Glover: he was a whole man, truthful, generous, wise and brave, a naval officer like Peel and Goodenough—a born leader of men. I first met him at Fernando Po, West Africa, June 22, 1857, when he arrived there in the "Dayspring" which was to convey the expedition under Dr. Baikie up the River Niger. Two months previously Dr. Baikie arrived at Sierra Leone, and I was discharged from H.M.S. " Hecla " for service as medical officer of the expedition. We remained a month at Sierra Leone, making preparations and selecting men likely to be useful as interpreters, and then proceeded in the mail steamer to Fernando Po. The members of the Government party were Dr. Baikie in command, Lieutenant Glover, Mr. May (second master for surveying purposes), Mr. Barter (botanist), Mr. Dalton (zoologist), and Fisher, Mr. Glover's servant. With Captain Grant and the officers of the " Dayspring," in all sixteen Englishmen, and a crew composed of Kroomen and other Africans, the total was 106.

'The objects of the expedition were to extend geographical knowledge of Central Africa, to cultivate friendly relations with the natives, to make treaties with them, to select sites for future towns or settlements, and, broadly speaking, to further British interests and the civilisation of Africa. The Rev. Dr. Crowther (now Bishop Crowther) and the Rev. Dr. Taylor (since dead), both natives of Yoruba, joined our party, with some lay agents to work under them.

'Dr. Baikie's first exploration of the River Binue and Kwarra, published by Murray in 1856, should be consulted, as no record of our expedition of 1857–58 was ever published, owing to the death of Dr. Baikie and absence of Lieutenant Glover.'

The following extracts from Mr. Glover's journal describes the voyage of the 'Dayspring' after she left Liverpool, and his life during the next few months in Africa, while he was engaged in the survey of the Niger, and in shooting a collection of birds for the expedition, which were sent home to the British Museum and afterwards placed in the South Kensington Museum. This journal was kept for and addressed to the lady mentioned at the end of the first chapter :—

'I sent you a letter by the pilot last night telling you of our sailing and the fair promise with which we commenced our voyage. We have had a fine breeze all day from the S.S.E., and the little "Dayspring," with wings outspread, is speeding gallantly on her way to the warm south. We have been most fortunate in our start; let us take it as a happy omen, and trust that the great Being, whose hand is in all, smiles upon our mission of mercy and peace, and that indeed our little vessel may be bearing, to those regions of ceaseless warfare and strife, the olive branch of peace. I did not write last night for, I believe, the first time for many days past; I rested. Just as Fisher had brought some tea and I was lying down, I was wakened by screams on deck. Rushing out of my cabin into the saloon, I felt a violent shock, which almost threw me on my face, at the same time the vessel's head was depressed. On gaining the deck I found that a large barque was under our bow. The little "Dayspring" bounded away some 20 yards, so light and buoyant is she on the water. The barque passed on, having knocked away our bow-sprit, jibboom and pretty figure-head, "the dove with the olive branch." Of course it has left us in a most crippled state, and it will detain us at Madeira while the defects are being made good. I went below again to assist the captain and crew to clear the deck. We are just off the Bay of Biscay, and the roughness of its waters seemed determined to compel our homage, for we had to reduce our sail before the freshening breeze, which soon increased to a gale from the south-west, with heavy seas and squalls of rain. I was at the helm all the forenoon, assisted by Fisher. We have only a few men, just enough to navigate the vessel to the coast, where we shall engage a regular crew of fifty men. There was not a dry bed on board. I slept on a sofa abaft, while Fisher found a dry place on the deck beside me, "Ven" (the dog) sleeping by his side. Most thankful was I to Him who rules the winds and waves when last night the storm broke.

'*Sunday.*—I have been thinking of all the plans

that must be carried out before I can return to England from this, our crusade against the Moslem, for so it really is, only, we will hope, a bloodless one. And while dressing, my eyes rested on my picture of the Saviour, and the thought came into my mind and the words to my lips : " That shall be the altar-piece for the first church in Central Africa, the seat at no distant time of the bishopric ; and I will build that church at our trading station, the very centre of this hitherto sealed land, with its great wide rivers wandering out east and west; and all their small tributary streams which flow into them, north and south, and are navigable for the small canoes of the country, must bear from this central station the trade and civilisation of England, as the means to the end, that great end, for which I feel that God's blessing goes with us."

'At present all these regions depend entirely on caravans from Tripoli across the desert. Kano is the central emporium, the place where all the produce from all parts is collected before it is despatched to Tripoli, and where all goods are brought from Tripoli before being dispersed to all the countries of Central Africa. It takes fourteen months to get back the caravans from Tripoli with goods from Europe, while from our station, Kano, it is only thirty days' easy travelling, and that without risk. See what Laird's Town must become, with splendid rivers running out for six hundred miles and more. I want an altar-cloth and a bell, and the church, small though it may be, will be ready when they arrive. I mean to make this specially my work; it will be the ground of a future great bishopric, and it will be something to have planted the first "mustard seed" in Laird's Town.

'*May* 29*th*.—I tried to get the doctor to join me in a lesson in Haussa. I find it so simple when we are together, and so heart-breaking alone. There are no rules, and the formation of the plural is most whimsical; for instance, " a great sheep " is " Baba Dunkia," the plural of which is " Maisaza Dumakia." We are sailing southward in such a summer sea, the tiny rippling waves glittering in the bright moonlight, just off Cape de Verd Island, and fairly within the tropics. Strange things come to the ship's side to look at us, the monsters of the deep, sperm whales and porpoises. This morning we sailed through a whole fleet of the beautiful nautilus, with their delicate sails of silver silk dancing merrily over the tiny waves. I had never seen anything like it before; well might the imagination of our first voyagers delight to fancy that they bore the souls of deceased mariners. Last night, attracted by our light, enough flying fishes flew on board to give us a fresh dish for breakfast.   But the strangest of all sea monsters was the sea-serpent which was floating lazily on the top of the water.   All at once it raised itself some feet out of the water and turned its snake-like head round to look at us.   I flew for my rifle, but we had passed out of gunshot by the time I returned, arriving only to see the creature sink slowly back into the sea.   To-night we have the Southern Cross shining in all its glorious splendour, and I have been gazing at it for hours.

'*Cape Palmas*.—Our decks have been all day covered with half-naked savages.   We have not been very successful amongst them.   They are somewhat grasping in their demands, as the bargain is for what they call " war palaver," not " palm-oil palaver," that is, instead of their being required to go on the rivers and load our ship with palm oil, we are taking them to the war-country.   I hardly know whether to call the whole scene ridiculous or sad : perhaps the latter.   They are nearly always at war with their neighbours on either side of them, and the fair sex are invariably the cause.   They asked for muskets and powder, as they are at war at the present moment, and told us that they had killed six of the next town "this moon"; pretty well, considering that this is only the 12th, and their fighting is more demonstrative than sanguinary. The word " chop " with them means something to eat, and stands for breakfast, dinner, or supper, according to the time of the day. The captain asked them if they had made "chop" of the six; upon which a tall gentleman, whose full dress consisted of six or seven ivory armlets reaching from the left wrist to the elbow, a piece of cloth round the loins, and an English beaver hat, covered with a coloured silk handkerchief to protect it from the rain, said, "No, sir, we gentleman, we kill, we no make much chop."

'And now to give you as good an idea as I can of the hooting, screaming, fighting, and bargaining by which we have been surrounded these two days. At early dawn, about twenty or thirty canoes were seen coming from the shore, each bearing from four to seven men. The men sitting at the bottom of the canoe facing the bow propel it with paddles, which they use in the water as you may have seen a gardener use his spade while filling up a hole back-handed. Swarms of canoes come alongside and the crew climb up. The greater number jump overboard and swim to the ship, and come towards you shaking you by the hand, assuring you that "Prince Albert" is glad to see you, or it may be "King Tom," "Jack Smoke," "Black Bill," "Seabreeze," "Bottle of Beer," and such like dignified names which distinguish their head men. These are "gentlemen" who, having saved enough to buy from two to four wives, are rich men, and have given up the sea. They came on this occasion to hire out their sons, who, when they are engaged, receive two months' pay in advance—that is, two pieces of cotton cloth like pocket handkerchiefs, each piece containing fourteen yards, and five shillings. The whole of this these affectionate fathers take to themselves, and as soon as the bargain is complete, the sons are locked up until the canoes are gone, and the ship at sea, else they would jump overboard and be off. Such is the custom of the country. Once started they must remain with us, for if they were to run away the people amongst whom we are going would make slaves of them.

'*Fernando Po, June* 17*th.*—At last, after forty-seven days' passage, we arrived at Fernando Po. Doctor Baikie carried me on shore to dine with the Spanish Governor, a Dutchman. I liked Mr. Crowther's [afterwards Bishop Crowther] appearance very much, as well as that of a Dr. Taylor, also black, who goes with us.

'We walked beneath palms and cedars, orange, lemons, limes, and guava trees forming a mass of tangled underwood to the splendid forest of stately cedars and the rich cotton trees, looking such monsters of the wood.

'I was up at daybreak taking angles and sights for our chronometers, and had a visit from Captain

Close and one of his lieutenants, who was " mid " of my watch in the " Winchester." It has been raining as it only can in the tropics. I found Dr. Baikie with an attack of fever. I am the only one, out of a party of eleven, not sick ; even the captain is ill.

' *Sunday, July 5th.*—Our last day at sea, for to-night we get to the bar of Rio Bento in St. John's river, called by the English traders the Brass, by which we are to enter Africa. We have still large bunches of bananas hanging to the beams to ripen, while opposite to me are great baskets of oranges and lemons. It is so strange that I have come back to all this. I like it so much, this summer land of fruit and flowers. The harbour is very pretty, and the trees which grow quite into the water are most luxuriant. There are five English vessels taking in palm oil, and the English Cask Houses on shore, dotted among the splendid foliage, give an air of life and movement to this otherwise solitary and deserted scenery. Will it always be so ? This must eventually be the centre port of Central Africa. I have been busy all yesterday making a plan to send to Lord Clarendon for the ease of the many ships which we hope will soon follow us up the Niger. It poured most piteously the whole time, and I was away from early dawn and did not return till late in the evening.

'*July* 20*th*.—We entered the creek which unites the two rivers, the Niger and the Brass. It is too narrow for vessels to pass in the channel. I must endeavour to give you an idea of the—well, I can hardly give a name to it, for from the one river to the other I could find no spot of ground on which to land. The whole is one entire swamp, covered at high water and exposed at low water, about the width of five feet, of the most stinking mud the earth ever produced, so densely covered with mangrove trees as to be quite impenetrable. I believe this describes every feature of its scenery, and yet withal it is very pretty, sometimes even beautiful. The trees are of the most intense green, almost meeting overhead, their fantastically-shaped stems and roots, with the branches and many creepers, hanging gracefully into the stream, forming pretty vistas through which little vessels can make their way. Innumerable parrots overhead screamed in discord all their own, and the long-legged cranes and graceful white egrets were disturbed, perhaps for the first time, in their joint fishing preserves. I never go out of the ship without a gun or rifle, and seldom return with less than a brace of some new variety or pelicans, and hope to have a fine collection of tropical birds to send home.

'From river to river is ten miles, and the lagoon stretches half-way. The entire country is one delta, with its countless palms and large silk-cotton trees, but the scenery tires the eyes.

'Dr. Baikie was evidently most anxious to get into the open waters of the Niger, and asked if I would attempt the creek. I said "Yes," though I thought it just possible we should stick in the mud, which we did. The morning tide floated us again. How shall I describe the tortures of that night! The mosquitos and sand flies devoured us, and, tired as I was, I walked the deck the entire night and smoked, by which I kept my face at least free from them. We started again early and found it, even in the daylight, difficult getting the vessel through this creek. After making a plan of the ditch, at high tide we got her off and proceeded up the river. Since then, my time has been occupied in one incessant chaining and fixing the various points and windings of the river as we ascend. We weigh anchor as soon as it is light enough for me to see, and I sketch till dark.

'On Saturday Dr. Baikie came to me and said that, owing to the lateness of the season, he wished to weigh anchor and go on after Morning Service on Sunday. I said "Very well"; but if I had been chief I would not have done it; so another Sunday passed working hard, and I have not found time to write, except for a few minutes when anchoring at a village yesterday, where we met his sable majesty of Abo, a very tall man of about thirty-five, dressed in the scarlet coat like what is worn by a mail-coach guard, parti-coloured trousers, the whole surmounted by a cardinal's hat. The buttons on the coat had a crown with a " V.R.," as had also his sword, which was carried before him. He brought with him his favourite wife, a girl about sixteen, rather pretty, whose duties in public seemed to be to sit at his feet and fan him, and when he spat, which he continually did over her, she carefully wiped the deck clean. I had written thus far when his majesty made his appearance for a second visit, bringing this time seven wives, his brother's and his own, as well as his brother's suite.

' *August* 16*th*.—I have not had a single moment to write since July 26. I have had a sharp attack of fever and ague, accompanied by wretched sickness. Now I am much better, and do not feel greatly weakened by my illness. On our first stoppage on the left bank of the river, I received a message from Dr. Baikie asking me to bring my rifle and shoot a bullock which the king had given us. Presents are the custom all over Africa. Very nice, you will say, but a return is always expected, and you may put it down as a rule that it is a very expensive mode of buying things. These bullocks all run wild in the bush, and when they give you one you must get it the best way you can. I have begged Dr. Baikie always to call me in on those occasions, as it gives me practice for nobler game. When the king gave the bullock he thought that of course we should not go to look for it, and when I, quite different in costume and appearance from those who had preceded me, entered his yard, rifle in hand, with half the town following at my heels, his majesty seemed not at all sure that I had not come to shoot him. His uneasiness appeared rather to increase when I said I had come to shoot the bullock, and there was some demur. At last, thinking it might be the easiest way to get rid of his visitors, he said he would show me the way himself, but assured me the bullock was a very wild one. This is a land of war, distrust, and rapine : you never take a cup of water without making the donor taste it before you. He led the way with the greatest distrust as we approached near the ground. I cocked my gun to examine the priming, and you would have laughed to have seen the start his poor frightened majesty gave. After all, I lost my sport. An eagle soared over our heads and my ball brought it to the ground. The people who were with me screamed and ran into the town, and when I entered it all avoided me as if I had the plague. They have not the slightest idea of attempting to

shoot a bird on the wing; a bullock or any wild
animal always takes about ten or twelve shots
before it is brought down, so that I had performed
a feat which, in their eyes, stamped me at once as
a magician.

' *September 9th.*—My trip up the mountain
yesterday was very successful, the party consisting
of Dr. Davis and Dr. Barter, the naturalist, with
five blacks to carry my instruments and our neces-
saries, and a guide, spear in hand. On landing, I
shot a white vulture which was sent on board to
be preserved. Our path lay over a pleasant upland
country for about five miles, until we came to the
base of the mountain, and after ascending about
five hundred feet we arrived at a pretty little plain,
nicely cultivated and studded with trees. A ditch
'and mud wall, loop-holed for shooting arrows,
barred our further progress, and beyond it the top
of some huts, comprising a town, peeped through
the trees. I proposed staying for breakfast under
a shady tree, and sending to tell the king of the
mountains that we wished to call upon him.
Before our repast was ended, a messenger came
from the king bidding us welcome, and saying that
he had never seen a white man, and was delighted
that we had come. He received us most warmly,
and seated on leopard skins we drank his country
beer with great relish. This hut of audience was

soon crowded, and nothing escaped the most scrutinising admiration. By this time I am almost mahogany in colour and certainly not a white man, while my two companions are. The greatest compliment which my guide and admirer Abdul Kader can pay me is that I am an Arab. But I am glad to say I am quite well, and rather more slim than when I left England, though I shall return with an old face and grey hair. We remained on the mountain until the setting sun warned me to put up my sketch book and descend. The view was grand, extending over 400 square miles—we were then 1,300 feet above the sea-level. The river winding its way along brought some sad thoughts to my mind, since, from all its various sources, until its entrance into the sea, oppression, bloodshed, wrong, and darkness, mar with foul spots its splendid stream. A fatality seems to hang over it. May it please God that we shall aid in its removal, and that soon commerce, as a means to a greater end, may cover its waters with other burdens than slaves, and the results of war and depredation.

'Next day brought us to the mouth of the Kedisnia river where lives the dreaded Othanan Yacki, Dansatah, and Dando, three chiefs of the Fallanie or Fallana. The first of these was king of this country some fourteen years ago, but was driven from it by his half-brother Dansatah.   The Fallanie up to the end of the last century were wandering cow-herds, moving from place to place as their cattle required pasture, encamping always outside the walls of towns and villages, never mixing with the Kaffir or heathen people of the land. This was the history when Othanan Yacki sent messengers bringing us welcome and a basket of Kola nuts and an invitation to proceed to Bida.

'I had fever accompanied by ague for two days, but would not give in, being able to hold out.   Dr. Baikie being ill, I was obliged to go, as the king's messages were imperative.   Mr. Crowther said he would come too, and I felt a gallop would cure my fever.   The horses were fresh, and we had to wait for our lagging attendants before arriving at the huts the king had prepared for us.   We found the chief hut twenty feet in diameter, the very picture of comfort.   Large logs burnt clear and bright on the ground in the centre, beside it stood an earthen water-bottle holding a quart of hot water from which we were expected to wash like Mohammedans before prayer.   On one side of the fire a platform was raised, made of bamboo a foot and a half high, on which was spread skins and mats to sleep on.   Soon my saddle holsters and saddle bag were in their place, and the king sent a message of a hundred thousand welcomes by men bearing smoking dishes of food. Mr. Crowther and I talked together till he fell asleep, heels up, head down. It was strange, hearing the night noises of the camp, the occasional voices of women and the cries of the children, or the neighing of horses, as they stood tethered outside the hut, making music in my ears, while I, a sailor bearded and turbaned, was a guest in the camp of Othanan Yacki. The scene in the hut next day was amusing. There arrived a bevy of princes. Othanan Yacki has thirty children living, and his brother fifty. So my levee was a large and distinguished one. They admired my saddles, bits, stirrups, and guns. After they were gone, two princesses came and begged for a looking-glass. According to a custom of the country they knelt down before me, bending their heads to the ground, and then placed themselves at the foot of my mat. I offered them a seat. It seemed that Abdul Kader had placed some writing paper for safety under the mat, as this is a great article for barter and much prized. He wished to get at it, and was most unceremoniously proceeding to push off my princess; but I told him that for once in his life he must wait upon women; this tent was England, and he must see how we treated women, and wait till they should go away. He replied, " Then in England you are fools." A train of dishes now appeared for the mid-day meal, sent by the king. After this we visited a tent to see them tempering a sword-blade. One of the princesses in passing to her father's quarters had caught sight of the white stranger. In her dismay she had thrown away her upper garment and never ceased running until she had reached her father's enclosure. My admirer, Abdul Kader, told her, "He is good, he would not hurt you." "And does he pray to God?" "Yes." "And his arms! look at mine, look at mine, and God made them both; God is wonderful. But will not the sun melt him? Will he bear fatigue?" Abdul told her of the mountains we had ascended together, and that I had left him far behind. She only answered, "God is wonderful."

' *Camp Jeso, October 31st.*—Dr. Baikie has left the bag open for me. I have had fever for days, and then was busy examining the rocks to see if a passage is practicable. The "Dayspring" was wrecked the day after I last wrote, and I have been a heavy loser. I was ill at the time from ague. The vessel with her steam could not stem the current, and struck on a sunken rock. The ship filled, except the forecastle, and during the night went down. The captain was sick and the chief went off to save his dog. Somehow I found myself in possession, with a naked sword in my hand driving the wretches who would save their rags instead of getting sails and provisions on shore.   However, by dark we had pitched our tents and secured some of our things.

' Dr. Crowther and I have sent for horses to make a journey up the river.   I have been laid up for days with fever.   So long as the excitement and work consequent on the wreck lasted I shook it off, and had I gone to Lagos the change of air would have done me good, but the horses are so long coming that I fear being ill again.   We have no coffee, tea, sugar or chocolate, and of wine, flour, and all their attendant luxuries, we have none. We roast Indian corn and prepare it as a substitute for coffee without milk.   We must wait for the arrival of the " Sunbeam " for more supplies.   My object is to push up the river as soon as possible, accompanied by Mr. Barter, the botanist.   Dr. Baikie expects me back in December, and has given me only a fortnight's provisions and presents for the chiefs.'

CHAPTER IV

First survey of the Niger, 1857-1861—Account of the wreck by
General Davis—Interview with King Abo—Rabba—Good reception at Boussa—Finding of Mungo Park's book—Return from surveying the Niger—Expedition to Lagos—First experience with the
Haussas—Palavers with the Chiefs—Return to camp—Finish of
survey—Return to England—Commendation by Lord Clarendon.

THE following notes are taken from Mr. (afterwards General) Davis's journal :—

'We left Fernando Po on June 29 and crossed
the bar of the Brass river. Glover has been away
all day surveying the bar. Our progress is slow,
and the labour of the surveying officer most
arduous. We had some shooting at crocodiles and
hippopotami, and some weary nights watching
for big game. The land became higher, and hills
and mountains were seen on either side. To climb
these and ascertain their altitudes and survey the
surrounding country was a labour of love to Glover,
and I often assisted. We got horses and rode to
Bida, where Massaba the king was encamped with
20,000 soldiers and camp followers. Massaba is a
scourge to the country around, but he was polite to
us. We anchored off Rabba, the ruins of a fine
town situated on high sandstone cliffs. The people

came off confidently. The skull of Umora, lately overcome by Massaba, was a prominent object on a stake as we landed there in sun 149°. Caravans from Kano, bound for Ilorin, were crossing the river, and the skull of Umora was stolen. At first the suspicion fell on the innocent people from Kano, afterwards on us, when we were shipwrecked above the sacred island of Ketsa.

' We left Rabba and steamed up the river. At nine we anchored, and Glover went away to sound. We proceeded, but could not stem the current, and were carried against a sunken rock. The ship struck her starboard side with great force. Warps were laid out and efforts made to haul her off. This only increased the inrush of the water. She heeled over and sunk gradually. At first there was a slight panic among the Kroomen, but order was soon restored by Glover and others. The boats were lowered and the officers and crew, with such stores as could be saved, were landed. A site for an encampment was selected, and, all hands working, three tents were built and a watch set. The ship's bell struck the hours, and our dinner was prepared by the cook. He was drunk, and nearly capsized the dingy with the sick, in which I was. I hit him over the head with the tiller, and he fell overboard, greatly to my relief. I found him on a sand-bank when I was' pulling back to the ship. Glover and

Captain Grant were the last to leave. In the night a tornado came on. We were all wet through and in dull spirits, when Mackintosh, the mate, who had saved his flute, played " Cheer, boys, cheer," and made us all laugh. Early next day we went to look for the " Dayspring." She had gone down.'

When the ' Dayspring ' became a wreck, and the party were thus obliged to get on shore and camp, Mr. Glover had all his work to do, for the Krooboys, taking advantage of the ill-fortune of the expedition, became mutinous, and it was with great difficulty he could get their help to bring the stores from the foundered vessel. There the party were obliged to remain some months until relief was brought to them from Lagos. While waiting, Mr. Glover was engaged in surveying the country and in laying down charts of the Niger, being the first European who ever surveyed that renowned river. The king of that part of the country, the Emir of Nupe, took a great fancy to him, and gave him numberless presents as a mark of honour, and a bodyguard of his fighting men to accompany him in his excursions into the surrounding country. Mr. Barter, the botanist, went with him, and was engaged in collecting specimens. When at Peteska Island, the extreme northern possession of Warra, Mr. Glover says, ' I have discovered that our proceedings here are most jealously watched. The island is in a high state of cultivation, and supplies Warra with palm wine, which must prove a source of great profit to the people. Mr. Barter was prevented from collecting botanical specimens, but I battled it out with the king, and, on condition that he did not strip the bark from the large trees that are held sacred, he was allowed to continue his pursuits, although most strictly watched. I was constantly receiving complaints of his infringing the contract, which I need hardly say were entirely without foundation. The cause of all this annoyance was their belief in charms, and their fear of our proficiency in the dark science made them keep this espionage on all our movements. Nothing could shake their conviction that if I put all their country down upon paper, and Mr. Barter took pieces of all their trees and shrubs home, we should make charms of these things to use against them, and then return and take their country from them. I found the people of Warra suspicious, captious liars and thieves, who asked for all that you possessed.'

'*Friday*, 10*th*.—Still very ill from fever. In evening went to see king and delivered message and presents. I found him seated outside the palace gates watching a dance by women dressed in strips of coloured cotton, a performance in honour of our arrival. The king and people profuse in compliments, but we are little better than prisoners, as we are not allowed to move outside our huts without one or two of the head men of the town ; but it matters little, as I am too ill with fever to do more than crawl to the king's hut and back, and this knocks me up for the whole day, and I had no sleep at night.

' 14*th*.—I packed up everything ready for a start, and moved all our belongings out of the yard under a large tree in the street, and waited for Bak (the chief told off to attend on strangers), who presently appeared, accompanied by the king's Ear and one or two others.   They were much annoyed at our readiness to set out. It seemed that last night the king and all his court got drunk, and did not break up till four o'clock this morning, consequently their heads were rather heavy for travelling. After spending two hours in useless endeavours to persuade me not to go, they gave it up, and left to procure bearers. They had brought presents from the king and queen. By the queen is understood the chief amongst the wives, and she is generally chosen from the family of the late king. I tried to get, if possible, a plan of the town, and had partly succeeded, when we were brought back and told we must stay under the tree, a head man remaining with us. At last Mr. Barter started with five bearers, and I followed, being in no humour to say good-bye to the king.

The head man who had been my guard, and was the public executioner, escorted me out of the town.

'The people here, as I found them, were nothing more than heathens, worshipping trees and rocks, and yet the name of God is ever in their mouths. They hope "that God will bring you safely on your journey, and that He will make you well," &c. I conclude they learn this from the Mohammedans scattered amongst them. They laugh at the idea of a future state.

'*Wednesday, 23rd.*—We started in good time, and found the predictions of yesterday as to the state of the road quite correct, it having been trodden down by elephants during the rainy season. About one o'clock we reached the site of old Boussa, and crossed the river, famous for its alligators. It had a few pools of deep water still remaining. There was no canoe at the usual ferry, and as that part is full of alligators, it would have been dangerous for horses and men. The country, just as yesterday, was entirely enveloped in fog, which has indeed been the case every day since I left the camp, preventing my seeing even the nearest objects, and the road lay amongst tall grass reaching above our heads when on horseback. Two hours' riding brought us to the beginning of the Boussa farms, which lasted for some miles, till the new Boussa came in sight, standing on a gentle eminence about 500 yards from the river, and surrounded by fine large cotton trees. We dismounted to send a messenger to announce our arrival to the king. He soon returned with permission to enter the town. His majesty came out of his palace to receive us.

' *Christmas Morning.*—Early came a large white cock from the king, with bowls of milk, fufu, and yams. Before I could get my breakfast came a message that the king wished to see me. I found his yard full of people, whom he was regaling with palm wine, from the effects of which many were already very drunk. He invited me into his hut, telling me that he was keeping company with his people, and wished his stranger friend to drink some palm wine with him. I took a meridian altitude, which brought on my fever of yesterday, and I was obliged to lie down for the rest of the afternoon. At five o'clock came another messenger from the king desiring my presence. I found him seated on an open space in front of his palace. The people kept flocking in until there could not have been less than 3,000, who then threw dust on their heads before him. Then came in six slave girls bearing on their heads calabashes filled with water. The ground having been plentifully sprinkled in front of his majesty, his band struck up. It consisted of six large drums, three smaller, and a brass horn at least six feet long, a fiddle with one string made of horse-hair, and two boys with calabashes filled with peas. I was seated on the right hand of the king, and as the band was within five yards of him, was almost stunned by the noise. When this had lasted about half an hour, he presented each of the musicians with a handful of coins and a Kola nut. The band having retired to a more agreeable distance, dancing began. This was of the rudest kind, kept up by single dancers. In the meantime a plentiful supply of palm wine was served out. The object of the dancers was to please the king and company, and to obtain cowries which were given by them to the band. The king asked me if " the Queen of England danced," and on my saying " Yes," said he would dance before me. In compliment to his majesty's dancing I sent him two handfuls of cowries, which act of mine was acknowledged by the surrounding crowd with shouts of applause. He then begged I should bring my revolver, which I did, and fired it off, and this closed the proceedings with *éclat*. The king seemed in love with his own dancing, telling me that he was going to dance home, which he accordingly did. At the gate of the palace he bade me good-bye, and said that he would visit me in the evening. I then paid a visit to his brother the " Dando." The king is a sociable man, always surrounded by his people, and accessible to them. He is very abstemious, and indeed quite a gentleman.

'Early next morning came a large Muscovy duck, with yams, fufu, and bowls of fresh milk. Visitors all day, and in the evening the king came bringing palm wine and honey. He said "all that he had was at my service, and that I must inform him in time whether I wished for horses or a canoe." On my saying I wished for a canoe, he said I "should have a large and good one," and that I "might keep it altogether" if I liked. I told him the expedition would visit him at Sokoto, and would then bring horses. He showed me a fine stud of twelve, and said I might buy any of these, even the horse that he rode himself.

'*Monday*, 28*th*.—The king came early, before I had packed up. He was mounted on a splendid horse, the head covered with bells. I was obliged to tell him I was not ready, which, he said, did not matter, he would come again when I was. I asked for a private audience, which he immediately gave, telling me it was his wish that trade and a missionary should come to him. I complained of the treatment I had received at Warra, and he said I must think nothing of it, as they were all fools, the meaning of the word Warra being "foolish." I told him that his gracious reception wiped out everything. He said "he loved me not a little, and that the whole people of Boussa did the same," and that he had tried in every way to prove this. On my subsequent visit I found that this was correct, for they refused to let me wait outside the gate, and, to judge from the crowd that welcomed my arrival, my entry was quite triumphal. My visit ended, the king mounted his horse, and half the town accompanied me to the canoe. Our parting was most warm, and I told him " the Suaki was Suaki," he had been a father to me during my stay, and I was sorry to leave Boussa. He said he would not leave the wharf till I was out of sight, and remained till the point shut me from his view. I was much disappointed I could not follow the main channel of the river, as the Wassi people on the opposite bank are at war with Boussa. I visited old Boussa, and in vain tried to discover the wreck of Mungo Park's canoe.'

The following extracts describe the journey from camp at Jeba to Boussa and back, from January 18 to February 4, 1858 :—

'*January 20th.*—We left the little village of Baha on the left, and came to the walled town of Qoom. It is of some extent, the River Lofa passing through it. I waited outside the town while Abdul Kader went to Louchi, who is governor of the whole upper district of Nushi, to say I had arrived. He returned with a message of welcome, and I was conducted to his own quarters, where I found huts already prepared. Louchi came to visit me with a large suite, and before I had an idea what he was about to do, seized my beard and kissed it. Soon I was in the midst of a long and loud controversy. Abdul Kader had discovered, on a woman whom he remembered to have seen at Warra, a piece of silk which he had lost at the time of the wreck. He immediately seized it, and the woman came to make her complaint. There was no doubt about the theft, but my friend Louchi, who is a great rogue, took the woman's part, and begged that because he loved me I should make Abdul Kader give up the piece of silk. This I refused, and because I was tired begged that the cause might be deferred till to-morrow.

' *January* 21*st.*—Louchi came early to inquire how I slept, and finding that I was going to buy horses of the King of Boussa, he insisted that I must buy them of him, because " he loved me." It was a poor stud, but I chose a small bay horse that pleased me. As I was going out of the yard in the evening a man slipped out of the crowd and offered me a book for sale. I saw at once that it was one that had belonged to poor Mungo Park. I asked the price, which was four hundred cowries, and offered half, upon which he indignantly carried off the book. I went for my ride, feeling quite con-

tented that it would be brought to me again.
Having by the purchase of the horse reduced my
loads to six, I started in the morning to Boussa.
Louchi had directed me by a long circuitous way
in order that the chief of the town might have the
pickings of the strangers' loads; but being as well
up in the geography of his province as himself, I
refused, and requested I might be put on the
straight road to Deako, where I wished to cross
the Niger. We did not reach Edemogu till 2.30,
travelling through an open and cultivated country.
On the way I was overtaken by a handsome man
on horseback, carrying a child on the pommel of
his saddle, and the people as we passed all addressed
him as " Dando," or prince. I wanted some fresh
bearers, but the chief of Edemogu said it was too
late, I must sleep there. This I refused to do, and
with the assistance of Dando, and a small bribe,
we were again on the road by three o'clock. Just as
I was parting with Dando, who had presented me
with a large calabash of beer, he produced from the
breast-pocket of his robe Mungo Park's book, and
asked what I would give him for it. Great value
was evidently attached to this book, but as my
apparent interest was very little, he begged that I
would accept it from him. I thanked him, and in
return gave him a spear-pointed knife, with which
he was greatly delighted.'

The country now became hilly, and volcanic mountains rose out of a plain of stone. Their road lay up the steep side of an extinct crater five hundred feet high, under a peak which towered two hundred feet above them. Lumps of cinder and iron, bigger than a man could lift, cut the horses' unshod feet. At last they reached the village of Bale, where they found blacksmiths' shops and smelting furnaces. Here the bearers refused to go any further. An old Mallam came to their rescue and got them fresh carriers.

'We travelled till dark and arrived at a river about fifteen yards wide. On the opposite bank we saw the roofs of a village in the bright moonlight. Visions of a smoking supper and rest arose from the peaceful scene, which were quickly dispelled. I sent one of my bearers to inform the head man of my arrival, and ask for shelter and a canoe to cross the river, which was deep and rapid. Suddenly there arose cries for help. My bearers took to their heels, leaving me with my servant to stand the brunt of whatever might happen. Above the shouts of men rose the shrill screams of women. It struck me at once this was the boundary of Nushi.

'We removed the loads to the rear, and sending my servant into the bush out of sight waited for what might follow. Though the people were frightened, they did not know our number, therefore I felt quite sure they would not venture to cross the stream to molest me during the night. Had they done so, I should have had a very defensible position, with a revolver and double-barrelled gun, and my servant to load. I should not have feared the result, as this would have been their first introduction to English powder. In about twenty minutes some twenty men rushed down to the opposite banks with spears, bows, and arrows. In vain we called out " Bullisi, Bullisi! " meaning "white man." They only vociferated, "Be off, be off, all Nushis are liars ! " At last, after both sides had bawled at each other till they were hoarse, they desired that " the white man should show himself." I went down, and by the light of the moon discovering that I really was white, they sent a man over to look at me. The scene became so ridiculous that I could not help laughing. There stood the man in the water, his head only visible, while I had to stoop down that he might see my face, which certainly was not a white one. Peeping out of the jungle in the rear were my frightened followers, while on the opposite bank spears gleamed in the moonlight and arrows were strung in the hands of men equally frightened.

' At last, after much questioning and answering had taken place between the man in the water and his friends on the bank, shouts of delight told me that all was right. The man emerged from the river, and with many salaams hoped that I would forgive the manner in which they had received me, and begged that I should come to the village. Soon I found myself in a comfortable hut, and an old cock, which I fortunately had in my possession, was quickly boiling in the pot. They brought me corn for my horse, and I lay down at last, tired out.

'*25th.*—I found my friends of last night a rough set, but at last I got my bearers under weigh, and in a few hours saw the Niger, which seemed like an old friend. On the opposite bank stood the little Bangui village. A canoe was sent over, but being a small one would only hold half my loads and servant. While counting out cowries to pay my carriers, there arose another disturbance. They were not satisfied, and on my servant attempting to cross with my things they rushed down and seized the canoe. Taking the revolver from my holster, which was in the canoe, I explained to them that five barrels represented one for each, and then drawing my knife I showed its point to the sixth. They seemed perfectly to understand this mode of reasoning, for quickly taking up their cowries they walked off. The canoe returned for me and my horse, which, swimming by the side, at first struck out well, but when half way over turned on his side, and I had great difficulty in saving him. The head man of Bangui received me most kindly. I found here a woman who had seen me at Warra, and appeared to have some influence in the village. She was of great use to me, sent boys to cut grass for my horse, brought me forward and took entire charge of my culinary arrangements. Leaving next day for Anapa I was now again on my old road, and arrived at Boussa, with an attack of fever.

'During my last visit the people of Boussa told me how much I pleased them, and I was now to find the truth of the Mallam's words. While waiting outside the town I perceived a stream of people issuing from the gates. They rushed towards me, and with loud shouts welcomed my arrival. It was in vain that I remonstrated. Seizing my bridle on each side they hurried me into the town, giving me quite a triumphal entry.'

This concludes the extracts from a very careful and elaborate journal, which is too full to be produced *in extenso*.

After Mr. Glover's journey to Boussa he returned by river to Rabba, shooting the rapids in a canoe, and found that Dr. Baikie and the remainder of the expedition had been unable to get any assistance during the time he had been away surveying.

Remaining here some further time without any

prospect of relief, he at last volunteered to go alone and bring the relief himself. He was given horses by a chief, and went overland to Lagos, being the first European who ever made the *down* journey, not the *up* one, be it remembered. It was on his way to Lagos that he passed Ibadan, where he made the acquaintance of the missionary and his wife, Mr. and Mrs. Hindres. Here he was taken ill with dysentery, and Mr. Hindres acted as nurse till he recovered. He then went to Lagos, and from Lagos got ship to Sierra Leone.

At Sierra Leone he came into contact with certain Africans who wished to return to their part of the country. These men bore the name of Haussas, a name evidently of German origin, and in many respects these Haussas resembled German soldiers. They would not venture to go back again by themselves, because of the risk of capture and slavery. There seemed to be for them no chance of getting a passage up the river. When Lieutenant Glover offered to take these poor fellows with his party they at once gladly accepted it. One, named Harry Maxwell, became much attached to him, and was faithful in his service for many years. At this time he also made the acquaintance of Selim Oga, an African, who had gained some little reputation for himself, and it is believed that, after being some time with Sir Richard Burton, he was

at length killed while attending to the wounded
after a tribal battle somewhere in Liberia.

With the Haussas, Mr. Glover returned to
Lagos. While waiting the completion of his preparations at Lagos to return overland to the camp
on the Niger, he worked hard surveying the lagoons,
and this occupation undoubtedly caused the fever
which attacked him with great severity.

Some exciting scenes took place at Lagos, when
it became known that many of the natives of the
Haussa country had joined the returning party.
These men, who were in slavery, tried to escape
from their masters. The Haussas would give notice
that on such a night they would attempt to run
away, and on trying to escape they were often
pursued and captured. The horses to be used for
the journey were sent from the island of Lagos
to the mainland opposite, to get fit for work, and
as soon as they were in condition the start was
arranged. It then became known that the owners
of the runaway slaves had formed a party to dispute
his passage by force. Mr. Glover was, however,
quite prepared to run the risk on the appointed
day. The opponents of his passage did indeed
assemble with a view to barring his path, but
apparently thought they might get the worst of it
if they fought, so let him go. In due time he
arrived at Abeokuta, where the native authorities

were by no means disposed to give him a free passage. Considerable excitement occurred here, as a slave amongst his party was recognised and claimed by Madam Tinubu, who was a very influential person in this town. But on his giving this sharp-sighted lady a large roll of cloth, she abandoned her claim. When Mr. Glover prepared to leave the next day the gates were closed against him. He had fortunately sent all his carriers and escort outside the walls before this was done. Hemmed in on all sides by armed men brandishing their weapons and thirsting for his blood, yet not daring to touch him, he remained sitting alone on his horse waiting for what appeared to be his doom. The animal he was riding was a powerful one, which had been given him by a chief, but as all the gates were closed, with armed men guarding them, there seemed little chance of escape. Just then he noticed a gap in the wall, where a number of men stood with spears. Some of the fighting men made a rush to seize his bridle. He drove his spurs into the horse's flanks and turned him to the break in the wall, the suddenness of the movement dispersing the crowd. But a row of spears barred his way, and there was nothing to do but to make a dash for it, and the horse responding to his rider broke over the formidable array of spears, and was out into the country beyond. This was one of the most exciting of the many hair-breadth escapes in his West African career. Some years after he came back to this town and cut a wide road up to its gates to replace the tortuous paths which led to the settlement.

At another halting place on his journey towards the Niger, he was anxious to purchase one or more horses, but the authorities for a long time refused to sell him an animal. At last a big white horse, with long flowing mane and pink eyes, was brought out, and he was informed that this animal could be bought provided he could ride it. Quite a scene took place over the matter. One of the chiefs sneeringly remarked as to 'the poor white man's' ability to ride the animal around which they clustered, when 'the poor white man,' suddenly seizing the bit and backing the horse on to the knees of the town authorities who were sitting close by looking on, dispersed them in affright. After this the chiefs agreed that he was a fit and proper person to ride it.

A chief once said to him, ' I know that happens to our poor country. First comes missionary—well, he very good man ; he write book. Then come Consul ; he write home. Then come merchant ; he very good man, he buy nuts. Then come governor ; he—well, he writes to Queeny, she send him back—

she send man-o'-war.   Our country done spoil—no
more of our poor place left.'

In his negotiations with the natives he had to
communicate with them through the 'palaver,'
which is the well-known and usual method of
discussion between the native Africans, and in the
course of his dealings with them he found the
most effectual aid to his diplomacy was a medicine-
chest which he invariably carried with him.   It
contained some lime juice and oil and some eau-
de-Cologne.   At night, when sitting round the
camp fires engaged in the ' palaver,' he would produce his chest, and with that delight in simple
things which is so characteristic of the Africans,
the natives would rub themselves with the oil till
they fairly shone again.   If he gave them lime
juice and soda, their joy was unbounded when the
compound in its effervescence bubbled over their
faces.   The eau-de-Cologne was for the use of his
own hands and face.   He pointed out to the
natives that if he opened up their country they
would possess these things in abundance.   Certain
it is that the natives literally laid the flattering
unction to themselves, and his 'oily' diplomacy
led to their complete satisfaction with the white
man.   'He very good man ; he can take nuts and
eberything,' was the opinion which the medicine-
chest earned.

While on this journey from Lagos to the camp of his shipwrecked party there was a conspiracy to murder him. He told the Haussas that in case of a sudden attack they were to lay down their loads so as to form a circular breastwork, and kneel behind them. He was struck with the ready way in which these men took his instructions and understood what he wished them to do, and it was from the opinion he formed of their capabilities as soldiers when on this march that in after years, when he was Governor of Lagos, he induced the Secretary of State to allow him to enrol a hundred of them as a beginning, and call them the Cape Coast Constabulary, now so well known in Western Africa. Perhaps the peculiar attachment to him of these Haussas was not only one of personal affection, but probably also caused by his insight into the character of the people themselves. Knowing well their Arab nature, he calmed their nomadic spirit, or rather quelled it by itself. He continually moved his men about the country, keeping them always occupied, and never long in one place. By a system of fines every fault received its punishment, and the money so obtained grew at length into a fund which was used for the benefit of any needy Haussa who wanted a grant from it. For instance, if a man had the authority from his fellows to build a new hut, and wanted

money to help his enterprise, the fund was at his
disposal, or when a birth occurred, or when anything of a nature happened that might require aid.
In managing this force he fully identified himself
with the interests of the people and endeared
himself to them, which enabled him to get them to
carry out his wishes and obey his will, earning for
him the title of the ' Father of the Haussas.'

After a tedious and weary march, with these runaway slaves as his only escort, at length he regained
the Niger, bringing with him supplies for the little
camp where the men were anxiously awaiting his
approach.

In March 1861, Mr. Glover returned to England,
after his long and zealous researches in various
parts of the Niger, which was till then un-
surveyed. He was looking thin and ill from the
repeated attacks of fever which he had contracted
while on this service. After his return he was
employed till June in finishing the charts and maps
for the Foreign Office, when he received the thanks
of Lord Clarendon, for the able manner in which
his work had been carried out, in the following
terms :—

To Dr. Baikie

' Foreign Office, January 14, 1858.

' Sir,—I have received your despatch reporting
the loss of the " Dayspring " in the rapids near

Jeba, and I have to express to you my great regret at this most unfortunate occurrence, which for the time has put a stop to the progress of the Ishadda Expedition. You will convey the approval of Her Majesty's Government to the officers of this expedition, and most especially to Lieutenant Glover of the Royal Navy, to whose excellent conduct on every occasion, as well as his zeal and ability, I have had much pleasure in calling the attention of the Lords of the Admiralty.

'CLARENDON.'

CHAPTER V

1861–1863

The Gold Coast of Western Africa—Lieutenant Glover commanding H.M.S. 'Handy'—Letter to Lord Alfred Churchill—The Settlement of Lagos—Neighbouring Tribes—Porto Novo—Egbas and Ibadans—Departure of Mr. Freeman—Lieutenant Glover acting Governor of Lagos—His despatch to the Secretary of State on the Settlement—His promotion to rank of Commander.

ON the completion of his work in connection with the Niger Expedition, Lieutenant Glover was appointed to the 'Aboukir' in the Channel Squadron, but was only borne on her books for a month. He then joined the 'Arrogant' while waiting for the command of the 'Handy,' which was specially commissioned for service in the Lagos Lagoons, and took over his command of her in October 1861. This was the last ship in which he served, for soon after his promotion as commander, he received his first commission under the Colonial Office and was appointed Administrator of Lagos. It would appear from the following extracts from a letter to Lord Alfred Churchill, M.P., that the people on the West Coast of Africa were not aware that Mr. Glover was being sent out on special service to them, but were anxious for this appointment : ' We desire further to interest your Lordship in Lieutenant Glover, R.N., well known in these parts of Africa through his indefatigable work for knowledge and civilisation. During his stay at Lagos and in the surrounding country he gained the love and confidence of every European resident, as well as the esteem of the native chiefs. When the late Consul died the residents of Lagos petitioned Commodore Wise to recommend Mr. Glover as Consul at Lagos, but then he went with Dr. Baikie into the interior of Africa for an uncertain time. At present Mr. Glover is in England, and your Lordship is in communication with the Government in respect of the Yoruba Consulate. We beg you to use your influence with the Government in favour of a man like Lieutenant Glover, whose appointment as representative of Her Majesty in Yoruba would doubtless be a boon to the country and to the prosperity of civilisation and commerce.'

Before leaving England in the 'Handy' he made the acquaintance of Mr. Freeman, who expressed himself pleased to meet an officer who possessed such local experience as Mr. Glover, which would serve him in good stead in helping to establish the authority of the very crude government existing then. The reason for these appointments being made were as follows :—The Consul at Lagos fearing an outbreak had sent off a despatch to Captain Bedingfield, of H.M.S. 'Prometheus,' then in harbour, by a black crew through a heavy surf to solicit his aid, as a rising of the black population under King Kosoko was imminent, and the lives of the small European population were in danger. The ship was with great difficulty brought through the surf, and lay off the King's Palace about two miles from Lagos, with her guns brought to bear upon it. This prevented the outbreak; but on Captain Bedingfield's reporting the circumstance to the home authorities, it was thought advisable to send Mr. Freeman out as Administrator, and Lieutenant Glover was despatched in the 'Handy.' After the arrival of the 'Handy' at Lagos a war broke out between the Egbas and the men of Ikorodu. Abeokuta, the home of the Egbas, was a town of recent origin, and when driven out of Yoruba they chose it for their settlement. English missionaries and merchants went among them, and as the Egbas increased in wealth and numbers they also increased in pride and presumption. Unfortunately, the English residents at Abeokuta, fearing to lose the influence they had acquired, took their side in every question, notwithstanding their adversaries had also a strong reason for believing themselves to be in the right. Thus arose the war with Ibadan, undertaken by the

Egbas professedly to retrieve the town of Ijaye besieged by the Abadano, but in reality to obtain a monopoly of all the commerce by closing all roads from Lagos to the interior except by Abeokuta. They kidnapped numbers of people, and sent them to be sold as slaves on the coast. Lagos was then the most renowned slave depôt in Western Africa.

Mr. Glover was despatched on a mission to Ibadan to try and obtain peace. He was accompanied by ten men of the West Indian Regiment, besides an armed escort of carriers. He entered the first village without the slightest opposition. The old chief received him well, but, unfortunately, an Egba was discovered in his party and the whole place was in commotion. All the men turned out with guns, spears, and bows and arrows. During the night drums were beating and the young men called to arms, and it was with difficulty they saved the Egba's life. This was the beginning of their troubles in endeavouring to obtain a passage through the country to Ibadan. Here he heard that Mrs. Hindres was very ill, and it was necessary that she should be removed to the coast if her life was to be saved. He never forgot her kind attention to him when he was suffering from dysentery the first time he visited that town. He managed with considerable difficulty to get some European food and comforts for her without creating suspicion, by having them stowed away among the bales of ordinary merchandise, but, considering the warlike attitude of the tribes, it was almost impossible to undertake her removal with safety. However, he sent a detachment of natives to meet her party and escort them to a spot which he had previously arranged. Before Mrs. Hindres could arrive at the appointed place his second party got there, and were made prisoners by a band of Ikorodu spies and taken before the chief, who wanted to know if they were communicating with the enemy. The party forming Mrs. Hindres' escort arriving shortly after were thus enabled to pass unmolested down the river, and get her on board the steamer while the band of spies were engaged with their prisoners. Altogether this expedition was a risky affair, the whole country being in open revolt, while one white man and a few native followers were trying to pass through the most hostile tribes into the interior. Doubtless there were many plots to murder him, as there had been on his journey from Lagos to the Niger when bringing relief to the shipwrecked crew of the 'Dayspring.' Among his own followers there were none he could depend on in case of attack, nor trust that poison was not given in his food. Sleeping on a ram skin at night, with a revolver as his most trusted companion, the dark tropical sky his roof, a log for his pillow, and a wide spreading tree for shelter, he could hear the beating of the tom-toms and the cries of the warriors at their war dances, preparing for the morrow, while he could see the dusky forms of the spies by the fire-light flitting from tree to tree round his camp, ready for marauding or bloodshed. But, notwithstanding these difficulties, his mission was a successful one.   When he returned to Lagos he found that Mr. Freeman was obliged by ill health to leave for England.   Lieutenant Glover was therefore appointed to act as the Administrator. Accordingly he was installed in Government House, and entered on a phase of his career more important than any he had yet passed through. Although Lagos was in those days the most notorious slave mart in Western Africa, it is now one of the most important centres of trade on the West Coast, being hailed by many as the 'Liverpool of West Africa,' and this was brought about mainly by his exertions.   It was in those days a miserable place, struggling with difficulties.   How he surmounted them may be seen by the following extracts from a despatch which he addressed to the Duke of Newcastle, Secretary of State, setting forth the situation as it then existed. This is one of the first despatches of importance which he wrote, and it indicates the proficiency he had already acquired in dealing with political situations :—

'I would beg leave to represent to your Grace the position of affairs of this settlement at the time of my entering upon the administration of the Government.

'A feeling of discontent was arising from the stoppage of trade, consequent upon the war in the interior and the robberies committed on Lagos property by the Egbas. Great dissatisfaction existed against the local Government on the part of both Europeans and coloured residents, while the king, his chiefs, and party, still brooding over the loss of their power and consequence, had requested the French Admiral to do for them as they had done at Porto Novo. In the farms, and, indeed, beyond the circle of five miles, kidnapping, robbery, and transit of slaves were rampant, in defiance of a Government which had neither force nor organisation to deal with the one, or to check the other. Part of Badagri was in a state of rebellion, having driven out the police, intriguing with Porto Novo, and openly declaring their right to French protection, though receiving from this Government a pension in lieu of duties which they (the chiefs) formerly had levied. While in sight of the town was hoisted the French flag on territory which had belonged to the natives of Badagri, who were in favour of British rule, and who had remained true to this Government while the rest of the inhabitants were in open revolt.   Such was the state of the settlement on the day of my landing, and our outward relations, as well as the state of affairs beyond the settlements, were in a great degree the cause of this internal disquietude. My object has been, while removing or subduing the effect, to carry out a policy which should also remove the cause, viz., to bring the war to an end.

'The exasperation of Abeokuta at the check given to the slave trade by the occupation of Lagos, the wish of this Government for another road for commerce to and from the interior (besides that of Abeokuta), the non-rendering of slaves who sought protection in this settlement, their rejection of Her Majesty's Vice-Consul, and the murders and robberies committed by them on the persons and properties of British subjects, their reverses in the war with Ibadan, and our refusal to allow them to destroy the town of Ikorodu—all these were causes sufficient in themselves to prevent any relations of close friendship existing between them and ourselves.

'A fine river, with a depth of four and a half fathoms, washed the banks of Oki Odun, the great slave market of the Egbas.   The King of Pokra added his request to those of Addo and Oki Odun, and I visited those places to ascertain personally the feeling of the people, intending to report the same to Her Majesty's Government; but I found that the French authorities at Porto Novo, were seeking to absorb all the surrounding country to their flag, and thus reduce Lagos to a mere town upon a sandy island, insignificant in itself, and contemptible for all time (as it was then) in the eyes of the surrounding tribes, to destroy its revenue, and cause it to be a constant burden upon the mother country.

' After I had restored order at Badagri, and the people had returned peacefully, the French flag was introduced into the town, and large presents made to induce them to hoist the flag and declare for its protection. At the same time I received Monsieur Daumas' despatch, claiming not only Appa but eastward of Badagri; and at a later date I was assured by Monsieur Baron Brossard that their claims extended to Beshi, nine miles from Lagos. At this time it was being discussed in Abeokuta to bring up the French from Porto Novo, and I hesitated no longer in accepting the Protectorate, which shut off alike the French from Abeokuta and the Egbas from the coast. This, my Lord Duke, was the first impression that we have succeeded in making upon the Egbas, and they have left nothing undone to complicate our position at Oki Odun. I am happy to report to your Grace that they have failed. It now became evident to them that a persistence in their present policy might at some future day induce Her Majesty's Government to put on a blockade, and for the first time they felt that a severe check could be placed upon them, for they had laughed at the last stoppage of their roads, as it only injured Lagos, they having a road by the Addo river, and through Addo and Badagri. A blockade I had no authority to put on, after receiving your Grace's despatch of March 20, 1863, but recent events in Lagos compelled me to prohibit altogether the sale of powder.

'Consequently, the Egbas can procure no supplies, although it is not prohibited expressly on their account.

'I explained at great length to Oyodu the opinion of Her Majesty's Government and their wish for peace between the Egbas and Ibadans; their wish to be in friendly relations with the Egbas and all the surrounding tribes; that within the settlement we intended to be strong; that the increased armed force was intended for the protection of the settlement, and in the event of Dahomey attacking Oki Odun (unless orders to the contrary were received from Her Majesty's Government) a force of 600 men would proceed to Oki Odun for its defence; that they ought to be glad of this, because if Dahomey again attacked Abeokuta, the Dahomians would have an enemy in the rear.

'If I have taken the liberty of expressing my feelings so freely and at such length, it is because of the near arrival of Governor Freeman, and this may be the last opportunity afforded me of placing before your Grace the state of affairs both within and without the settlement at the time of my arrival. If it shall be shown that I have restored confidence in the government of this colony where none was felt, if I have made Lagos and its position respected by timely interference, have suppressed two revolts, caused law and order to be respected and maintained, have brought the Egbas to listen to reason, and shortly to end the war without spilling one drop of blood, I would respectfully hope that I shall have shown to your Grace that, had I hesitated until I had obtained the sanction of Her Majesty's Government, I could have obtained none of these ends. Badagri lost to us, the French at our doors, our prestige gone, the discontent in Lagos might then have been well excused if they had thought that indeed the time had come when they (as they believed) are again to drive us to our ships.

'Such, my Lord Duke, up to this time is the result of the policy which was forced upon me, first, by the French, and secondly, by King Docemo.

With all respect, I presume to remind your Grace of the only instructions which I remember to have received—viz., we have got war, obtain for us peace. I cannot report to your Grace that I have obtained that peace, but the confidence of all European merchants, as well as the influential native traders, is strong in the belief that peace is at hand, if the measures I have adopted be adhered to, and they have one and all cheerfully assented to the stopping of their powder trade.'

The foregoing despatch is of considerable interest, because it shows that from the outset in his colonial career Mr. Glover was obliged by circumstances, forced upon him at the moment, to act on his own judgment and resources. It is well known during his African experience that he never flinched in acting as he considered right for the good of the colony, even when he encountered a good deal of opposition. In a letter from Sir Gilbert Carter, the popular Governor of Lagos, in the year 1896, this is so well brought out that the following extract is given :

' Government House, Lagos : April 8, 1896.

' In Mr. Glover's time Ibadan was an unknown land, though he did not fail to preach the policy of opening up the Hinterland as the only means of properly developing the colony, but in those days

H

there was no money, and colonial extension was looked upon with horror in high places. If you will read the despatches you will find that Mr. Glover's advanced views earned him many a wigging. It is his policy that I have been carrying out, and I am very proud that it has been left for me to do.'

After being relieved of his acting appointment on Mr. Freeman's return, Mr. Glover was promoted to the rank of commander, and thus was ended his naval career, which had been laborious, varied, and fruitful in results. He then proceeded to England, and while there, in March 1864, addressed a despatch to the Secretary of State. From that some extracts may be made in order to illustrate further the condition of Lagos and its surroundings.

' Since 1860 a war has been raging between the Egbas or Abeokutans and Ijebus Odes on the one hand, and the Ibadans on the other, the result of which has been that no less than thirty towns and villages have been swept from the face of the country. One of these towns—viz., Ijaye, contained upwards of 60,000 inhabitants. This town was in alliance with Abeokuta when the Egbas went to war with Ibadan. As the war progressed the Egbas sold their friends from Ijaye' (who had sought refuge in Abeokuta) into slavery, in order, as they said, to purchase the means of continuing the war; and when at length the greater part of the young population had been sold, the rest were abandoned to the Ibadans. At the same time in like manner the smaller villages have disappeared, overcome by treachery rather than by fighting. Their chief offered up a sacrifice, and the entire remnant of their population was sold in the slave-market of the coast.

'One grievance alleged against us is our protection of Ikorodu, a town in which the remnant of the tribe of Ijebu Ramos have taken refuge, and only nine miles distant from Lagos; another is our sympathy with the Ibadans, who are fighting in the cause of the Ijebu Ramos, and to maintain the road which, passing through the country of Ramos, would bring our markets the produce not only of the country of the Ibadans, but of all Yoruba, which extends northwards to the banks of the Niger. It is for this line of communication, so desirable for British commerce and the peaceable development of the resources of the interior, that the Egbas are now fighting. Up to the commencement of the present war they possessed the only road between Lagos and the Niger which was available for commerce. Since that time this road has been closed by them, not against their avowed enemies, but against us. They refuse to allow us to become mediators between themselves and the Ibadans, who are desirous to place the settlement of the war in our hands, and have, moreover, informed us that "they will make peace when the Egbas are tired of war." Under these circumstances, my Lord, it is for Her Majesty's Government to consider, first, whether the object for which Lagos was annexed to the British Crown shall be obtained—viz., to put an end to these continual wars and suppress the slave trade, or, on the other hand, to allow the attainment of this most important object to be defeated by the opposition of the Egbas. Secondly, whether Lagos shall be allowed to become a self-supporting settlement independent of the Imperial revenue, a prosperous emporium of commerce, and the future Liverpool of Africa, or a deplorable failure like all our other forts and settlements on the Gold Coast, and a continual drain upon the Imperial treasury. Up to the present Her Majesty's Government has abstained from assuming any very decided tone or attitude towards the Egbas. And if the town of Ikorodu be occupied by the armed local force as a military demonstration to add weight to the communication of her Majesty's Government, I am convinced that the arbitration of the existing difficulties, and, indeed, the entire settlement of the war, will be placed in our hands.'

Captain Glover remained only a very short time in England, returning as Colonial Secretary

to Lagos, and received very high praise from Lord
Clarendon while acting in this capacity.   Soon
after this Mr. Freeman, being obliged to leave on
account of ill-health caused by constant fevers,
Captain Glover was appointed Governor of Lagos.

CHAPTER VI

1863–1872

Life in Lagos—The settlement of Lagos—Expedition to the interior—
Burton on Government House—An African love letter—'Gunner
—The 'Victory' horse—The Queen's birthday receptions—Death
of the Governor's brothers—Sir Andrew Clarke's reminiscences
—Farewell addresses—Return home.

THIS part of Captain Glover's life was, perhaps, the
most interesting, though the least known to the
outer world.   He was now Governor of a new
Crown colony with a large native population, where
there were few Europeans.   These latter were
merchants or officials, sent out, often to die in a
few weeks or months, on this fever-stricken coast.
There were no police, and only a small number of
men belonging to a West India regiment to protect
this young settlement, surrounded as it was on all
sides by hostile tribes; no roads—except the tortuous tracks by which the natives carry their
burdens and food from the interior; no laws; no
ideas of sanitary arrangements; no religion except
Mohammedanism, heathenism, and 'Obeah,' which
was conducted by the native medicine-men, who
possessed secrets and undiscoverable poisons, and

who held their superstitious witchcrafts and charms like a sword of terror over the people.

About this time Dr. Eales, then surgeon of the 'Prometheus,' surveying at Lagos, writes as follows :—'The loss of Mr. Freeman would have been a very great misfortune to the colony (which, by his tact and energy, he had done much to improve during his short sojourn) had he not been succeeded by a man so capable as Captain Glover. Now commenced in earnest the improvements of the town. A splendid esplanade was laid out the entire length of the settlement, about a mile long and eighty yards broad, parallel with the lagoon, and planted the whole way with trees. Long, broad streets were made through the native portions of the town. A fine court-house was built, a jetty thrown out into the lagoon. A colonial hospital, one Church of England and two large Nonconformist churches erected. By this example public enterprise was awakened. Several fine houses, on European models, were constructed, and the colony, which only a couple of years before was, with trifling exceptions, a collection of native houses and a few better edifices owned by English, French, Italian and Portuguese merchants, became one of the chief settlements on the West Coast.'

In 1863 Captain Glover was sent for to confer with the home authorities in England. On his

return to Lagos an expedition up the Niger was
despatched in the 'Investigator' (Commander
Sands) with the object of keeping up friendly relations with the kings and chiefs, and the usual
presents were sent from the Queen to King Masaba
—velvets, musical boxes, pictures, etc. The king in
his speech said: 'Tell the Queen that I am pleased
with the beautiful things she has sent, which I shall
present to my wives; but that I hope in her next
present she will remember that I am a warrior with
a large army to keep up in the field, and that the
best present she can send me is plenty of guns and
powder.' On the way they stayed at Lokoja, a lovely
spot at the confluence of the Binue and Kwarra,
a tributary of the Niger, the object being to see
the Consul, Dr. Baikie, and give him his orders
to present himself before the Colonial Office. On
their arrival Dr. Baikie came off dressed in native
costume, and on returning his visit they found him
luxuriously living as ruler of his kingdom under the
protection of King Masaba. It was with great
reluctance that Dr. Baikie was compelled to return
when he realised that he must proceed to England.
When he left Lokoja he was a strong man in
perfect health, but he took fever at Lagos and
died before reaching Sierra Leone.

A description of Government House, where
Captain Glover spent so much of his time, is

alluded to by the late Sir Richard Burton in one of his books, as an ' iron coffin with generally a dead consul inside.' It was made of iron, and was exceedingly hot. To obtain sleep at night in it was difficult, almost impossible. The consequence was that the Governor and his guests frequently met each other wandering from one part to another in quest of sleep with mattress and pillow in hand, having implicitly obeyed the scriptural instructions to ' take up their beds and walk.' On one occasion his Excellency, as was his wont, having tried in vain to rest before the break of day, compromised the matter of sleeping either indoors or out by lying down with his head and shoulders in the passage and the rest of his body in the room. The dusky constable on duty as guard came across the Governor in that position, and attributing it to a physical inability to move, and alarmed lest his condition should become known, shook him roughly by the shoulders. The weary Governor vainly attempted to make him go away, but that zealous official, thinking only of the supposed cause of his Excellency's position, shook him till he thoroughly roused him up, and sleep for that night was impossible. The passage which separated the rooms was used as the armoury for the Haussa troops, and the presence of these weapons added much to the peace of this and the surrounding districts, as the native chiefs, on visiting Government House, were much awed by the fact of the Governor sleeping with arms all round him.

Government House in the morning was indeed a busy scene. After breakfast for two or three hours ' Obba Golobar ' (as his people called him) was to be seen sitting on the verandah smoking a cigarette and listening to their grievances. He had always a native interpreter, and patiently listened to both sides of the question being explained to him amid the loud clamour of the aggrieved parties. Here, as in the East, every native speaks in parables, and in the most extravagant poetical language. If a case of breach of promise of marriage was brought forward against one of these dusky-skinned warriors, his friends and also those of the disconsolate lady were loud in their expressions of disapproval, and on these occasions the love letters would be handed up for inspection. These remarkable epistles were always written by the wise men in the market-place seated under the tall palm trees, which were held almost sacred by the natives. Nothing short of the Song of Solomon can describe the language of an African's letter addressed to his dusky bride ; for example : ' Were the firmament my sheet of paper and the sea my ink, it would be inadequate to express the love and adoration I feel for thee.' After sending a number of these productions the enamoured Romeo declines to pay the stipulated price to the father of his betrothed. This causes an exciting interview with the enraged parents, which ends with 'We go to Governor,' and so next day the whole party present themselves to have justice done. After hearing both sides, 'Golobar' asked to have the young lady brought before him, and if he found that she liked the man, and that it was not a question of her being bought by the highest bidder, he pointed out her beauty and charms to the sulky bridegroom, and asked if he could for one moment desert such an adorable lady for the consideration of a few extra head of cattle. This generally settled the matter, and all present cried 'Shame, shame!' and without further persuasion the youth handed over the necessary payment and carried off his bride. As a rule, these women were most faithful wives, and far better workers and carriers than the male portion of the community. In a letter written by Mr. Glover to a friend, he alludes to witchcraft, which is such a common superstition among the natives. He says: 'I have been employed for hours in the morning investigating a case of witchcraft with all the solemnity which would have been required five centuries ago.'

The Government House at Lagos contained

many pets; some of the 'Harness' antelopes [1] were brought to England and placed in the Zoological gardens. Besides an ostrich and a secretary bird kept for killing snakes, there was a curious bird called the 'clock bird,' who used to march out regularly with the horses as far as the town gates, but was never known to go past them. The favourite companion of this bird was the celebrated horse 'Gunner.' This horse was offered as a present to the Governor by the chiefs of Ikorodu on account of his having routed the Egbas, and 'Gunner' was always known as a 'Victory' horse. Before accepting this present, the Governor wrote home and explained that it would be expedient to allow him to do so, and leave was granted him; so 'Gunner' became an inmate of the Government House stable, and no one but the Governor was allowed to mount him. The animal remained in the stables after Captain Glover left the colony, as he considered the horse more of a present to the Government than to himself. A succeeding Governor relegated him to the brick-fields, which so enraged the natives that they made an appeal on his behalf to the new authorities, and he was bought by 'Obukiti,' one of the chiefs.

As much entertaining as was possible in a

---

[1] So called from stripes over their body, looking as if they were covered with a harness.

small society went on in Government House, and there were many pleasant croquet parties and receptions, besides dinners and dances which were very popular. An amusing incident occurred at one of the Queen's birthday dinners, to which the Governor invited one of the native chiefs. On the invitation card the usual formula requesting 'the pleasure of your company' was printed. The chief duly arrived, but attended by fifty of his followers. As dinner was only laid for twenty the Private Secretary rushed to the Governor to know what was to be done, and some light refreshment was offered to the unexpected guests; but the chief seemed a little hurt, and said, 'You invite me and my company to dinner, and no! not one man stay away when "Golobar" sends for him.' On one occasion the flag-ship from the Cape of Good Hope arrived off the roadstead, and Commodore Hornby, with some of his officers, were guests. A great native chief, 'Bologun Kere,' was also invited. While at breakfast, in course of conversation, the Governor asked the chief how old he thought he (the Governor) was? The Bologun answered 'A hundred years,' which remark was received with much laughter. He was then asked how old he thought the Commodore was, and he replied 'Fifty years.' Being questioned as to his reason for thinking so, said that '"Obba Golobar"' had beard and getting grey from hard work, while the Commodore had no beard.' The Governor told him that the Commodore was his senior officer in the navy, and had much care and anxiety about the men in the squadron under his command. The chief laughed and said, 'There is not much need to care for men, the greatest need is to care for women, because man is born of woman, and the governor had a greater care protecting men, women, and children; men could fight for themselves, but women needed protection as they could not fight.' The chief was much applauded for his chivalrous sentiments.

On another of these occasions the mail came in, bringing the sad news of the death of the Governor's two brothers in the Forty-third Light Infantry, who were both killed the same day at the Gate Pah in the New Zealand war, but the dinner went on as usual. The guests thought that the Governor had not had time to read his letters, and was unaware of the fact. After dinner one of them inquired if he knew of his loss? He was greatly touched by the kind feeling expressed by all, and told them 'He was well aware of it, but that they had died as brave soldiers for their country,' and he could not let his private sorrow interfere with his public duty; he hoped his friends would not hurry away on his account, although

he would retire from their society for that evening. A sum of money which came to him after
the death of his brothers he devoted to the education of some natives at Lagos.

One of his attributes which impressed the
people was his great strength and capacity of
enduring long marches and great hardships, with
only country food to eat, and that often of a
meagre kind. He wore no covering on his head
except a small dark-blue forage cap, while other
Europeans were obliged to seek protection from the
sun. They were, also struck by his endurance in
remaining for hours in the saddle by day, when by
night he had only his black ram-skin rug to rest
on, if not the guest of some chief.

All the 'war palavers' used to be carried
on under the great palm trees, which are the
principal feature in the market-place of every
native village, and which are held sacred by the
people. On one occasion, when 'Golobar' had
much trouble with a hostile and warlike town in
the interior, whither he had made a long and
tedious march to put down a revolt and settle
disputes, knowing that as soon as he had left for
Lagos their 'war palavers' would begin again, he
threatened to cut down the palm trees in their
market-place. So great was the consternation of
the chiefs and principal men of the town that they

came on bended knees, throwing dust on their heads, to beg of him to spare their sacred trees. ' Golobar ' said he would think it over ; and when they came to know his decision, replied : ' Yes, I will spare these trees ; but, mark you, I will put a white fowl's feather in the topmost branches, and when at night you sit by your firelight and talk of the Great White Queen in the North, and say that man's blood must flow, that your warriors will go forth on their war-paths, then this fowl's feather will whisper into my ear and tell me what you will do, and I will come, I and my chiefs, with the army of the " Great White Queen," and will wipe you out of the land, and there will be wailing in your camp.' After this, never again did the chiefs palaver under these trees. They knew that ' Golobar ' would come as he had said, and he had no further trouble with that town. It was his knowledge of their superstitions and their way of talking in parables, as well as his courage, that gave him such a personal power when dealing with the natives, together with a strong magnetism which few could resist. They seemed to be governed by what they called ' the power of the eye.'

In his study of these natives he discovered the existence of a secret bond among them, which he concluded was a form of free-masonry as it had been handed down to them through the black Arabs

whose legends lead us to the supposition that th
craft had its origin in the days of Solomon. Their
measures for grain are all of Hebrew origin, made
in the form of conical baskets. After his return to
England, Captain Glover was installed as a mason,
with the view of proving how far freemasonry was
known in these obscure tribes.

Another of their peculiarities was their method
of communication by symbols. For instance, a
native envoy would arrive from the interior bearing
a piece of stick with a cleft in it, or a joint of bamboo, which would signify the hostile or friendly
state of the country he represented. The tongs
was symbolical that nothing is so hot that cannot
be held by them, *i.e.*, that, however difficult the
treaty, the Ibadans will keep it. The gnarl or
knot in the cane, that the understanding is from
God, made by His will, and that man cannot untie
it. A messenger bringing a bullet and flint in his
mouth means 'War.' All this was perfectly in-
telligible to the Governor, who respected such laws,
customs, and manners of the natives, as were not
repugnant to conscience and good feeling.

Constant jealousy—often breaking out into
warfare—was rife among all the neighbouring
tribes, many of whom misrepresented the attitude
of the Lagos Government, and there was but one
effectual way of putting a stop to this friction,

namely, by keeping the roads to the interior open with a firm hand, so as to allow the produce to come down to the coast. For this purpose the Governor caused a large market to be made at Lagos where all could sell their goods.

As time moved on, there began to be a general desire among the chiefs for peaceable relations, but there was, as in all African palavers, the stumbling-block of ' who shall advance first ? ' It is difficult to say how long they would have continued in their state of hostility had not the Governor undertaken the office of peacemaker. Several chiefs were brought together, and the opening of the market at Ogudu was the occasion on which he succeeded in arranging matters.

Afterwards, when the peace of the country was established, and the King of Dahomey had sent him a flag symbolic of allied friends, when the British subjects could travel anywhere in the interior without fear of molestation, the very name ' Golo-bar afrai ogun ' (Glover the mighty warrior) giving facility to all who used it, he induced the home Government to reward the kings and chiefs who had helped him to restore peace. Mr. Cardwell, then Secretary of State, sent him two swords with Arabic inscriptions, to be presented to Ex-King Kosoko and Chief Tappa, and also two others to be handed down in the Yoruba tribe, and held by their representatives for the time being. The ceremony took place on the race-course, where a large crowd was assembled. With the thermometer at 130° in the sun, a company of the Third West Indian Regiment was drawn up in line, while a company of artillery with three field-pieces, and two or three hundred Haussas were present, dressed in their dark blue tunics with red Turkish trousers, and close fitting caps, their band playing.

Meanwhile King Kosoko arrived on the ground attended by a large retinue, and was escorted to a shed reserved for the ceremonies of the day. His Majesty was arrayed in a robe of brocade, with a beaver hat trimmed with gold lace. The several chiefs approached and paid him homage. As soon as the Governor arrived and was seated, King Kosoko and the chiefs advanced and were placed on his left. After the salute was fired the companies marched past in review. The Ex-King was called and presented with a sword, bearing the inscription 'Presented by the Government of Queen Victoria to the Ex-King Kosoko in commemoration of loyal services rendered by him to the Government of Lagos.' In handing it to him, the Governor sheathed the sword, saying, 'There was now peace in the country, if there was still war he would have presented it drawn.'

Among the chiefs one of the most powerful was

'Tappa,' an Egba, and the war minister of King Kosoko. This chief was reported to be very rich, and a portion of the town of Lagos was named after him in which the people of his tribe lived. Tappa was always a great friend of 'Golobar's,' and helped him on every possible occasion. When he was dying he sent to ask the Governor to come and see him once more, and during that last interview, while holding the hand of the dying man, the medicine-men came in with their idols to perform the last rites. Tappa turned towards the Governor and said, 'Send them away, I have done with all that, and I believe in the white man's God.' This was the only native he ever knew who, when death was approaching, demanded that the idols and medicine-men should be sent away. Tappa's death is supposed to have been caused by poison, and so subtle are these native vegetable extracts, that it is impossible to detect traces of the poison, even by a post-mortem examination.

At this point it may be convenient to incorporate in the narrative the following interesting reminiscences contributed by General Sir Andrew Clarke :—

'In 1862 I was sent as Commissioner to the West Coast of Africa, especially to inquire into questions concerning the Ashantis. Captain Glover was then Governor of Lagos ; and was identifying himself with the interests of the Colony and the policy of developing the Hinterland.

'When I arrived at Cape Coast Castle I was struck with the sounds of yelling and shouting that was going on, evidently caused by natives suffering from some deadly panic. On inquiry I found the cause of this disturbance arose from the friends of a powerful Ashanti chief, who had been sent as an envoy to Cape Coast Castle, and who had been thrown into prison by Sir Benjamin Pine. They feared that I had come to cause the execution of their chief. On my sending for the prisoner he proved to be a fine specimen of humanity, very intelligent, and quite an African gentleman. When interviewing him I found he had been put into prison because of his alleged cruelties to his people. On my investigating the matter, the chief turned to me and said, "I know the history of your country; you, too, put to death for evil deeds and for far less crimes than we do. Was it not at the beginning of this century, when George III. was your king, that daily two or three men were hanged for sheep stealing, poaching, or some other similar offences? We keep all our criminals till some festival or occasion when we can meet together, perhaps once a year, perhaps only once in two or three years, as it is difficult to collect in large numbers in our country, and then all the men

who have done wrong and who are condemned to
suffer death, are brought out and executed for
others to see and be warned.   And there is not one
of those men so condemned who is not worthy of
death, over and over again, for the crimes that
have been committed by them."[1]   I found on
inquiry into the matter that this was true, and I
discovered that one of the reasons why Glover had
such a strong hold over the natives was that he
always inquired closely into every question, and
could understand their difficulties, from a native
point of view as well as from ours.   He could thus
treat them with fairness and justice, and he was
not led away by the exaggerated stories which often
reached England, or were believed by Englishmen
who were sent out only for a short time to the
coast.

'I went on to Lagos, and there was taken very
ill with fever and dysentery.   Dr. Rowe, afterwards
Sir Samuel Rowe, was the medical officer attending
me, and I was staying at Government House with
Captain Glover, who nursed me himself day and
night, and hardly ever left me.   On Christmas-eve
I was lying on the bed in Glover's room, which he
had placed at my disposal, while he was opening
a parcel of pink spun silk vests which I had brought

[1] This chief was afterwards killed by Sir Garnet Wolseley's force
during the Ashanti War.

him from Cape Coast Castle. This he did principally to arouse my attention from the languor and
inert state I was in ; and after trying them on to see
and admire their fit, he went into the adjoining
room to finish mixing a Christmas pudding. On
this task being completed he proceeded to open a
case of champagne for his guests. The popping of
the corks awoke me from my dozing condition, and
I heard him ask Dr. Rowe if he might give a glass
of champagne to Clarke ? Dr. Rowe replied, "You
may give him anything you like, he can't last till
morning." At that moment a gun fired ; I knew it
meant that H.M.S. "Investigator" had crossed the
bar, and I said, in response to Dr. Rowe's remark,
"I'll be d—— if I don't." Glover brought me a tum-
bler full of champagne, which I roused myself to
take, for that gun had brought me hope when all
hope for life had gone. I called my boy, and told
him that when Lieutenant Gambier, the commander
of the gunboat, came on shore, he was to report
himself to me, and I dozed off again. The next
thing I was conscious of was the " click, click " of
Lieutenant Gambier's sword on the stairs. By a
bit of luck he came into the room, followed by
Glover, for the black boy had fallen asleep and forgot to give my message. I roused up on seeing
them and said, " I want you to take me to sea to-
night." Gambier replied : " Impossible, I must coal

first.''   Glover remarked there would be no impossibility or difficulty about that, for he would see to it
himself.   And he stayed up all the night to see the
work was done and assistance given, otherwise it
would not have been possible to go to sea by daybreak.   The last thing I can remember was finding
myself on deck, and I afterwards heard that Glover
had carried me on board himself. By twelve o'clock
we were out of sight of land, and the fever had left
me.   It was the energy and promptness he displayed in getting the gunboat ready for sea to
which I owed my life.'

When the duties of his government prevented
Captain Glover from leaving Lagos to visit
distant portions of the Hinterland in that colony,
he was continually employing natives to collect information concerning the surrounding country, and
thus we find a record of a journey from Lagos to
Benin when the messenger was refused admittance
into that city, though he was able to approach it
and learn the distances to the various towns in the
neighbourhood, and particulars concerning the
kings, chiefs, or 'bales' who governed the people
around.   The inhabitants of Benin were noted for
their cruelties and the barbarity of their human
sacrifices.   A mystery hung over the city, and the
gates were sealed to other Africans as well as to
the 'white man's' envoys. Still the information col-

lected was sufficient to enable maps to be made locating various places in this unknown district. A portion near Benin remained unexplored, but the route to the coast was developed.

The formation of the Haussa force, called the Gold Coast constabulary, became one of considerable importance. Nominally police, they are the local soldiers at Lagos. From the kindness that Captain Glover had always shown to this tribe, which he found in slavery during his first visit to that colony, there sprung up a deep respect and personal attachment towards him, and this enabled him to induce them to enlist. He found, under discipline, he could tame their Arab restlessness, which made them utterly useless as traders and agriculturists, because they were never happy long in one place. While not above cattle lifting and running away with the wives of the neighbouring tribes, they became valuable and steady soldiers with European officers to lead them, learning their drill quickly and well, and becoming good shots. The Governor's opinion of the capabilities of these men was fully justified, the Haussas having continued to do good service from the formation of the force to the present time. In a London paper, dated February 5, 1896, speaking of the late Ashanti expedition, it says, 'The services rendered by the Haussa force are specially commented upon, their obedience and soldierly conduct in general being most praiseworthy.'

In these early days, when the colony was in its infancy, the office of Governor was no sinecure ; discretion, judgment, and firm administrative qualities being necessary to keep peace among the neighbouring tribes. In addition to these demands on the mental and moral qualities of a ruler, there was constant hard work and worry, and malarial fever to contend with, in a climate which enervates the strongest men. The Governor encouraged all sports and outdoor games and gatherings, to prevent the depression which assailed new comers, and give as much recreation as was possible to those whose lot was cast on the West Coast of Africa.

At the end of his five years' term of government he returned to England, universally regretted by the people of Lagos, and received many farewell addresses from its inhabitants. Soon after his departure they sent a petition to the Colonial Office, asking that he should be sent back again as Governor, and offering to pay a large increase of salary if he would accept a second term. The Colonial Office at once acceded to this request, and assented to his receiving an increase of emolument. All his friends in England were strenuous in their efforts to dissuade him from returning to such a pestilential climate ; but their advice was

of no avail. It might be that he was influenced
at that time by a disappointment, which had
destroyed the hopes of many years, or that his
love for Africa was stronger than any personal
interest. Whatever his motive was, he accepted
the Governorship for the second time, and returned
to Lagos, where he continued the improvements
he had begun.   He received many addresses of
welcome on his return, and among others, one from
Akorodu, from the chief of all Egbas, saying ' that
during his absence he had had much trouble with
his domestic affairs, in consequence of his wives
running away with Lagos men, and refusing to
return.' His letter was accompanied with the
amusing request that ' the Governor should cause
the return of the runaway wives.' What means
Captain Glover employed to induce these ladies
to go back to their lords and masters we have
no record to prove ; but it is clear that he generally
arranged the difficulties, and kept the Lagos men in
pretty good order.

CHAPTER VII

MR. POPE HENNESSEY IN WESTERN AFRICA

Captain Glover's return to Lagos—Survey of the ' Volta '—Egba disturbances—Mr. Goldsworthy's mission to Porto Novo—Mr. Pope Hennessey arrives in Lagos—Dispatch to the Secretary of State—Policy of the Hinterland—Stoppage of roads—Slavery question—Letter to the Editor of the ' Manchester Courier '—Letter from Captain Glover to Mr. Pope Hennessey—Sir George Berkeley appointed Governor—Fresh disturbances on the Gold Coast.

AFTER the Governor's return for his second term of office, he again had occasion to take up his old work of surveying. The River ' Volta ' was till then unexplored for navigating purposes, and he was anxious to ascertain whether it would prove a suitable water-way for commercial purposes into the interior. Life at Lagos continued much the same during the next few years as was described in the last chapter. Trade had considerably increased. The town had been much improved by new churches, schools, public buildings, and private dwelling-houses. Feuds still continued among neighbouring tribes. The Egbas once more tried to prevent trade being carried on with Lagos, except through their country. Abeokuta, their home, was the largest and most cultivated district beyond Lagos. Some sons of liberated Africans induced the native authorities of that town to drive out the white missionaries and merchants, so as to have it in their own hands. The result of the mismanagement of these semi-civilised Creoles was such that the rising Abeokuta bade fair to become a disgrace to Christianity and civilisation. From trade relations with Lagos the Egbas of Abeokuta gained control of several thousands of pounds belonging to the merchants of Lagos, which they refused to pay up, and used in the Ijaye war, where they squandered the whole of it, but were repulsed and beaten. Then, to retrieve their loss, they went to war with Ikorodu, which is near Lagos, and had they succeeded Abeokuta would have tried to invade Lagos also. Captain Glover realised this, and was determined to teach Abeokuta people to live and let live, and not to allow them to debar other tribes from direct communication with Lagos by stopping up the roads, and capturing, killing, or making slaves of the people who passed through. He also saw that the best solution of the difficulty would be to effect the opening up of a new pass through the rich and unexplored countries of the Ondos and Ifeis to Ibadan. Accordingly, Mr. Goldsworthy was sent by this route on a mission to the king and chief of

the many towns in this extensive country, and the
new route became more free and available for trade
than the old one from the Egba country. This
alarmed the Egbas, who made a solemn league to
thwart our policy. More than a hundred Abeokuta chiefs got Awujale the king to enter into a
compact, made binding by the blood of a human
sacrifice, to stop trade coming to Lagos, their
object being to upset the Government of Lagos,
and use the port for themselves. In this case
they would have been free to revive the slave trade.
But some of the powerful Egba chiefs saw the
futility of this scheme, and were anxious for peace,
and to maintain their friendship with ' Golobar.'
In consequence of its having been discovered that
some of the letters to the Governor, sent from
Abeokuta, accompanied by the usual symbol, the
staff of the Bashorun, were not authorised by him,
they made a law forbidding any sticks or staves to
accompany letters representing the true sentiments
of the Egba Government; and they ordered from
England a proper stamp and official envelope,
bearing the inscription of the Egba united board
of management, and a cross to represent the
four united kings of Abeokuta. The following
letter was sent to the Governor from the Abeokuta
chiefs, of which a translation is here given :—' In
the name of God the Merciful. Praise be to God the

Creator of the Universe. This epistle comes from the "Alatise," or he who makes kings good, to him whom the great God does bless on this earth. I am your friend as well as you are mine in truth. May the great God help you in all your undertakings.

'I received all the messages you sent to me, for which I am thankful; experience shows me that your views are mine. May you have long life. Observe always that I shall hold to your words in the letter to me, as from my best of friends. The contents of the letter incline me to write to praise and thank you. I heard that you sent to Jebba. I am inclined to suggest that you should study the circumstances of the times, and act accordingly.

'I, however, will intreat that you will not allow powder to leave your territory for any other place than Abeokuta.

'It is said in the Koran that mankind comes from the same parent stock; whatever other foolish nations do ignorantly should excite the compassion of the wise, who should help to remedy that which went wrong. You should therefore make matters good for the Egbas, Ijebus, as well as other people.

'I say the above to you from facts which are felt everywhere. Here, in the black man's country, your wise proceedings and plans make your influence great, and all of us feel it ; therefore we consider you the Head, the power made to stop further troubles, and regulate our affairs. We feel that we had never had the like white man to deal thus with us before. I therefore send you salutations, which the above sentiments draw from me.

' Therefore, I say again, that whatever messengers, with whatever messages from the countries around come to you, use your great knowledge to make them go for the general good.

' Whatever good, however small, is done by any person will surely redound on the donor ; you must continue to do good, as surely reward is in life as well as after life.

' It is not new to you that further in the interior peoples and towns allow no powder to go from them to other places. Lagos and Abeokuta are the exceptions. We in Abeokuta stop this now ; may God direct us all to do things in the right way.

' I ask you, my own friend, to use the great power you possess to put the country to rights. Forget not that we here are all brethren. You have power. There are many ungovernable ones among us in the surrounding countries, but you could put all things to rights.

' Continue to act as you are acting now, and God will help you.

'I want to call to your recollection the difference existing between Taivo and Captain Davies. Do make things right again between them.

'Let God be with him who has power to make the world quiet and peaceful.'

It will be seen by the above letter what strong personal friendship existed between many of the powerful Egba chiefs and the Governors, though some others were not so easily influenced. But while the younger men were restless and ready to fight, their elders recognised that in the end nothing was to be gained by adopting a hostile attitude towards a Government under whose protection they had secured peace and trade. Nor could they forget that the chief representative of that Government had, at the risk of his life, marched through a hostile country, with only a few natives, to make peace between two tribes whose constant wars interfered with the trade of the surrounding country.

At this time Mepon the King of Porto Novo, a most cruel and barbarous monarch, had been ruling for nine years. Rapine, murders, and robberies were of such frequent occurrence that the native princes and chiefs determined no longer to submit to his rule, and sent a petition to Lagos, signed by all their most influential men, to beg the Governor to protect them from his tyranny. He sent the Government steamer 'Eko,' with some Haussas on

K

board, under the command of Captain Goldsworthy, to see what state the town was in. He found things were even worse than was represented. In a despatch to the Governor, dated January 1872, he says : ' I cannot but express my opinion that the Government should, in the cause of humanity, if not for political reasons, interfere and put an end to this continual sacrifice of human life. . . . The instances of the cruelties of King Mepon would be too many to enumerate ; but it is not too much to say that two or more human beings are sacrificed by his orders every day, and the mode of the executions is as varied as are the pretexts on which the poor creatures suffer—some for supposed witchcraft, another for attempt to escape from slavery, while others are tortured in such a way that death itself is preferable. If the British Government does not interfere and put an end to the barbarities practised in a town bordering on one of our own colonies, it will be a foul disgrace to a country which boasts of freeing enslaved Africa, and yet permits atrocities scarcely paralleled to take place on the borders of its territories.'

The French had a strong footing at Porto Novo, and were not anxious for English rule. It was, therefore, a matter that required very judicious handling before the question could be finally settled. That every care was taken to avoid disturbing the friendly relations that existed between Great Britain and France, and that, at the same time, a firm front was shown towards the Porto Novians, will be seen by the orders given by the Governor to Captain Goldsworthy, when sending him on this mission.

' Government House, Lagos : December 6, 1871.

' Sir,—1. It is my direction that you proceed to Porto Novo in the colonial steamer " Eko," which vessel is provisioned for thirty days, for the purpose of giving protection to the lives and property of British subjects and all others who may have occasion to pass on the Lagoon.

' 2. You will particularly pay attention to the Lagos market canoes, which have been instructed to keep together, and give them such escort from time to time as you may consider necessary, and to other canoes when applied for.

' 3. You will be careful to hold no communication with the King of Porto Novo, and if the king wishes to communicate with you, refer him to me, offering to submit to me any communications he may send to you. You will understand that the present situation of affairs is not to be altered by any action of the king, the princes, or the government, until instructions are received from Her Majesty's Government.'

K 2

A firm hand in this, as in all important matters, was needed, and before long the Porto Novians put themselves under the protection of the British Crown, and a treaty was made between the king and the Government. Thus slavery and cruelty was suppressed, while, on the other side of the country, the new road to the interior was kept open and the Egbas prevented from thwarting trading facilities between Lagos and the surrounding tribes. Such was the state of the country when the Governor-in-Chief of the West African settlements came to visit Lagos.

In May 1872 Captain Glover went on six months' leave to England, his term of government at Lagos coming to an end in November of that year. He did not return, owing to a still more important occupation to be hereafter described. There were special causes inducing him to take this leave, for both before and after his departure events occurred in Western Africa which I must, however reluctantly, recount.

Mr. Pope Hennessey was sent by Her Majesty's Government, in the spring of 1872, to visit several settlements on the West Coast in the capacity of Governor-in-Chief. On coming to Lagos he made certain inquiries of his own, in consequence of which he proceeded first to impugn and then to modify Captain Glover's policy. Mr. Pope Hennessey only remained two months at Lagos, but his visit caused a veritable interregnum in the British and patriotic policy which had heretofore prevailed, and which, after a cessation for a short time, greatly to the detriment of British interests, was happily restored. My object being to set forth Captain Glover's proceedings, I am unwilling to say more than can be helped regarding Mr. Pope Hennessey; nevertheless, the attitude of the Governor-in-Chief towards the Governor of Lagos was such that an explanation cannot be avoided. He conceived the very erroneous idea that Captain Glover entertained a personal hatred of the Egbas, and that they were a down-trodden and oppressed people. That this was untrue is self-evident; but it has been necessary in the foregoing pages to explain the position of the tribes at a greater length than would otherwise have been necessary.

In his letter granting leave of absence to Captain Glover, Mr. Pope Hennessey writes : 'Looking to your long and valuable service in the settlement of Lagos, and to the comparatively short time you have been away from the active discharge of your official duties, I have no hesitation in granting you the six months' leave you require.'

The expressions are formally courteous, and may so far be appreciated; nevertheless, he had, in a letter to the Secretary of State, impugned

Captain Glover's policy, and was causing its reversal on the spot. This is clear from an important draft of a despatch written by Captain Glover to the Secretary of State. I have the original draft in his own handwriting, stating the circumstances of the case, which, however interesting they may be, are too long to print. From this despatch it is clear that the trade of Lagos had been principally with certain tribes on the coast, notably with the Egbas and with Abeokuta their principal town; but there was a far more important Hinterland, namely, that of the Yoruba's; and the Governor's policy was to open up communication with the Yoruba country, partly to increase lawful traffic, and partly to stop unlawful traffic in slaves. To this the Egbas and half-breed Egbas, from their narrow point of view, objected, and they induced Mr. Pope Hennessey to adopt their views. This he did without making any inquiries from the Governor or from the principal people at Lagos, ignoring his own countrymen, namely, the British representative and the principal officers who had been in Lagos for many years. Among the consequences was the marked and immediate diminution of British trade, which naturally caused anxiety in Lancashire, where there was a large and growing trade with Lagos.

This feeling is displayed by the following

extracts from a letter written by Mr. Leigh Clair in the 'Manchester Courier,' dated November 5, 1872 :—

'Lagos, as you are aware, is the great port for cotton and palm oil in the West Coast of Africa. Situated in a Lagoon in the bight of Benin, it is the chief port for the large and rich country between the bight of Benin and the River Niger. It has a British Governor and a Legislative Council, and it has hitherto been a prosperous and progressive colony, as is shown by the following statistics :—1864 the Customs revenue was 9,039*l.* 15*s.* 6*d.* ; in 1871, 33,264*l.* 4*s.* 11*d.* In 1864 the value of its imports was 120,796*l.* ; and in 1871, 391,553*l.* In 1864 the value of exports was 166,093*l.* 8*s.* 1*d.* ; in 1871, 589,802*l.* 9*s.* 6*d.* The great increase in its prosperity is owing to the judicious government of Captain Glover. He, to my certain knowledge, has spent not only his official pay, but also his private resources in furthering the prosperity of the colony. Lagos is surrounded by three coast tribes—the Porto Novians, the Egbas, and the Ijebus—who wish to keep all the trade in their own hands, and it is difficult for the vast Yoruba country, which extends to within a few miles of the Niger, to send down its produce to the seaboard, or to receive goods in return. This Yoruba country teems with wealth, and its people are anxious to trade with England. Governor Glover, judging from years of experience of the country and its people, has constantly had before him the desirability of opening fresh roads into the interior. In 1869 he sent a messenger with instructions to pass through the Yoruba country, and make his way by the proposed new route to the coast; this was successfully carried out, and the messengers were everywhere joyfully received by the king's " bales " and chiefs. He found the country rich with produce, which was lying rotting in the ground for want of a market to sell it in. Many of the tribes had neither seen or heard of a white man; they said : " We are all thieves, and never at peace, because we cannot make trade and sell our produce." All the tribes agreed that they did not want to buy and sell slaves; all they wanted was trade with the white man. Directly it was known at Lagos that the road was opened and safe, caravans of slaves and refugees prepared to return joyfully to their long-lost homes, taking with them the property they had accumulated by honest labour. The Governor in person then left Lagos for Odi, the river considered most desirable for the purpose, in order that, by his presence, he might insure the safe starting of the first caravan under a European, Captain Goldsworthy, the district magistrate. He was joyfully received everywhere, even by chiefs who he had supposed might not be friendly. All seemed a success, and Governor Glover then found that, taking advantage of his absence, the Egbas and the Ijebus, being roused by fear of losing the monopoly of the Lagos trade, had spread all sorts of reports with a view of preventing the new road being a success ; they said it would injure their trade, they would lose their slaves, and that the British Government would seize their country. The Egbas had already chosen their roads, and the Ijebus did the same, and the trade of Lagos came to a stand. The Egbas said the English had taken their country, and had interfered with the allegiance of their subjects, and they wanted the English sent away, and wished Lagos to return to the government of their native king. The Egbas shut their roads, on the plea that guns and powder were prohibited to them, and also because the Governor had insisted upon the use of a standard measure by which palm kernels should be sold, instead of the deceitful and uncertain sale by bag, which had given rise to endless disputes and trickery. Their real object was, however, to force the Government into allowing them the right to seize slaves at Ebuta-Mela, within half a mile of Lagos, on British territory, and they wished to replace the Government by that of a native king. The Egbas were assisted in their demands by the worthless portion of the Lagos people—people who have nothing to lose, and who have been everlastingly crying out against our laws and the abolition of the slave trade. A little firmness and patience would have righted all this, and the new law have become a success, as the markets in the interior were gradually becoming overstocked with produce, and the stock of goods was being consumed, and fresh supplies could not be got until the roads were opened ; in other words, trade would have forced the opening of the roads. Unfortunately, at this point, however, Mr. Pope Hennessey arrived upon the scene as Governor-in-Chief, and without knowing anything of the country or the people, listened to the idle statements of the party opposed to Governor Glover, and in a few days undid all the work it had taken Captain Glover years to do. He removed the steamer " Eko," which had been sent to Porto Novo to protect British interests, and, more particularly, the opening of the new roads. He withdrew the steamer protecting the Lagoon at Odi, and ordered the Government House built there to be destroyed. Guns and powder were already free, the brickmaking machinery was to be sold, the Government steamer sold, and the engineers and apprentices discharged, and all the expensive Government workshops allowed to be idle. Governor Glover, whose period of service was just expiring, could not countenance these proceedings; therefore he applied for leave of absence to come home. I now come to the result of all this. The trade of Lagos has been stopped since March, and the roads are still shut, although trade may force them open any day. Cotton, palm oil, and other produce, are locked up in the interior, and goods are lying idle at Lagos. A large number of English vessels have been lying months in Lagos roads without cargo, or have had to leave for other ports. The loss to merchants is large, and so is the loss of revenue to the Government. Strange to say, the new road established by Governor Glover is still open, and oil is coming down, although slowly, and this, in the face of difficulties, and the opposition of Mr. Pope Hennessey and the present acting Governor Fowler. The slave trade is gaining ground, and the British flag is no longer a protection to the slaves. Slaves have been allowed to be seized, lives have been sacrificed, and people have been thrown into prison, without trial, for preventing slaves being taken from under the protection of the British flag. You will thus see how the hopes of a rising colony may be blighted by Government appointments made from political motives.'

Some of the results of the revival of the slave trade at Lagos are lamentable to relate. More than one poor woman drowned herself and her children in the river, preferring for them a watery grave rather than the bonds of cruel captors. A touching story is told by Dr. Rowe of the capture of the wife of a Haussa, who was sold for 8*l.* She came to him to intercede on her behalf, with the tears rolling down her face, accompanied by her husband, a powerfully built man, who had armed himself with a knife, vowing he would kill her owner sooner than let his wife be dragged away into slavery. I have in my possession authentic letters from Captain Goldsworthy, and other persons of undoubted veracity, describing many scenes like these, and others giving account of such barbarous cruelties committed at Porto Novo, that I consider them to be unfit for publication ; and yet it was to protect the people from such outrages occurring that the steamer 'Eko' was sent by Captain Glover, which was withdrawn by Mr. Pope Hennessey.

That Captain Glover had endeavoured to indicate to the Governor-in-Chief the reason for the policy that he had pursued, with the view of preventing an unfortunate change, will be apparent from the following draft in his own handwriting:—

To his Excellency John Pope Hennessey

'Government House, Lagos : June 9, 1872.

'Sir,—(1) I have the honour to acknowledge the receipt of your Excellency's despatch No. 37 of May 16.

'(2) In reference to paragraphs 2 and 3, I must observe to your Excellency that the stoppage of trade by the Egbas and Ijebus was not occasioned by prohibition of arms by this Government, but on account of the slave question ; and that my intercourse with the interior tribes has been conducted wholly and entirely in the cause of peace, friendly intercourse, and the extension of commerce and Christianity.

'(3) In regard to paragraphs 4, 5, 6, and 7, all I have to observe is that the steamer " Eko " was employed for the protection of our trade on the Lagoon against the piratical acts of the slaves of the King of Porto Novo ; that I do not consider that she was intermeddling in the affairs of Porto Novo, and that the instructions, dated December 6, 1871, and given by me to Captain Goldsworthy (see inclosure No. 1) were in accordance with the concluding paragraph of Lord Kimberley's despatch of February 23, 1872, namely, " That you will quietly abstain from interfering with the affairs of that town, without directions from home," my instructions to Captain Goldsworthy being dated December 6, 1871, nearly three months anterior to Lord Kimberley's instructions on the subject. I moreover abstain from endeavouring "to obtain redress" even "by peaceable means" for robberies committed on the Lagoon (see despatch, Downing Street, 137, of March 1, 1872) until your Excellency shall visit Lagos. (Reported in my despatch No. 31, of March 26, 1872). "That the presence of the steamer 'Eko' caused great commotion and inconvenience" has no foundation in fact, and on further inquiry your Excellency will find my statement to be correct; and, furthermore, I considered I was carrying out the instructions contained in paragraph 35, page 10, of the Colonial Regulations on the subject of the suppression of piracy.

'(4) In reference to paragraphs 8 and 9, I am confident that when your Excellency shall have had time to go more into the affairs of Lagos than was afforded by your recent short visit, between the dates of April 25 and April 30 (one day of which was a Sunday), that your Excellency will not attach to me "the responsibility for a state of affairs brought about by the factious intrigues of a local clique."

'(5) On the subject of recruiting the Haussa force, I have to inform your Excellency that recruiting has been going on since November 8, 1871 (see inclosure No. 2), and that upon the receipt of Lord Kimberley's despatch, February 12, 1872, I hastened to increase the force by inducing them to join for six months, when there was a hesitation displayed in enlisting for three years with a prospect of serving on the Gold Coast.

'(6) In regard to the concluding paragraph of your Excellency's despatch, I am quite prepared to await the result of your Excellency's investigation on your return to Lagos.'

I refrain from mentioning numerous unpleasant incidents connected with this period which must have been most galling to any English gentleman in Captain Glover's position, as they were not of a purely political character; nor could Government House be any longer a place for him when the Governor-in-Chief's committees, composed of half-breeds selected from the lowest class of people in the town, pervaded every room and relieved the Governor of any portable plate that might be within reach. Suffice it to say, that those who are cognisant of Mr. Pope Hennessey's career in Labuan, the Mauritius, and Hong Kong, will form their own estimate of the policy pursued by him on the West Coast of Africa. Numbers of letters and petitions were sent to England. At last

Bishop Crowther, strongly supported by his own countrymen, came home to represent matters in the cause of humanity.

In 1873 Sir George Berkeley became Governor of Lagos, when Captain Glover's policy was resumed, and, consequently, British trade revived. Lagos began to grow and flourish once more; slavery was checked; the coast tribes were kept in their proper place; communication with the tribes in the interior was resumed. But the process was slow, and it was long before the country recovered the check it had received.

While Captain Glover was still on leave in England, new complications arose in Africa, which led to war with Ashanti; and it will be seen in the next Chapter how he was sent for by the War Office to advise the authorities with regard to raising native troops, and utilising the rivers and roads into the interior through which they must pass.

CHAPTER VIII

NATIVE EXPEDITION AGAINST THE ASHANTIS BY
SIR JOHN HAWLEY GLOVER

Causes of the Ashanti War—Cession of Elmina—Testimony of Sir Gilbert Carter and Sir Andrew Clarke—Circumstances in which Captain Glover's Report was drawn up—Interview of Captain Glover with Mr. Cardwell—Description of country round the Volta—Lord Kimberley informs Captain Glover his offer is accepted to raise native troops—Sir Garnet Wolseley is given military command of Ashanti Expedition—Captain Glover proceeds to Cape Coast to enlist Haussas and native allies.

[BEFORE proceeding to give the unfinished report of the Native Expedition against the Ashantis drawn up by Sir John Glover, it may be as well to indicate briefly the causes which led to the outbreak of hostilities on the West Coast.

There can be no question that the main exciting cause of the Ashanti War of 1872–73 was the cession by the Dutch to the British Crown of Elmina and their other settlements on the Gold Coast in April 1872. In spite of the fact that prior to the ratification of the Convention by which the Dutch surrendered their rights, the British Government had ascertained from the King of Ashanti that he

L

possessed no claim to Elmina, there is no doubt that the Ashantis strongly objected to the change of ownership. They had long been accustomed to Dutch methods, which they contrasted with those of the English in the neighbouring settlement of Cape Coast Castle; and there were many reasons for preferring the Dutch, who, from the Governor downwards, all had native wives, and made no secret of their existence.

The Elminas themselves were by no means pleased with the change, and this feeling was greatly intensified by the indiscreet action of Her Majesty's Commissioner who negotiated the transfer—Mr. John Pope Hennessey. This officer, with amazing ineptitude, immediately after the cession appointed a native, named Eminsang, to be the civil commandant of the fort and responsible head of the settlement. When it is considered that a Dutch officer of high rank had held the post of Governor, and that Admiral de Ruyter's staff had always been held by the Governors of Elmina as a symbol of their office, it will readily be understood that the appointment of Eminsang was resented on all sides. Moreover, this man, who had held a comparatively minor office under the Dutch Government, was intensely disliked by the whole community. In these circumstances it is not surprising that almost immediately after the departure of the Commissioner a serious riot took place, and an attempt was made to shoot Eminsang; unfortunately the shot took effect upon a Dutch officer named Joost, who was killed. Eminsang, after this episode, ran away, and another commandant was appointed, this time an European doctor, with no qualifications for the post except that he was an Irishman and a Roman Catholic. The official version made it appear that Joost had made himself obnoxious to certain labourers whose pay had been withheld, and that in consequence his life had been attempted. Eminsang's sudden departure, however, is a sufficient answer to this allegation.

This episode is only mentioned to show the feeling which existed in Elmina at the time of the transfer, and the Elminas were only too glad to encourage the feeling which existed amongst the Ashantis, to invade the Protectorate and to obtain a port, which had long been desired by the Ashanti authorities.

The Ashantis undoubtedly were in constant communication with the disaffected Elminas, and from the latter they obtained information as to the proceedings of the British.

The Ashanti army was dispatched from Kumasi in December 1872, and in January of the following year crossed the River Prah and from thence spread over the Protectorate. In April it met and defeated the Fanti allies at Dunkwa, and subsequently at a place called Jukwa, and from thence proceeded to Elmina, where it was defeated by the seamen and marines of the Fleet, combined with the Colonial Forces, under Sir Francis Festing, R.M.L.I.

Mr. Carter—now Sir Gilbert Carter—to whom I am indebted for the foregoing summary of the pre-disposing causes of the Ashanti War, was at that time employed on the West Coast, and has assured me that he retains a very clear recollection of the events which occurred at Elmina in 1872. As one of the Commissioners appointed by Mr. Pope Hennessey to take over the stores left behind by the Dutch, he was present at the transfer. Curiously enough it was a descendant of the famous Admiral Van Tromp who told him the story of the riot, which was subsequently confirmed from other sources.

Sir Andrew Clarke, whose intimate relations with Captain Glover eleven years earlier have been described in a previous chapter, was at this juncture in London. To quote his own words : ' When fresh difficulties had arisen with Ashanti, in consequence of the new arrangement between England and Holland, which gave to Holland the control of Sumatra, in the Straits of Malacca, in exchange for Elmina and Dutch interests on the Gold Coast, I was consulted by the Colonial Office, and from my previous experience of his character and his knowledge of Africa I advised that Captain Glover should be appointed and given a free hand in dealing with the whole question. My advice was eventually only partly adopted, for Captain Glover was given the command of the expedition up the Volta, and subsequently it was decided to send a British force from this country. This, however, was an afterthought, and wholly unnecessary for the permanent pacification of the West Coast, as events have since proved.'

The full story of the native expedition could hardly be elucidated except by Captain Glover himself, or by some one who was with him through that long and arduous undertaking. It was not fully told either by him or by anyone in his life-time. Thus it will never be adequately narrated. Indeed Captain Glover himself felt this, and on his death-bed said that the narrative was 'a work which he was leaving undone.'

In 1875, after the conclusion of the war, the subject was much upon his mind. On June 27 in that year he wrote thus to the Colonial Office: 'I believe no one can accuse me of either writing or talking about the proceedings of my force since my return from Ashanti—if I except the occasion of the banquet at Liverpool, when I mentioned the cordial relations which had throughout the

campaign existed between the General and myself
. . . . I think the time has come when our side of
the Ashanti force shall have full justice done to
it. Might I suggest that Captain Goldsworthy
or myself be authorised to draw up, under the
authority of the Colonial Office, an official report or
narrative of the Volta campaign, which might be
printed in the form of a Blue Book.'

In reply, he was instructed to prepare such an
account fully and categorically. He did accordingly
begin the preparation of this report, but had
advanced only a short way with it when he was
appointed Governor of Newfoundland. After that
he never found leisure to complete the work.
The beginning of the draft report remains in his
own handwriting, as a testamentary fragment. It
has a value of its own—as explaining how this important affair began—showing how he was first
consulted by the two Departments of State which
were concerned, and how, in consequence of that, he
made certain proposals to Her Majesty's Government, and how he thereon received certain instructions. All these things will be found to speak for
themselves. With this view the draft is here given,
so far as it goes, and exactly as he left it.—E.R.G.]

'On July 16, 1873, came the news of the defeat
of the Fanti army in Denkera. About this date Mr.
Goschen, then First Lord of the Admiralty, sent for

me, to give my opinion as to the possibility of getting stores up to the neighbourhood of Prahsu from the coast by the River Prah. My only knowledge of the Prah amounted to the certainty that it would not be found practicable to get up even empty canoes from the sea to Prahsu. This led to a conversation on the subject of the war generally, and of the eastern portion of the protected territory in particular, which had not been invaded by the Ashantis or its tribes called out for its defence by the Government.

' Some days after this interview I was sent for by Mr. Cardwell, then Secretary of State for War, and asked to repeat what I had said to Mr. Goschen. This resulted in my receiving a summons to attend a meeting at the Horse Guards on July 29; present, the Secretary of State for War, his Royal Highness the Commander-in-Chief, Admiral Sir Alexander Milne, General Sir Richard Airey, Major-General Sir Charles Ellice, Sir Andrew Clarke, and others.

' I put before the meeting the necessity of raising the eastern tribes and falling on the flank and rear of the invading force, and at the same time threatening Kumasi by a force to be assembled on the Prah in Western Akim, so as to compel the Ashantis to loosen their grip of Cape Coast Castle and its immediate neighbourhood, and thereby enable us to raise up the beaten down Fantis, who were crouching under the protection of our forts, and the small force then holding them, and give us time to organise a forward movement against the Ashantis and drive them beyond the Prah.

' To this was added an extended plan of operations up the Volta river, to raise the Mohammedan tribes north of the Volta, in the neighbourhood of Salaga, and to endeavour to communicate with and send supplies to the Gamans on the north-west of Kumasi, a tribe hostile to the Ashantis, who had been for several years endeavouring to enter into friendly relations with the Government at Cape Coast Castle.

' My proposal was to cause a diversion in the rear of the Ashantis and threaten Kumasi by a force assembled on the Prah in Western Akim. From Sir A. Clarke emanated the Volta proposition, to which I added Gaman and Salaga; but this necessitated the clearing of the Lower Volta, and securing the right of an extended base, viz., to bring to subjection the Awunas, without doing which it would be in vain to hope the seaboard tribes of the eastern portion of the Protectorate would move. It should be borne in mind that no idea existed in the minds of either Sir A. Clarke or myself that European troops were to be employed.

' The day after the meeting at the Horse Guards

I addressed a letter to the Secretary of State for the Colonies, dated July 30, offering my services to carry out the suggestion of the meeting.

' " The proposal to use the tribes of the Eastern district of the Protectorate in order to cause a diversion in the rear of the Ashanti army, and, at the same time, to threaten Kumasi," [1] suggested that the Haussa force of some three hundred and fifty men be increased to a thousand strong, to form a disciplined nucleus to the native levies. On August 2 I received a reply from Mr. Herbert, stating that Lord Kimberley was disposed to accept my offer, and desiring me to call at the Colonial Office on the following Monday. At this interview, on August 3, Lord Kimberley informed me my offer was accepted, and the utmost confidence placed in me ; that I was to choose my own staff, and settle with Mr. Herbert my salary, and that every detail of the expedition was left to my discretion. I was to send in a plan of the formation of the force to be raised. This I submitted on the 6th, and on the· 7th I furnished the commanding officer a list of the six officers whom I nominated for my staff—(Sec. 19 and 20, B.B. 2, pages 33 and 34.) Lieutenants Cameron and Barnard, of 19th Regiment, were subsequently substituted for Captain Buller, of the 60th Rifles, and Mr.

[1] No. 8, page 13, par. 2, B.B. 2, March 1874.

Tatham, late Quartermaster of 24th Regiment. Eventually, Mr. Blissett, then serving at Cape Coast Castle, was attached to my force as the control officer, and after my arrival at Akra a subsequent addition was made to the staff by Lieutenant Moore, R.N., of H.M.S. " Druid " ; Dr. Bale ; Mr. Ponsonby, Acting Sub-lieutenant of H.M.S. "Active"; Mr. Adamson, late Acting Sub-lieutenant, R.N. ; Dr. Parke, Army Medical Staff, and Dr. Thompson, from the oil rivers ; native commissioners, and Mr. Edward Bannerman ; a native gentleman as my private secretary, and Mr. Bannerman in charge of postal service and local agency at Akra.   I was instructed to procure a steamer, suitable for the navigation of the Volta, at Belfast, and purchased a steamer called the " Lady of the Lake," for 325*l.*, which subsequently proved admirably adapted for the purpose. On Friday, at an interview with Lord Kimberley, at which was present Major-General Sir Garnet Wolseley, I was informed by Lord Kimberley that Her Majesty had approved the appointment of Sir Garnet Wolseley to administer the government of the Gold Coast, with the chief military command.   I asked Lord Kimberley if this appointment of Sir Garnet Wolseley would make any alteration in the programme marked out for me by his Lordship.   Lord Kimberley replied, " None whatever."   I then said, " Then it appears to me, my Lord, that the only difference will be this, that I shall be serving under a distinguished soldier, instead of under any casual officer who might be for the time being administering the government of the Gold Coast." As neither Lord Kimberley nor Sir Garnet made any observation, I imagined something further was expected from me, and continued, "All I have further to say is that I trust when Sir Garnet returns to England he may be enabled to tell your Lordship that I never failed him." It was then settled—but against the wish of Sir Garnet—that I should still have the Haussa armed police whom I might find embodied at Cape Coast Castle on my arrival; but Lord Kimberley acquiesced in the request of Sir Garnet, that the 150 Haussas then at Lagos should be attached to the force under Sir Garnet.

'On August 19 I left England, and having purchased at Madeira six horses and three mules, arrived in due course at Cape Coast Castle on September 11, where I was detained until the evening of the 12th arranging for the withdrawal of the Haussas to Akra, and for the detaching of Messrs. Goldsworthy, Rowe, and Blissett to my headquarters at Akra.

'The officers who had accompanied me from England proceeded to Akra on the 11th, while I followed them in a steam cutter of H.M.S. "Simoon," landing at Akra on September 13, and Captain Larcom was dispatched to Lagos on the 14th, to enlist Haussa and Yoruba recruits.

' Colonel Harley had directed the civil command at Akra to summons the kings and chiefs of the Eastern district to meet me at Akra, and on my arrival I found that this order was only too consonant with the wishes of the two kings of Akra, who soon showed me they intended that nothing should be done without their approval and their means. Having had a taste of King Takia's obstructiveness during some active operations against the Ashantis on the Volta in 1870, I determined as much as possible to act directly with the separate kings and chiefs, and when I did succeed in getting them together, found that my determination met with general assent, and their satisfaction was loudly expressed when told that they would receive direct from myself or the Commissioners their several subsidies, arms, and ammunition.

' To hasten the meeting of the kings and chiefs, and for the special convenience of the kings of Eastern and Western Akim, whom I was most anxious to get first in motion, I summoned them to meet me at Akropong, as a more central point than Akra, and wrote that I would be there to meet them on the 22nd.

'On Tuesday, the 16th, Dr. Rowe arrived from Cape Coast Castle, with 200 Haussas, and the native Commissioners set out to the respective tribes to which they were accredited to notify to the kings and chiefs that they should meet me at Akropong on Monday, the 22nd. The kings of Eastern and Western Akim could not be expected to be there, but I hoped to see the rest, and thus to save time.

' The presence of the detachment of Haussas in Akra caused a stir among the Haussas, not only in Akra itself, but in the surrounding districts ; and to the apathy of the kings and chiefs was added their opposition and that of the inhabitants generally to the enlistment of their Haussa slaves.

'On the 17th Dr. Rowe had to return to Cape Coast Castle to make some final arrangements before permanently joining my force.

'A certain quantity of provisions had been brought out in the steamer with me, and having engaged the services of an English trader, I dispatched him in charge of a portion of these provisions, in a merchant ship, to form a depôt at Addah Fort, a trading station at the mouth of the Volta. This put the Akronahs on the eastern bank of the Volta in motion, and they at once demonstrated the nature of the attitude they intended to assume by seizing the Addahs.

'Before reaching Cape Coast Castle I had detailed Captain Sartorius to organise the Eastern and Western Akims, having relation to that part of my instructions indicated in Par. 9, B.B. 2, page 43, and in accordance with my original proposal to Lord Kimberley in Par. 2, No. 8, July 30, 1873, B.B.2, p. 13, and conformably with my suggestion to the meeting held at the Horse Guards on July 29, viz., to cause a diversion in the rear of the Ashanti army, and at the same time to threaten Kumasi. This ostensible object, and one on which so much stress was laid in my instructions, was not likely to fade out of remembrance on landing at Akra, nor was it probable that I should allow any future operations either on the Lower or Upper Volta to interfere with the attainment of this most essential and immediate object.   Captain Sartorius was therefore given orders to accompany me to Akropong, to make himself acquainted with the road, and to obtain such information of the Akims and their country as might be derived at interviews with natives and messengers from those countries, whom he would meet at that place.   The opposition on the part of Kings Takai and Solamon to accompany me to Akropong, was at last overcome by giving them each some money to enable them to appear in proper state at the meeting on the 20th.   Accompanied by Captain Sartorius, I left Akra for Akropong, and after a satisfactory meeting of all the chiefs, excepting the two Akim kings and the chief of Addah on the Volta, returned to Akra on the 26th. The distance from the chief towns of the kings of Eastern and Western Akim and the bad state of the roads sufficiently explained their absence, whilst the presence of Ashanti envoys at Aniako, the chief town of the Awunas, and the seizure of Addahs by these people, caused the absence of the chief of Addah.

'The absence of the two important kings before mentioned necessitated a second and general meeting at Akra when they could be present; it was not until October 8 that the King of Akim came to Akra, or till the 9th that the King of Kroboe made his appearance. On my return to Akra I found that Captain Goldsworthy had arrived from Cape Coast on the previous day, bringing with him a further detachment of 117 Haussas, at the request of Colonel Harley; this officer was for the present to act in the capacity of Civil Commandant of Akra, as well as my second in command.

'During my absence recruiting had been going on, to which was offered a daily increasing opposition on the part of the inhabitants of Akra, and the confinement of some Haussas in the king's prison (every man of local consequence having a domestic lock-up for his slaves) to prevent them going to the fort to be enlisted, resulted in the destruction of that African Bastille over which floated the British flag. Subsequent disturbances took place, and the manifestation of ill-feeling was so strong, both on the part of the townspeople and the Haussas, that I dreaded an entire collapse, not only of the undertaking to increase the Haussa force, but of the attempt that was then being made to raise the tribes in that portion of the Protectorate[1] ; I therefore authorised the payment of 5*l*. per head for every recruit for whom a claim substantiated might be put in, and this did not altogether end the difficulty. Haussa women wished to accompany the men, and at every embarkation of a detachment for the camp at Addah, the whole town came down to the beach to resist the departure of the women. In all this degradation through which I felt myself dragged and debased I had the one consoling assurance that my representations to the British Government must insure this blot upon our escutcheon being once and for ever removed, or our flag withdrawn from flying its protection over such shameless debasement and dishonour.

'On the 27th I detached by land Lieutenant Cameron, 19th Regt., with 50 Haussas, to Addah,

[1] See B.B. 4, page 19.

to cover that place from any attack of the Awunas. My transport not having arrived, I purchased 1,700*l.* worth of trade guns, powder, lead and flints, from a merchant ship in the roadstead. Also some rum and tobacco from an American ship, with which to make a beginning, and sent off 500*l.* worth of guns and ammunition to Western Akim, but no rum. Commander Larcom had also been despatched to Lagos to raise Haussa and Yoruba recruits, and to engage native seamen and firemen for the steamer and steam launches which were expected. In the meantime messengers, who had been waiting at Lagos to hear of my arrival at Akra, arrived—the one, announcing the accession of Omoro to the throne of Nupe in place of the late Mapaha, deceased; and from the king and war chief of Ondo to say that the king had gone back by my desire to rebuild the ancient capital. I availed myself of the opportune presence of these men to send news of the war to those countries, and to tell the Haussas in Nupe to join me at Salaga, and the Ondos to facilitate the passing down of Yorubas from Ibadan through their country to the lagoon eastward of Lagos. The opening of this route by Captain Goldsworthy had been repeatedly and most offensively denied by Mr. Pope Hennessey.

'If needed, here was proof of the success of Captain Goldsworthy's undertaking, which had cost me two years of tedious labour to conceive and carry through. Dr. Rowe, who returned from Cape Coast Castle on the morning of the 29th, left the same evening for Lagos, taking with him the messengers for Nupe and Ondo. He was to relieve Commander Larcom, R.N., who was to proceed to Sierra Leone and Cape Palmas to procure, if possible, 100 Kroomen, as those I had ordered at Cape Palmas on my way out had not arrived. I wished, if possible, to be independent of Akra canoe-men, and also as far as possible of Akra fighting men ; hence my object of getting one thousand disciplined Haussa and Yoruba fighting men, native crews from Lagos for the steamer and steam launches, and Kroo boys for the canoes which were coming from England. I had experienced the unreliability of Akras, both as fighting force and canoemen, in 1870 ; and when pointing this out to Lord Kimberley, his lordship replied, " I am aware of the difficulties ; if there were none, I should tell you to go on, and not stop until you reached Timbuctoo." '

CALIFORNIA

rradoe
In
S   S   I   N
Akim Swai
Accassie
Akropon Wakissi
Apradi
Faiabo
Braquah
Aftoh Insu
Adun
Sutah
Accrofoomu
Odobbim
Dadiasu
Adda Warra
Essecoomah
Mansu
Booicoom
Ayapay
Cocubino
T
Wonkorsu
Adjumacoe
Tuti
Darman
Barna
Ochesu
R. Amiss
Bissiassie
N
Yancoomassie
Eyeamin

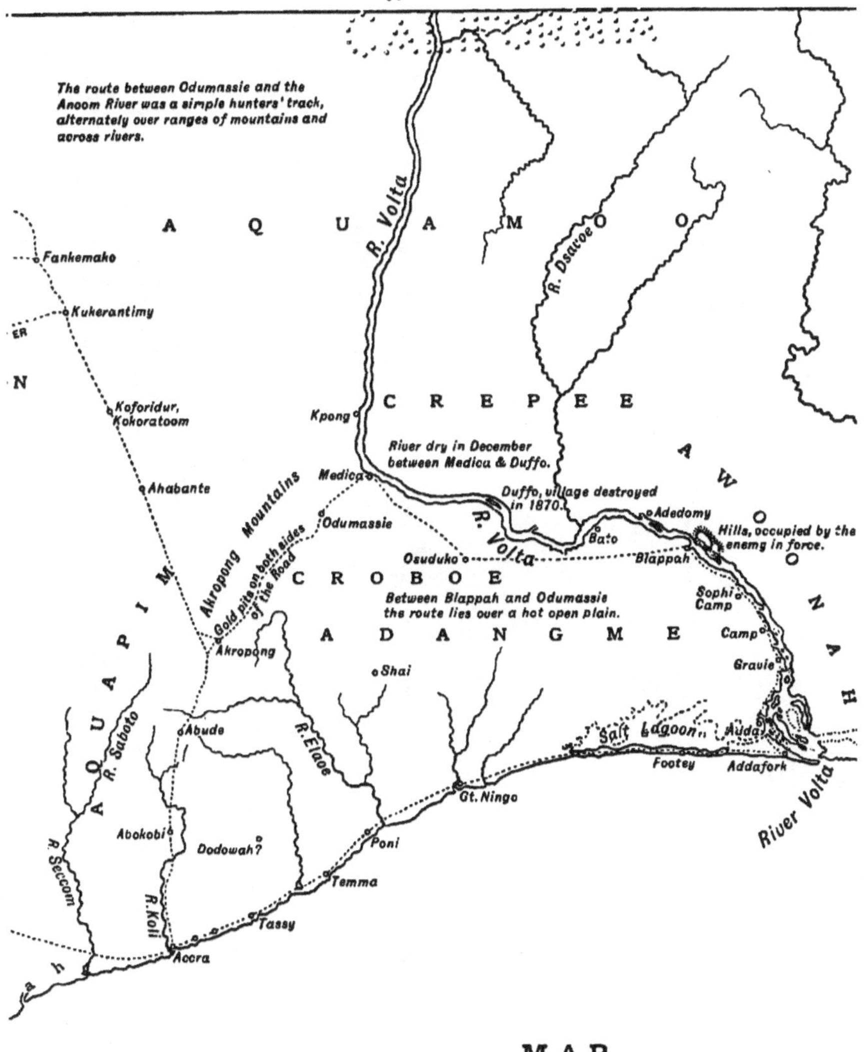
The route between Odumnassie and the
Anoom River was a simple hunters' track,
alternately over ranges of mountains and
across rivers.
Fankemake
Kukerantimy
ER
N
Koforidur,
Kokoratoom
Ahabante
A Q U A U A M O O
R. Volta
R. Dsacoe
C R E P E E
Kpong
River dry in December
between Medica & Duffo.
Medica
Duffo, village destroyed
in 1870.
A
W
Odumassie
R. Volta
Adedomy
Hills, occupied by the
enemy in force.
O
O
Osuduko
Bato
Blappah
C R O B O E
Between Blappah and Odumassie
the route lies over a hot open plain.
Sophi
Camp
Akropong Mountains
Gold pits on both sides
of the Road
A D A N G M E
Camp
Akropong
Gravie
N
A
H
Shai
A
Q
U
A
P
I
M.
R. Saboto
Abude
R. Elaoe
Salt Lagoon
Auda
Footey
Addafork
River Volta
Gt. Ningo
R. Seccom
Abokobi
Dodowah?
Poni
R. Koil
Temma
Tassy
Accra
ah
oe
MAP
to illustrate the
ASHANTI CAMPAIGN
1873-4.
English Statute Miles
5   0   5   10   15
Reduced, by permission, from the Journal of the
Royal United Service Institution, Vol. XVIII.
Walker & Boutall
Co. 15 Waterloo Place.

CHAPTER IX

THE ASHANTI WAR, 1873–1874

By SIR RICHARD TEMPLE

I APPROACH the most difficult and important passage in Captain Glover's career. He had begun to describe it for himself, as will have been seen from the preceding Chapter. But other duties prevented him from completing his description. Such completion I have now to attempt, collating and following the scattered but still explicit memoranda which he left behind. Indeed, I have, in some shape or other, his own authority for every fact or circumstance to be narrated.

The brilliant and decisive victory over the Ashantis won by the main British column, including the European troops under Sir Garnet Wolseley as Major-General, is a matter of history still fresh in the national memory. There was also an auxiliary native expedition, commanded by Captain Glover, also under the Major-General's orders. The object of the present narrative is to elucidate the conduct and the results of that expedition.

The outcome of the expedition was set forth in a despatch from Government House, Cape Coast, dated February 22, 1873, and addressed to the Secretary of State for the Colonies by Sir Garnet Wolseley, in which he used the following words :—

' Captain Glover has conducted these operations with great skill and ability, having overcome all the numerous difficulties that he had to encounter with the zeal and energy for which he is well known. . . . . The diversion effected by Captain Glover's force in favour of the main army operating direct upon Kumasi under my own immediate orders, contributed materially to the success that has been achieved in this war, and I have great pleasure in recommending Captain Glover and the officers serving under him to your Lordship's most favourable consideration.'

I proceed, then, to explain what Captain Glover did and how he did it; what effect he gave to the original instructions from the Secretary of State for the Colonies, and how he conformed to the orders subsequently received from Sir Garnet Wolseley; what were the difficulties which he is justly described by Sir Garnet as having overcome, and what was the nature of the material contribution which he is recognised as having afforded to the success of the war.

The theatre of imperial action was in the region behind or north of the Gold Coast. This portion of the African coast was thus named by reason of its auriferous character; it used to be called the Coast of Guinea. It runs for about two hundred miles from east to west, unlike the West Coast generally, which runs from north to south. The particular bend and trend of the West Coast— which causes the Gold Coast thus to run from east to west—has been explained in the Introduction to these Memoirs. Therein, also, the climatic disadvantages of the country have been set forth.

Along the Gold Coast are several British Settlements, beginning from the eastern end. First, Lagos; then Addah (mouth of the Volta); next Akra ; then Cape Coast Castle, and, further on, some other settlements which need not here be specified.

In the region north of and behind the Gold Coast there are two rivers to be remembered. Of these the eastern and the larger is the Volta. It rises in a range of mountains far to the north, and thence runs in a course mostly southwards to the sea. West of the Volta valley in the lesser mountains there rises the Prah, which runs for some distance from east to south-west, and then, for a short way, west, about a hundred miles from the coast. Then it turns southwards with a decided bend, and joins the sea to the west of Cape Coast Castle. A clear notion of the course, and the relative position, of these two rivers is essential to the comprehension of my narrative.

The country to the south and the south-east of the Prah, between the river and the coast, was inhabited by Protected tribes, and was called the British Protectorate. The Ashantis dwelt north of the Prah—their territory was considered to be a kingdom, and their capital was at Kumasi. They had, owing to causes set forth in the previous Chapter, been invading and harassing the Protectorate, and it was in consequence of this invasion that war against them was undertaken by the British. If they were to be attacked either from the British bases on the coast, or from the lower valley of the Volta, then the Prah must be crossed. Thus the Prah becomes the Rubicon of this story.

Cape Coast Castle was the base of Sir Garnet Wolseley's advance with the European troops, crossing the Prah at Prahsu, near the bend mentioned above. Captain Glover's sphere was to the east, first at Akra, and then on the Volta. It was at Akra, indeed, that he landed on his arrival from England, on September 11, 1873. His own narrative, given in the preceding Chapter, brings him to

Akra ; and from that point I have to take up the narration.

He had been appointed, in August 1873, by Her Majesty, to be ' Special Commissioner to the friendly Native Chiefs in the east of the Protected territories near or adjacent to our settlement on the Gold Coast.' The understanding with which he started from England has been stated in the last preceding Chapter by himself. But it was followed up by an important despatch to him from Lord Kimberley, dated August 18. He was informed thus :—

'The general object which you will keep in view is to create such a diversion on the rear and flank of the Ashantis as may force them to retreat from the Protectorate, or at all events, to so far harass and alarm them as to enable an attack to be made on them in front with better prospect of success.'

'9. The facilities which are afforded by a river, navigable as the Volta is, to a long distance from the coast, for carrying the war into the Ashanti territory, are unquestionable. . . .

'It must be left to you to judge for yourself on the spot, according to circumstances, how far it may be prudent to attempt to penetrate into the Ashanti territory in the direction of Kumasi. . . .

'11. You will, of course, bear in mind that the

resources of the Ashantis are said to be very considerable, and that an advance to a great distance from the Volta must necessarily be attended with much risk, unless, indeed, you should succeed in obtaining assistance from the tribes in the eastern part of the Ashanti dominions.'

In accordance with this despatch, a river steamer, with several steam launches, had been ordered to join him for service on the Volta, by Her Majesty's Government. Undoubtedly, then, his base was at the mouth of the Volta, and his base line was on the lower course of that river. Whatever may, or may not, have been the merits of that course, it certainly was prescribed to him; and his instructions were similarly understood at the Major-General's headquarters as 'indicating a general line of operations by the Volta to the Ashanti kingdom.' ('Narrative,' i., 111.)

A consideration of the state of the tribes in that quarter will show that there were good reasons for this general instruction. The Ashanti kingdom proper was, at that time, beyond the Prah, that is, north and west of that river. The Ashantis were a disciplined and fighting race, much feared by the surrounding tribes. As was afterwards proved, they had at least three bodies of real soldiers, each more than ten thousand strong, besides other forces, which made up their total number to at least forty, perhaps even to fifty, thousand. They were adepts at shooting from behind the impenetrable cover of the immense forests which guarded their capital, Kumasi. They were formidable even to a European assailant; still more were they to be feared by all the surrounding tribes. But they never had been content to remain within their proper borders. They had claimed or exercised a suzerainty over the tribes on the south and east of the Prah, that is, between that river and the sea, which had been under British protection, and which they had recently been invading, thereby bringing down British force upon themselves. For the western part of the Protectorate Cape Coast Castle was the best centre of operations; for the eastern part, either Akra or Addah, at the Volta mouth. The fear of the Ashantis still lay heavy on the unwarlike tribes of the Eastern Protectorate—namely, the Eastern Akims, the Akwapims and the Kroboes; and these three are mentioned here because we shall hear more of them hereafter. Even after the war had been begun by the British, there were Ashanti leaders—called captains by the Europeans—or emissaries moving about among these tribes, and sometimes even promoting armed resistance to British officers. But the Ashanti influence did not end there. It was powerful on the north, that is, on the higher or middle course of the Volta, and more particularly on the eastern bank of that river. There were on the north the Akwamus, extending over both sides of the river, and close up to the Ashanti border. South of them, and on the eastern bank, were the Kripis, very much under their influence, perhaps even at their disposal. These Akwamus were quite ready to throw in their lot with the Ashantis, and to carry the Kripis with them. Below the Kripis, again, and on the eastern bank, were the Awunas, extending to the coast, well-known to be on the side of the Ashantis, and eager to subjugate the Eastern Protectorate for the Ashanti dominion. So far as the protected tribes were concerned, there was nothing to prevent the Akwamus and Awunas from marching right through the Protectorate to succour the Ashantis, to hang on the right flank of the main European column advancing from Cape Coast Castle towards Kumasi, and so to enable the Ashantis to oppose that advance with all their might, and harass its return to the coast after striking the blow against Kumasi. Further, even if the Akwamus were held in check by a British demonstration on the Volta, still, the tribes in the Eastern Protectorate could not be expected to move under British leadership towards the Ashanti border, unless the Awunas were either driven back, or suppressed altogether. Otherwise, when the

Protectorate had been left undefended by the departure of its fighting men for Ashanti-land, the Awunas would have turned it into an unhappy hunting-ground, with horrors innumerable—clearing fertile fields, burning houses, carrying off families into bondage, ' feeding fat every grudge,' every vendetta, every inter-tribal feud. Naturally, the Protectorate dreaded this beyond measure; and the most competent European observers on the spot attested that such dread was well-founded. Further, the Protectorate itself might be loyal to the British in sentiment; but if, from the absence of British authority on the Volta, they were left at the mercy of the Akwamus and the Awunas, allies of the Ashantis—while the European column was advancing on another line—then they might perforce have to join the Ashanti cause. Indeed, there were already many Ashantis flitting about, and doubtless urging them to this very course.

Now, in this situation of the tribes it was essential that British authority, in some tangible shape, should be established on the Volta—first, to hold the Akwamus in check and indirectly to prevent them from helping the Ashantis; secondly, forcibly to hold back the Awunas both from aiding the Ashantis and from harrying the Protectorate; thirdly, to keep the protected tribes loyal to the British cause, and to obtain some assistance from them as against the Ashantis ; fourthly, to secure the right flank of the European advance free from any foe, from any allies or friends of the Ashantis, so that European energy might be concentrated on the enemy in front, that is, the Ashantis proper.

The British policy was, as might be expected, masterly. Its object was to deliver a swift, deadly, and decisive assault on the Ashanti kingdom, with the European strength, under the eye of the Major-General. For the furtherance of this object, it was essential to conduct collateral operations, distracting the Ashantis, spoiling their possible alliances, and so facilitating the European advance. The greater part of these collateral operations with native Africans, which contributed materially to the ultimate result, was entrusted to Captain Glover.

Such, then, was the policy which Captain Glover had to pursue, and such were the causes that brought it about.

His first care was to collect as many hundreds of the Haussa tribe as possible. Some bodies of these men, already under discipline, were thus collected, with the co-operation of the British authorities, in the Coast Settlements ; and he enlisted some more of them, though with difficulty, in the tracts between Akra and the Volta mouth. He also obtained the services of some hundreds of the

Yoruba tribe and at once trained them. The total of men from both tribes exceeded a thousand, and they were to form the backbone of his expedition. His special acquaintance with these two interesting and valuable tribes has been explained in the Introduction to these Memoirs, and in several passages of the Memoirs themselves.

He might have enlisted a far greater number of Haussas, had it not been for the existence of slavery all along this coast. Soldierly men of this tribe who wished to enlist with him were prevented from doing so by slave-owners, with violence and often with bodily hurt; very many were cast into irons; others who escaped for enlistment bore marks of the stakes by which they had been fixed to the ground to prevent their decamping. Sometimes the Haussas rose on their jailers and felled the chiefs to the ground, with surface wounds which he had to plaster up. Once they broke open a slave prison, which he described as an African Bastille. This question caused him infinite anxiety, for if in consequence of it a hostile feeling were to be aroused among the tribes, his chance of obtaining aid from them would be gone. In vain did he remind the slave-masters that they were under British protection, and that the war was being undertaken to prevent bloody and destructive incursions on them by the Ashantis. The gravity of this obstacle was set forth by himself on two occasions after his return to England. In April 1874 he said (at Liverpool) : ' The system of slavery was brought into operation to impede the force which I was sent out to raise.' In May of the same year (in London) he stated : ' Our first difficulty—I may say, our difficulty to the end—was the system of slavery. . . . The masters of the slaves were our most confirmed enemies. . . . Instead of assisting us with their slaves to fight their battles, they immediately put all their slaves in chains to prevent them joining the Queen's forces.'

His next care was to induce the tribes between Akra and the Volta to join him, that is, the tribes officially styled those of the Eastern Protectorate already mentioned. He explained to these chiefs, with all his skill in African diplomacy, that their interest was identical with his as British representative. Sometimes they came to his camp with semi-barbaric pomp, announcing their arrival with joyous volleys of musketry, with drum-beating and horn-blowing. He knew of old that with a certain exuberance of imagination—in the absence of reasoning power—and some rude virtues, they were quite childish in many respects, with all the vanities and foibles of spoilt children—and, as might be expected, the bondsmen of superstition. To a man of his habits their impatience of, indeed incapacity for, discipline was grievous. He had found them occasionally forward—even daring ; but too often cowardly from lack of pride or shame, though they sometimes braved danger from the fear of punishment. What agreeably surprised him was the superiority of the women over the men in all manly virtues and in the willingness to endure physical fatigue. There seemed to be a public opinion among the women, so that, when the men were hesitating, his last appeal to them would be to remember what their women would say at home. So long as healthy sentiment prevailed in the homes he would not despair of keeping the men more or less in the proper line of action.

After coming in with some state, the chiefs gave him the usual assurances, swore their grotesque oaths, and received some payments in advance or presents. But soon he found that they would not march very far up the Volta, nor from the west bank of that river, towards Ashanti-land, till their rear on their own coast was made safe. Their meaning was this, that he must overcome or over-awe a certain tribe on the east bank of the Volta. This was the mischievous tribe of Awunas, whom he knew to have been the purveyors of gunpowder to the Ashantis—a matter of consequence to the Ashanti kingdom, which had no coastline of its own. The lands of his allied, or protected, tribes

would, on their marching away with him, be left
exposed to Awuna depredation, if that tribe were
left unsubdued. Thus he was obliged to recognise
the necessity of subduing them. Consequently he
had to keep his attention personally fixed eastwards
on the Lower Volta.

At the same time he strove to make a positive
demonstration against the Ashantis on his west
front. For this purpose he dispatched his able
deputy, Captain Sartorius. He instructed that
excellent officer to keep the country between the
Volta and the Prah under warlike supervision right
up to the eastern frontier of Ashanti-land; to
threaten that border, especially on the upper course of
the Prah ; to clear the left or west bank of the Volta
from hostile tribes, and, if possible, to establish some
posts and stations inland from that river westwards.
The practical value and suitability of the instructions thus given were acknowledged and commended
by Sir Garnet Wolseley's Military Secretary.—
(' Narrative,' i., p. 392.)

His persuasion was so far effective with his
coast tribes that before the end of the autumn he
was able to assemble about twenty thousand men at
Addah near the Volta mouth—African undisciplined
levies, including also a thousand, more disciplined,
Haussas and Yorubas. By this time his river
steamer 'The Lady of the Lake ' and three steam

launches were available to him for navigating the lower reach of that river. He next proceeded some distance up stream, establishing depôts, stations, and posts from point to point with detached bodies from his levies.

Regarding his position and proceedings on the Volta at this time, there is excellent evidence recorded at the moment by Mr. H. M. Stanley, then Correspondent of the 'New York Herald.' The first sight of his camp is thus described :—

'The trimly-set bell-tents, the well-ordered arrays of cloth houses, the lines of sable soldiery at drill, the out-door piles of Government stores, the row of cannon, open-mouthed, pointed towards the distant enemy, and the constant incoming and out-going of military orderlies.'

The interview with him is thus described by Mr. Stanley :—

'I discerned the sturdy form of Governor Glover striding hither and thither, and recognised his cool, calm voice giving orders. He was superintending personally the loading of " The Lady of the Lake " for an up-river trip with ammunition ; he was giving orders to a blacksmith ; he was showing a carpenter what his day duties were to be ; he was speaking to the engineer about his boilers ; he was telling the coloured captain at what hour to be ready, and what sand-bars to avoid ; he was assisting a man

N

to lift a box of ammunition on to his shoulders ; he
was listening to a Yoruba complaint about some
unfairness in the distribution of accoutrements ; he
was inspecting the crews of the steam launches ;
he was directing some of the steamboat men how
to treat the wild bullocks ; he was questioning the
commissariat officers about his supplies ; he was
rebuking the Akra king, Tarkey, for dilatoriness
of his men ; he was specifying the day's duties to
a Haussa sergeant ; he was here, there, and everywhere—alert, active, prompt, industrious.   He
was general-in-chief, quartermaster-general, commissariat officer, military secretary, pilot, captain,
engineer, general supervisor of all things, over-
seer over all men, conductor of great and small
things ; and, in short, the impellent force of his
army. . . . I am glad I undertook to discover
Glover's whereabouts. It has been a pleasure to
me to have seen this great man in camp, where a
great man may best be seen. I shall ever think
of the kindly face, the massive features, with the
genius of commanding men lighting up every
lineament, and the sturdy form so full of energy, as
an event.'

Mr. Stanley paints a dark picture of the banks
of the Volta, near its mouth :—' The black vegetable
mould of the morass is still in a state of chaos. . . .
at present man flies the vicinity. . . . Though we

on board the steamer hurry by the fatal district, the wind wafts the deadly exhalation towards us. . . . Even while we hurry by we feel the influence of the forbidden region, we feel unusual lassitude of frame, are conscious that a veil of death hangs over us, and sensible that for breathing that noxious air we shall suffer.'

Captain Glover pushed his military stations up the river from point to point. At some distance inland was a comparatively healthy hill, named Akropong, then occupied by some Bâle missionaries. He spoke of them before the Royal Geographical Society, in London, in 1874, thus : 'I am delighted to have the opportunity of bearing testimony in public to the kindness with which they received me at all their stations, the hospitality they were enabled to afford us, the assistance they gave us in providing skilled artificers for our force, in the shape of carpenters, blacksmiths, farriers, shoemakers ; and also for putting into the field two hundred very capital soldiers ; indeed, the only reliable men that I raised in the Protectorate, except the Haussas. Their mission stations along the whole line of march as far as Kibbi were always open to us ; their cleared ground always formed our camp. At Akropong they had large plantations of coffee and tobacco.'

After delays unconscionable, pretexts interminable, palavers, parleys, excuses with the Africans, he induced them to move a little. Their plan with him was to find the way how not to fight—first to promise, without actually bringing any men into camp ; when pressed, to bring in some men, without moving any more ; when further pressed, then just to move their men to some military post without compromising themselves by any military move- ment ; when urged to show something like fight, to make objections, to refuse point blank, and at last to desert. If one tribe feared to march till its neighbours had also marched, lest its lands should be left at their mercy, he would get them to all move together ; but in the end they would collec- tively decline to face a campaign against the Ashantis. He recorded in the very severest terms his sense of their cowardly conduct. But he doubtless knew that there was method in all this feigned madness of theirs ; besides their cowardice, there existed disaffection ; for though they hated the Ashantis, they dreaded the British as being the foes of slavery.

However, by diplomatic skill and moral authority, exercised with amazing patience and persistency, he succeeded, early in September, in moving his African allies—irrespective of his dis- ciplined Haussas and Yorubas—to the several stations or posts on the Volta, some 3,000 at one place, 6,000 at another, 4,500 at another, 5,500 at another, and at one place 11,000. Altogether the total of his force was 25,000 men, strongly holding the line of the Volta. Then he caused operations to be conducted against the tribes on the eastern bank, who were now declared enemies, and in this work his excellent deputy, Captain (now Sir Roger) Goldsworthy, was honourably concerned. His enemies were encamped on some hills, right on the tops, near to the eastern bank. But from a steam launch he shelled them out of their camp; and during several days in December actions were fought successfully. On December 25, indeed, the fighting was so severe that his deputy, Captain Goldsworthy, received two wounds, and had his horse shot under him. He was rejoined here by Captain Sartorius, who had been working beyond the west bank, as already explained. With him he dined in comparative comfort on Christmas Day, in a camp from which the enemy had been driven. He found his men the next morning too exhausted to march; still he expected to make an early movement. He hoped that, after their successes, his native allies would feel sufficiently safe from Awuna aggression to follow him towards Ashanti-land, especially as he would leave a goodly part of his native force with Mr. Goldsworthy to hold the Awunas down. His plans became, however, somewhat interrupted by the military exigencies arising from the movements of the main or European column.

On December 14, he, being then at the mouth of the Volta, had received from Sir Garnet Wolseley a despatch of the 11th, explaining the intended movements of the European troops from Cape Coast Castle towards Kumasi, and requesting him to co-operate by crossing the Upper Prah by January 15 (1874). He at once replied that, advancing from the Volta, he would be established on the bank of the Upper Prah by that date with all the available force he could assemble—and he quite hoped to bring a goodly part of his African levies with him. From the Prah he would advance on Juabin, or Duabin, a place to the north of, and in the rear of, Kumasi, and belonging to a feudatory of the Ashanti king, which, indeed, was the second place in the Ashanti kingdom, next after Kumasi. He then proceeded up the river to arrange for the simultaneous movement of his several bodies of men from their positions on the Volta towards the Prah. But the experience with African levies, as already described, was renewed in a still worse form; and even his personal presence from station to station failed to induce these incorrigible Africans to stir. So, to his grief, he had to report, just before Christmas, to Sir Garnet Wolseley how, despite his utmost efforts, he found his Africans so slow to be moved that he could not promise to bring them on to the Prah before the beginning of February, and that with such people in his train he could not feel assured of being with a specified force on a given date at a certain point.

He thereon received an order from Sir Garnet Wolseley to take with him what disciplined troops—Haussas, Yorubas, and others—he might have, and whatever African levies he could get to follow him, and to be on the Prah by January 15. Private as well as official explanation was given to him of the military exigencies which had dictated this order, with special reference to the European troops. He was assured that if he appeared across that river, on the date prescribed, with a force small, but good, he would be rendering material aid to the British expedition. In reply, he undertook immediate compliance to the utmost of his ability. It was a disappointment to him thus unavoidably to leave his officers, his men, and his allies, on the east of the Volta, just after some days of successful fighting, which, with a few more days of similar operations, might have disposed of the Awunas finally, so as to enable the bulk of his allies to follow him to Ashanti-land. He foresaw that, at the best, only a portion could fairly be expected to follow him then, and that a portion must, without blame to themselves, stay behind to watch the Awunas. But he appreciated the military necessities relating to the European troops which had obliged the Major-General to resume his presence on the Prah by a certain date. He felt the importance of his being there just then, inasmuch as Kumasi was to be attacked within the first week of February—perhaps after a severe effort by the European troops—and that he ought to be helping on the flank or the rear. He understood that, in these circumstances, the Major-General was constrained to fix January 15 by an absolute order not to be departed from, save under the impossibility of compliance.

Forthwith he caused some bodies of his men to cross to the left or west bank, facing towards Ashanti-land—despite the opposition of Ashantis who had advanced thither some way from their own proper boundary, or from local allies of theirs. By light guns and rockets he rapidly overcame that resistance. He directed Captain Goldsworthy, with a considerable force of African levies, to continue the operations, already described, on the east bank against the Awunas. He was anxious regarding the safety of his magazines near the Volta mouth, and the Major-General providently asked for the services of a war vessel for their protection.

His reply was received by Sir Garnet Wolseley on December 31, and at once acknowledged. He was informed that if he could cross the Prah by December 15, with his small force of disciplined troops, he would still be able to do much towards carrying out the general object of his operations, and to so far harass and alarm the Ashantis as to enable an attack to be made on them in front with better prospect of success. After crossing the Prah, he was to operate in the direction of Juabin as quickly as possible. Then the instructions to him embodied the following explicit direction—'Under no circumstance whatever will you allow any men of the force under your command to cross the Dah river, which flows to the westward of Juabin, or to advance towards Kumasi without the distinct orders of the Major-General.'

The military secretary to Sir Garnet Wolseley thus wrote shortly afterwards ('Narrative,' ii., p. 422) :—

'It is impossible to pass on without commenting upon the loyal spirit which Captain Glover had from first to last shown in carrying out the instructions of the Major-General. . . . Captain Glover's position can be easily understood by all who have learnt the utter futility of relying upon native promises. Now he was about to depend on these promises no more, but to act on his own account with his few disciplined troops; and the successful operations which he had already carried out in the few days between the 23rd and the 28th (of December) were an earnest of the skill which he would show on his advance into the enemy's territory.'

Captain Glover then prepared for the most arduous of the many enterprises he had undertaken during his busy life. He maintained bodies of troops at his several stations on the Volta banks, to preserve that river as his military base, and to keep a certain check on the Akwamo tribe on the north which abutted on the east of the Ashanti tributaries, and was probably hostile to the British. He left Captain Goldsworthy in his rear, and on the east side of the Volta, to continue the operations which had more than once proved successful against the Awunas, to hold that tribe in restraint and, if possible, to subdue them—at all events, to prevent their harrying the lands of any tribe on the west bank who might follow their leader to Ashanti-land. Though his advance cut him off from communication with the trans-Volta region, he rejoiced afterwards to learn that his deputy carried out this mission to a successful issue, despite the hindrance from the wounds previously received. Undaunted by all previous disappointments, he let his native allies see that he was going to Ashanti-land, whether they followed or not; leaving upon them the responsibility of refusing or failing to accompany him. Among them all there were three men, one, the chief of the Kroboes—quite the best personally, and commanding some good tribesmen, too; the second, the chief of the Akwapims; the third, the chief of the Eastern Akims, who was personally forceful in character, though his tribesmen were deficient in good qualities. Still, these three at least were men of whom something could be made, and who could command the services of some among their followers. It was fated happily that these three, at least, should not fail him; indeed, as will be seen presently, they did follow him more or less closely, with insufficient numbers, indeed, but still with some appreciable force. Lastly, he deputed his trusted coadjutor, Captain Sartorius, to do whatever could be done with the tribes between the Volta and the Prah, and to join him hereafter, if possible, on or about the Prah.

Then, on December 27, 1873, he started alone for the hardest of his many journeys—a march for nearly three weeks of two hundred miles over three ranges of rugged hills from 1,200 to 1,500 feet in height. He was within a very few days joined by Lieutenant Barnard. With him were his Haussas and Yorubas, in number, on the whole, about equal to the strength of a battalion. He had only their weapons to depend on, for there had not been time to transport the light guns and the rockets from the east side of the Volta. Rockets were useful to him in clearing from invisible foes the bush that beset his route. Fortunately he, and each officer with him, had either a horse or a mule, and sufficient grass for these indispensable animals was found in the forests around. Though he and his were in the very lightest marching order, still the supplies of food for tracts mostly foodless, the scantiest shelter, and the ammunition for infantry, alone constituted a burdensome amount of impedimenta. The carriers for these things must, as usual, outnumber the combatants, and had to be obtained from his allies on the Volta. The men thus engaged by him were but too prone to desert. Fortunately, the African women had endurance, resolution, and fidelity equal even to such service, and he cordially acknowledged their priceless aid in his hour of need. His light guns and rockets would, it was hoped, follow him closely under convoy of some among his native chiefs.

His line of march could not be called even a bridle road. At first he found it to be a path of miners for long-disused gold diggings; after that it became a hunter's track of the rudest kind. Trying as the track was to his infantry, the old paths of the gold miners were the most dangerous ; for he thus described them :—

'About seven miles from Akropong we came to

the gold pits, and one of our great difficulties along the road was to prevent our horses and men going down these pits. On one occasion I jumped my mare over a very large tree, and how she escaped going down a hole I do not know, for she landed with her forefoot close to it. I pulled her up, and put her a little to the right; but there was another gold pit on the other side, and we very nearly went down that.'[1]

When subsequently thanking his officers, together with the Haussas and Yorubas, for 'their cheerfulness and perseverance on the toilsome march,' he thus described the expedition :—

'Our march from the Volta to the Prah, from December 27 to January 15, was over a precipitous and densely wooded country, covered by an almost impenetrable jungle of undergrowth and trees of the largest size. Our track for long distances was with difficulty traced through this, and our progress constantly impeded by bog and morass, by trees, and streams with steep banks and without bridges; the mountain paths being merely water-courses with large granite boulders, from which torrents caused by tropical rains had washed the soil.'

In common with other military observers at that time, he declared that ' the timber of these forests is most magnificent—you see trees.... which tower up

[1] Lecture before Royal United Service Institution, May 1874.

180 feet before you come to a single branch.'   His testimony was borne out by another witness,[1] who spoke of these forests of gigantic trees, often 200 feet high, laced together with creepers, supporting foliage so thick as to shut out the sun. . . . The system of African cultivation afforded good cover to our enemies ; clearing the ground by fire, they sow in the ashes, and when the soil is exhausted they abandon the spot for another clearing. On these deserted fields there rises lofty vegetation, impenetrable, save to naked savages, who crawl through it on their faces.'

Rightly did he praise the alacrity of his people amidst the depressing gloom of this all-pervading forest.   He was corroborated by another witness of authority, who wrote thus :—' To live always shut in by . . . the same luxuriant growth of huge ferns, palms, and creepers . . . never catching a glimpse of a real horizon—ever enclosed by these walls, which none the less imprison because they are of leaves and not of stone—to live thus palls upon the senses with a deadly and depressing weight.'

On the other hand, the nerves of himself and his coadjutors were ceaselessly strained by watchfulness against ambush and ambuscade, or stray shots from the thicket. The utmost economy of ammunition was necessary for him, for the sake of

---

[1] Sir Evelyn Wood, United Service Institution.

gunpowder; the food was stinted, and the rations doled out scantily; clothing and equipments were often left behind. He had also to contemplate the grave risk of being opposed when his troops were weary, with feet worn by the rough stones, and at the same time short of ammunition. Nearly midway on this arduous route was Kibbi, where he hoped to find native allies from the neighbourhood, with depôts of supplies and relays of carriers. But he was hardly surprised when these provident arrangements were largely belied by results. Still he pressed onwards, leaving at the halting places in the rear of his advance a long string of supplies which it was hoped might be brought on by the native chiefs who ought very shortly to be following him. Meanwhile he was receiving help from his native allies in the rear, and their promises had not wholly failed. In an imperfectly kept journal of his staff officer there is this entry for January 8 :—'Had a formal interview with the Queen of Akwapim, the head women and the Queen of Kripi,—resulted in getting all the load carried onwards by the women.' As immediate payment was necessary from time to time, this journal is interspersed with references to the anxieties respecting the transporting, guarding, and escorting of specie. Indeed, the success of his transport and supply arrangements generally was a wonder among the many wonders of this march. He was admirably assisted by the chief of his staff, Surgeon-Major Rowe, who was coming up from the Volta, having established a transport basis there, and organised depôts at stages as he passed on to join his principal. Every lesser consideration was subordinated, even sacrificed, to the object of keeping his promise, and being on the Prah by January 15.

In the same journal of his is a sad entry—'Cameron falls sick, and lies down on the road, and has to be sent for. Bale goes on with the men.' Lieutenant Cameron, despite sickness, pressed on and joined him in camp, but only to die; Dr. Bale, too, came up, but died also. On January 10 he welcomed Captain Sartorius in camp, and had the great benefit onwards of that excellent officer's assistance.

Heretofore he had been traversing country over which the Ashantis had claimed dominion, which, however, had of late been lost to them, but where they still had scattered men of their own or local allies. Yet he felt that these people were quite prepared to rejoin the Ashanti kingdom, or desert it finally, according as its star should be rising or falling. His traversing their country at this juncture, then, detached them from the Ashanti cause. There was one chief (at Assouam) of some local consequence, and of very doubtful temper, near the Prah, whom he kept on the British side by his timely presence. He was now to cross the Prah and invade the kingdom of Ashanti proper.

About this time, owing to geographical position, his communication with the Major-General was fairly quick. On the 11th he received a despatch from the Major-General of the 8th, authorising him to cross the Prah even before the 15th if he could. He replied in two letters, written on or about the 13th, stating that, after crossing the Prah, his object would be to advance either on Kumasi or on Juabin. Then he received a despatch from Sir Garnet Wolseley—whose main column was advancing from the other direction—with a reiterated instruction that 'no portion of his force was to advance beyond Juabin, or, should he be unable to reach that place, no nearer than six miles from Kumasi.'

Thus, on the evening of January 14, 1874, he encamped near the left or eastern bank of the Upper Prah. Early on the morning of the 15th— the day appointed by Sir Garnet Wolseley—he sent his vanguard across the river, under Lieutenant Barnard, and before noon he himself crossed with the remainder of his force. His brave men were there, if not in perfect health after their tremendous march, still in full strength and spirits, and fit for any duty. None of them had failed

him from any fault of their own ; and their hardened
feet had withstood the miles and miles of jagged
stones. As was acknowledged in the ' Narrative,' he
crossed ' keeping his tryst to a moment.' Rarely
indeed has a hard tryst been kept under harder
circumstances. The point of his passage over the
river was about forty-five miles to the east, perhaps slightly to the south-east of Kumasi—that is
to say, on a latitude nearly level with the capital
of the Ashanti king. That night he bivouacked
on Ashanti soil.

The next morning, the 16th, he made his first
advance into Ashanti-land. His first Ashanti
prisoner proved to be a man who was about to be
made a local chief by the Ashanti king, and on
whose installation some forty slaves were to be
sacrificed. The installation was thus stopped, and
the forty intended victims were saved by falling
into his hands. The first Ashanti village taken by
him was Abugu. That he carried by a rush under
the enemy's fire, by which three of his men were
mortally wounded and others stricken down. They
here found two hundred sheep, and quantities of
vegetables, forming a welcome spoil to his poorly-
fed soldiery. Here, also, he took some Ashanti
prisoners ; but they were so far loyal to their own
side that they would tell him nothing about men or
places.

Hoping that some means of communication might still be available for the main column, he sent a despatch on the 17th to the Major-General, reporting that he had established himself in Ashanti-land, and would move forwards as soon as his ammunition should come up. This was the last despatch that he was able to send.

He had to wait at Abugu for a few days for his light guns, rockets, and musketry ammunition. These came up under convoy; and with the convoy there arrived nearly three thousand men, in a certain sense combatants, mainly under the Chief of Akim, whom he had adjured to follow up from the Volta, partly under local chiefs on the line of march in the rear. Thus, with his disciplined troops and his native allies he must have had nearly four thousand men in camp. He forthwith tested the mettle of his Akim chief and men by setting them to take an Ashanti village, and the service was performed with some slight loss to themselves in killed and wounded. Meanwhile he had consolidated his position round Abugu by capturing all the villages in its vicinity. Thus he was in military possession of a tract in Ashanti territory by January 20.

On January 22 he resumed his route towards Juabin—the point for which Sir Garnet Wolseley had directed him to make. The point at which he immediately aimed was Konomo a commanding position on the Juabin route. Having detached Lieutenant Barnard to take some villages which threatened the left of the line, and to seize Udumasi also on the left—he himself marched straight for Konomo. Meanwhile Lieutenant Barnard was hotly engaged at Udumasi, carrying it with a rush under fire. The sound of all this firing reached Konomo in the afternoon, which place was evidently held in some force by the Ashantis. Seeing that Udumasi, on their right, was being assaulted, and knowing that Captain Glover was himself coming upon them from their front, the Ashantis decamped, leaving Konomo to him. In the evening he cautiously approached (not knowing what ambush might await him), with the Chief of Akim at his side, who, with African cleverness, and doubtless at great risk, crept into the place and found it deserted.

This January 22 was an eventful day for him— Udumasi, on the road towards Kumasi, taken by his lieutenant, together with other villages ; Konomo, commanding the road towards Juabin, the second place in the Ashanti kingdom, occupied by himself ; and the Ashanti troops from several points retreating before him westwards and north-westwards. Their retreat was rendered certain by the discovery of several among their camps, which, by a calculation of space, were reckoned to have contained several thousand men in all.

On the 26th he joined Lieutenant Barnard at Udumasi, which was close to Konomo. His entire force in camp might be under three thousand men in all, but then he was obliged to guard his rear line, which had become extended by his recent advance. Though now only two days' march from Kumasi, still he had to hold his successful hand for a while. He explicitly stated—after giving reasons—'to go on with the small force I had, and with only enough ammunition to carry us through one or two days' fighting, was not to be thought of.' (Lecture, United Service Institution, May 1874.)

At Udumasi, then, he halted for a while, for several reasons. In the first place, his force of real combatants was small. His disciplined men— Haussas and Yorubas—were truly admirable ; but their number had been diminished by casualties. His native allies had one good chief, and on their arrival had done an act of service ; but since that date had proved themselves not only cowardly but untrustworthy ; so much so, that once he had been forced to threaten them with measures ordinarily applicable to mutineers. Still he kept them in line with him before the enemy, and there was the moral effect, in part at least ; for the troubles in his camp would hardly be known to the Ashantis. The paucity of trustworthy men made it difficult for him to guard against the cutting off of the communications in his rear. Such a disruption would be fatal to him, as his men had ammunition enough for only two days' fighting. Wintery rain storms had descended, to render the river in front of him, the Anum, hard to cross. On his right were the Ashanti troops, who had left their encampments for him to occupy, and who were probably then resting on Juabin as their base. On his left front, between him and Kumasi, was, as he had learned from prisoners, an important section of the Ashanti forces, in communication with their king and their capital.

Thus he had pushed so far and so fast into Ashanti-land in his anxiety to carry out the Major-General's instructions, in spirit as well as in letter, that theoretically his position might be deemed critical. These several Ashanti forces might, perhaps, converge upon him ; but for commanders like him the first thing was rightly to estimate the temper of the enemy. He had learnt how the Ashantis were saying among themselves that it were vain for them to contend against a Haussa force led by Europeans. So they were not likely to attack him while he stopped and held his own.

Meanwhile his halting was in a strategic situation of much advantage. It was on the left flank of the Ashantis, with a tendency towards their left rear, and it gave him about an equal distance of twenty-five miles either from Juabin or Kumasi. He was thus about two military marches only from Kumasi—a distance which could be accomplished by a few men in a forced march of one day. An Ashanti woman prisoner told him that starting from Udumasi in the morning with a load upon her head she could reach Kumasi in the evening; and had often done it in company with her mistress. Naturally he was anxious to communicate with the British column, which was known to be advancing from the other side towards the Ashanti front. But such communication by any direct route was impossible, as the main Ashanti army intervened; and if he sent a communication by a comparatively safe and circuitous route it could not be in time. He had then been over eleven days in Ashanti territory, had advanced full twenty miles inside the border, had taken two considerable villages, and also lesser villages within about five miles of his line on the right and on the left, causing bodies of Ashanti troops to retire. Thus he had occupied something under two hundred square miles of country, an appreciable slice, so to speak, of the Ashanti kingdom. All this must evidently have produced some effect favourable to the British main expedition advancing on Kumasi.

As he had reported himself and his force to the Major-General, from his camp at Abugu, on the 17th, he naturally became anxious to do the same from Udumasi on the 26th. This was to him a primary object; but its accomplishment was becoming difficult or impossible. The main column was advancing, and he was doing the same—both were moving towards the same point, Kumasi; and now, between the two—namely, the British main or European column and the British native force—about two-thirds of the Ashanti army intervened. Of that army one division was watching him, and another, probably the flower of Ashanti manhood, was preparing to meet Sir Garnet Wolseley. The Ashanti forces were, as usual, ensconced in their sylvan fastnesses; and through these forests, alive with sharpshooters, no messenger of his could have attempted to carry a letter and survived the attempt. He could, indeed, have sent a despatch round by the south of the Prah safely enough; but, by that circuitous route, it would not have been in time. For he was sure that Sir Garnet Wolseley would be victoriously in Kumasi within the first week of February. Thus he could not know precisely what the successes of the main column were, nor what the Major-General's orders for him would be in the event of the expected victory being won ; and the Major-General could not know how he was faring with the Ashantis on all sides of him.   His latest despatch from the Major-General was dated January 23, when the headquarters were at Mainsu.

But he employed his halting days at Udumasi in notable efforts to establish communication with the main column, or with the native force under Captain Butler, which was believed to be operating between his position and that column. On his left flank, that is, on the south-west, there lay the lake Busum Etshui.   It was thought that if some of his officers and men could penetrate so far, some chain of connexion might be formed ; and this might be done without crossing the Anum in front.   So he caused an attempt to be made on the 29th, but, after a progress of some miles, the forest proved impenetrable, and the lake was not sighted.   On February 1 he organised another attempt to communicate with Captain Butler by crossing the Anum and working along its bank south-westwards, under Captain Sartorius and Commander Larcom.   This was a brilliant, though dangerous, enterprise, which caused him much anxiety.   First, his officers captured the venison in a hunting camp, a welcome spoil in their underfed condition ; then they fell in with an armed Ashanti camp; the Ashantis came down upon them singing their war song, a rare instance of their attacking in this overt way. Commander Larcom placed his rocket-trough on the pathway, and the attack was repelled. The main story shall, however, be told in Captain Glover's own words. He said: 'Captain Sartorius marched a small force of 130 men through two camps (of the Ashantis). . . . The Ashantis were as much surprised as he was. . . . But his rear was completely cut off, and he might have been prevented from rejoining my force at Udumasi. So he dispatched forty Haussas back, who went through these two camps with only one man wounded in the head, and they rejoined me at five in the evening. But very anxious was I about Captain Sartorius, and I sent Lieutenant Barnard, at ten o'clock that night, with all the men I could spare— only 150—to reinforce him. . . . He encamped very close to their (Ashanti) camp that night. . . . In the morning he heard the friendly sound of firing, and Lieutenant Barnard's force was coming up. They joined, drove the enemy out of their camp, and occupied it with their small force, having five men killed and eleven wounded.'—(Lecture, Royal United Service Institution, May 1894.) So impressed was he with the risks which had been run that he added these soldierly words: 'They ought never to have got where they did, and they ought never to have come back.'

Thus the impossibility of establishing communication was proved; still, he wrote to the Major-General on January 28, and again on February 3, but these letters had to go by an indirect route.

The effects following from these movements can best be measured by a comparison of dates. On January 15, when Captain Glover crossed the Upper Prah, forty to forty-five miles from Kumasi, and on its left flank, Sir Garnet Wolseley was himself at Prahsu, near the southerly bend of the Prah, about forty-five to fifty miles from Kumasi and from the front of the Ashanti position, preparing for the arrival of the European troops, and for their crossing the river on the 19th. At the first, then, the auxiliary column was nearer to the Ashanti than the main British column, and had crossed the Prah four days sooner. The native force, though its line of transport was far longer, had greater resources for transport to draw upon than the European force, and had much less to carry, the efforts of the European officers with both forces being equally admirable. By January 20, Captain Glover had advanced nearly ten miles inside the Ashanti border, had taken Abugu and the surrounding villages, and was in military possession of a certain tract of country. On that date the British main column had done much the same on its side. On the 21st the king wrote from Kumasi to the Major-General, accepting a part of the British claim, including the surrender of his white prisoners; and so important was this deemed, that the news was dispatched by a special war vessel to England. This concession on the king's part was, possibly, indeed, probably, dictated by the knowledge that his flank, as well as his front, was now menaced. On the 22nd, when Captain Glover took the two places, Konomo and Udumasi—the latter distant twenty-five miles from Kumasi—the main British column had advanced to Mainsu, thirty miles from that capital. On the 26th, when Captain Glover took up his position for a while at Udumasi, the king wrote from Kumasi to Sir Garnet Wolseley that all his chiefs had gone out to guard their roads; and this remarkable statement must have related to Captain Glover's presence in force on his left flank. On the 31st the decisive battle between the main British column and the Ashantis under their king was victoriously fought at Amoaful, twelve miles distant from Kumasi. On that day, at least, two considerable bodies of Ashanti troops must have been detached to watch Captain Glover, one near Udumasi, to oppose his marching towards Kumasi, the other to check his possible movement on Juabin. Indeed, the Juabin force, instead of being with the king at Kumasi, was at its own place to prevent its possible capture by Captain Glover. The same conditions existed on February 3 and 4, when the conclusive attack was delivered and Kumasi fell to British arms. For this, indeed, he was expressly commended by Sir Garnet Wolseley. The 'Narrative' states (ii. 261) that on the day of the battle of Amoaful, and also on the day when we (the British) entered Kumasi, Captain Glover was holding the Juabin force in check on the River Anum, thus drawing it off from opposition to the main body (that is, from the British column). Further, Sir Garnet Wolseley himself wrote to Captain Glover, on February 7, that the Juabin tribe had not been engaged in the action along the main line, 'having been engaged in watching you.' From subsequent inquiries, Captain Glover himself learnt that the Ashantis engaged in watching him at that critical time, on the side not only of Juabin, but of Kumasi, amounted in all to some number between fifteen and twenty thousand men.

I revert to Captain Glover, halting with his force at Udumasi on and after January 26, till over February 4, when Kumasi fell. His position was strengthened on February 6 by the arrival of Lieutenant Moore, who had marched all the way from the Volta with about two thousand native allies, Kroboes and Akwapims, under the chiefs who had been adjured on the Volta to follow up. They had, so far, fulfilled their promise; and the Kroboes especially were good men under a capable chief. Together with them he received a convoy of small guns, rockets and ammunition. He had now the needful resources for moving onward, even in the teeth of opposition. Indeed, he had but too good reasons for doing so, inasmuch as his force had, in a sparsely populated country, consumed the available food, that is, had eaten up all the yams and plantains that could be got. So he must, if possible, march in order that his men might eat. Just then, however, he heard from native sources of the fall of Kumasi on the 4th, but the information was not trustworthy.

At all events, on the 8th, he marched from Udumasi for Kumasi, hoping to open communication with the British commander. He left a part of his native allies there in order to guard the passage of the Anum. Just after he had started these natives received a message from the Chief of Juabin which they sent on to him. He learnt from the message that the King of Kumasi was considered to have been very foolish, and to have consequently lost his capital; but that the Chief of Juabin would submit to the British Government. The chief begged him to accept the submission, and to send it on to the Major-General. This was the first authentic report he received of the fall of Kumasi. Afterwards he found that his natives at Udumasi, under the enterprising Chief of Akim, learning from the messengers the purport of the message—the fall of Kumasi, and the submission of Juabin—proceeded forthwith to Juabin, occupied the place for the British, and entered into transactions with local chiefs in British interests and against the Ashantis. This was extraordinary promptitude and energy on the part of the Akims, who had been hitherto backward rather than forward. But, in the circumstances, the enterprise was safe enough, and if it had not been so, the Akim chief would still have been equal to it. The occurrence proved to be of some interest and importance.

Marching from Udumasi, then, Captain Glover took the road for Kumasi, supposing the Major-General still to be there. After crossing the Anum river he came upon several camps deserted by Ashanti troops, and one of them was large enough for eight thousand men. The desertion must have taken place in hot haste, as he found the road strewn for miles with corn and corn-flour, to the delight of his followers after their scanty rations.

Once more he learned from the information of scouts and prisoners that, with his very moderate force, he was between two considerable Ashanti forces, with one of which was the king himself. But he rejoiced to think that he had reached a point which placed him between the king and Kumasi. But after the fall of their capital the Ashantis were not in heart to attack him. How welcome even the casual windfall of some grain from a deserted camp must have been, can be judged from a letter of his to Sir Garnet Wolseley three days later. He wrote: 'My men have had only one ounce of salt meat per man since January 18, and that one four days since.'

But that the king was in a position, if so minded, to attack him, or otherwise to show fight against the British cause, was fully believed by Mr. H. M. Stanley, who was at Kumasi till the 6th, and had much insight into African affairs. He wrote thus: 'The king was persuaded to believe, as he saw his summer palace of Amineeha surrounded by his still numerous adherents, and his force increased every moment by fugitives fresh from Kumasi, that his state was not yet hopeless, that he still had sufficient people to perhaps create a new kingdom.'

Indeed, the king was feeling the weight of his presence so much as to write a despatch, on the 8th, to Sir Garnet Wolseley, received in the British camp on the 9th, begging that the Major-General would halt Captain Glover's forces, which were advancing from the east.—('Narrative,' ii. 249.)

As he neared Kumasi, Captain Glover was mindful of his original order not to approach that place closer than six miles, and not to cross the River Dah (which was the same as the Ordah). At this point, then, he sent forward Captain Sartorius, with an escort of twenty Haussas, to take a letter to the Major-General at Kumasi, asking for orders, and to return the next day. He learnt afterwards that this mission was at first fraught with danger, as, despite their great defeat, the Ashantis were on the watch; for when Captain Sartorius and his little band wound their way through the forests they heard the rustling of invisible movement in the bush dogging them all the way; in the evening the enemy openly menaced them, and they had to halt in a slightly defensible position, and nothing but the Captain's personal forwardness induced the Haussas to move on in the morning.

But he became very anxious on finding that Captain Sartorius did not return. So he marched to look for his officer, and this search brought him close to Kumasi. From the condition of the villages, and the attitude of the villagers, he saw that the Ashanti authority had certainly departed. So he decided at once to proceed and report himself and his force to the Major-General, who might still be in the captured capital. Soon he found that the European troops, having victoriously entered on the 4th, had departed on the 6th for the march homewards. He did not then know that on leaving Kumasi the Major-General had sent him two despatches, the first apprising him of the victories, and directing him to fall back on the Prah, and the further one virtually leaving him to act for the best, according to his discretion, with his forces, under the surrounding circumstances.—('Narrative of Ashanti War,' vol. ii., pp. 262 and 263, by H. Brackenbury.) These despatches were never received. Thus he entered the place on the 12th, the town being partly burned. He learnt that the king had fled during the British advance on the capital, had since accepted Sir Garnet Wolseley's terms of peace, and had sent down the first instalment of the required gold.

He had found no signs of Captain Sartorius, but his anxiety was relieved by an incident which shall be presented in his own words: 'I came to the burly form of a man without his head, and, curiously enough, he was very white. I at once said, "There's poor Sartorius." I rode on half a mile and fell in with a wounded Haussa, whose thigh was broken. He was propped up against a tree, and had some bunches of plantains and calabashes of water ; evidently someone had made him, under the circumstances, comfortable. I told my Haussas to make a hurdle for him, and bring him down (with us). I said, " Who gave you these plantains? " He replied, " Oh ! a white man, who passed here two days ago with twenty Haussas." I need not describe the relief to my feelings, because that proved to me that it was not Captain Sartorius' body that I had seen headless on the road.' He did not yet know, however, that, in fact, Captain Sartorius had passed through Kumasi unmolested, and, after a brilliantly adventurous ride of thirty-five miles, had joined Sir Garnet Wolseley's camp, some three marches south of Kumasi—and, as regards the Captain, did not return to him ; no orders from the Major-General were received.

Captain Glover's stay in Kumasi did not last more than three hours, a few cowering inhabitants only being visible. He must perforce press onwards along the British line of march towards stations where supplies would be available. But as he rode through the deserted street, and drew up in the desolate square—recently the scene of barbaric power and circumstance—and overlooked his martial array, the impression on the imagination of himself and his officers must have been deep, and still more so on that of his African followers. As he proceeded with them through the forests, which had been the battlefields, with the main column, they became conscious that the bush must be thickly strewn with masses of corruption, though the corpses were unseen—proving that the Ashantis had bravely withstood the fire of the European troops.

The fact of his entrance into Kumasi at the head of 4,600 men, a force armed and equipped—of whom nearly one thousand were excellent soldiers inured to the march and the fight—must have deterred the king from returning thither at the time, and must have caused the reality of the Major-General's victory to be felt. It must have produced due effect on the Ashanti people. It made them feel that their political downfall was being witnessed by the several tribes represented in that force, some of the very tribes who had long suffered from Ashanti domination and oppression. Equally direct was the influence on the tribesmen in the force. Heretofore they had regarded Kumasi, not only with fear as the centre of armed power, but with a reverent superstition. Wise sayings were current among them that the place would never be taken by an enemy till this or that event of physical impossibility or improbability should occur. That the Ashantis had been beaten in battle, they might have believed; but the fall of Kumasi itself would have been beyond their belief, had they not seen it for themselves. Now it was seen by every man in the force, every eastern Akim, every Akwapim, every Kroboe, all fighting men of known tribes, and every carrier and camp follower, of other tribes, who was with them. All these returning to their homes would spread the tidings throughout the Eastern Protectorate, and to the districts beyond the Volta. Thus, the political consequences of the British victory were brought home to the African mind.

Soon a handsome gold present to him came from the King of Ashanti, with a request that he will withdraw his Akim forces from Juabin, and order them back again across the Prah. He declined to accept the present; but on entering into conversation with the messengers, he was informed that the Akim chief, while occupying Juabin, had been inducing the people there to submit to British authority, and also the local chiefs between the Prah and the Volta to hand over the symbols of office which they had originally received from the Ashanti king. Thus he saw the complete disruption of the Ashanti dominion, and recognised that this was among the many consequences of his march through these tribes in that country.

He might well feel thankful on the retrospect of having caused more than 6,000 armed men to cross the Prah, 4,600 of whom had entered Kumasi, while the remainder operated on Juabin.

Thus ended his famous march from the Volta to Kumasi, the Ashanti capital, which he reckoned at two hundred miles by straight lines on the map, with one hundred and fifty more for turnings and twistings in the path, or three hundred and fifty in all. His progress had been laborious, over the narrowest of ways, with the extremes of ruggedness in ascents and descents. From Kumasi onwards he met with roads recently engineered. He was then within reach of food suited for civilised men, instead of the hard and scanty fare which he had been cheerfully sharing with his African followers for several weeks, but which was unsuited to the European constitution. Indeed, the mode of life had reduced his strength and even somewhat emaciated his powerful frame.

Soon he was informed that his timely occupation of Kumasi had caused much satisfaction to the Major-General. Indeed, he received by the military telegraph line a telegram from Sir Garnet thus : 'Congratulate you most sincerely on all you have done.' In a letter from the British camp, Captain Sartorius wrote to him : 'The General has just drunk your health.'

He then sent orders to his Akim chief at Juabin, and to the officers on his rear line in that quarter, to recross the Prah and to return to the Volta. He himself proceeded to Essiaman, the store depôt station on the British line of march towards the coast. At length, after weeks of insufficient nourishment, he and his 4,600 men found plenty to eat. 'It had been a matter of grave consideration how the stores were ever to be cleared out of Essiaman. . . . Captain Glover's men saved all further trouble on that head.'— ('Narrative,' ii. 276.)

On February 20 he sent his natives eastwards towards Akra, and himself marched with the disciplined troops to the coast, near Cape Coast Castle, by the military road which had lately been made. I have heard that some of his officers—as they emerged from the overshadowing forests, with the oppressive sensation of confined vision during many weeks, and beheld the open coast—were reminded of the exclamation of Xenophon's soldiers, as they caught sight of the Euxine after their toils in Asia Minor : 'The sea ! the sea ! ' His Haussas were very properly to be retained in the British service. The conduct of these men was indeed to be preserved in British history. We had done everything for them, and they did their best for us, despite temptations, perils, fatigues, privations.

Landless, homeless, so scattered as to be defenceless, they sought refuge and respite from African
slavery by voluntary enlistment in our service, as
gallant natives, to live in the air of soldiers and
freemen. The discovery and development of a
military resource so valuable as this on the Gold
Coast is one among his many signal claims to
public gratitude. His Yorubas, however, who
had been nearly as good, were to be disbanded, and
the organisation of all his levies was to be broken
up. He consequently reverted to his old stations
on the River Volta; and at Blappa, the most
important of those stations, he indited a despatch
to Sir Garnet Wolseley which was full of interest.
In it he specified, with characteristic heartiness,
the achievements of the good men and true who
had been serving under him, and whose deeds will
be remembered by those Britons who love to dwell
on what their countrymen can do in times of trial
and suffering. They were Captain (now Sir Roger)
Goldsworthy; Captain (now General) Sartorius;
Commander Larcom; Sub-Lieutenant Ponsonby;
Surgeon-Major (afterwards Sir Samuel) Rowe;
Lieutenant Cameron; Lieutenant (now Brigadier-
General) Barnard; Lieutenant Moore (R.N.); Mr.
Blissett; Sub-Lieutenant Adamson; and Dr. Parke.
As regards the natives, while warmly commending
certain exceptions, he felt bound to report un-

favourably of the tribes of the Eastern Protectorate ; and, indeed, his well-informed evidence should be a warning to the British Government not to employ such people on warlike operations.   Nevertheless, in justice, it is to be remembered that some thousands of them did follow him to Ashanti as combatants, by the same severe march which he himself made with his disciplined troops.   Besides them he must have had a host of carriers who endured the same hardships—with less danger, perhaps, but with even more fatigue.   Of his combatant followers, some behaved well when they reached the scene of action, while others did badly ; though it so happened that some of the latter, Akims, did render a particular, perhaps an important, service.   The Akim chief, though only twenty-one years old, did evince valuable qualities on certain occasions.   The Akwapim chief marched to Kumasi, and was helpful in providing carriers. The only chief who was always able, willing, and ready to obey the orders he received was the Kroboe chief.   The best men of all the forces on the Volta were two companies of native Christians belonging to the Bâle Mission.

The brave deeds having been narrated, it may be well to make a summary comparison between what he undertook, or was ordered to undertake, on the one hand, and what he actually did on the other. He was, in the first place, instructed to induce the tribes in the Eastern Protectorate to raise their levies. In connexion therewith he was to create a diversion against the Ashantis by operating on the River Volta. All this he did most fully, and the levies took the field in great numbers. But his operations on the Volta grew in dimensions—they had to be conducted on the east or opposite side of the river; and they took up much time, which was a serious consideration, inasmuch as the main British attack on the Ashanti kingdom was emergent, and had to be carried out against time. Next, he had been instructed to harass and alarm the Ashantis all along their left flank; then his operations on the Volta, with his forward posts and emissaries towards the Prah, did effect that object. His work on the Volta, though unavoidably protracted, was ultimately successful; it suppressed the trans-Volta tribes who threatened our allies in the Protectorate; further, it held back these tribes, and also the north Volta tribes, from helping the Ashantis. At first it had been left to his discretion as to how far he should advance towards the River Prah and into Ashanti-land. Then he received an order to so advance; and that, too, by a date so early as to demand the most energetic promptitude. This order he executed, despite obstacles, physical and military, with a loyalty that was acknowledged by his superior, and an ability beyond praise. For this, too, he maintained a long line of transport communication in his rear—a line of such length as to be rare in the annals of the British in Africa.

Arrived in Ashanti-land, he kept two large bodies of the Ashanti forces in check, hindering their junction with the main force to resist the European troops who were moving on Kumasi from another direction. He held the road to Juabin, the second town next after the capital, in the Ashanti kingdom, and, keeping that place under observation, he prevented it from helping the king and the capital in the hour of extremity. Advancing to within three marches of Kumasi with such small force as he could take with him so far as that, he occupied a critically difficult position for many days, with the Ashanti forces all round him in their forests—all which conduced to facilitate the attack by the European troops, which was going on with the utmost brilliancy under Sir Garnet Wolseley at that very time. By the end of this short campaign he had brought 6,000 Africans into Ashanti-land, and some of them occupied Juabin for the British immediately after Kumasi had fallen to European arms. But he marched the greater part of them into Kumasi itself after the departure of the European troops on their return homewards, a proceeding of his which had a moral and political effect. Thus he not only threatened the flank of the Ashantis, according to his original instructions, but he effected much more by making an effectual demonstration in the heart of the Ashanti kingdom, incurring for himself and his men a risk which a real commander is ever ready to incur when dealing with Africans. In the end he fulfilled, and even more than fulfilled, the trust confided to him by his commission from the Sovereign.

The cordial and generous recognition of his services by Sir Garnet Wolseley has been already cited at the beginning of this Chapter.

On March 13, Lord Carnarvon requested that an expression be conveyed to Captain Glover of the high approval entertained by the Queen and by Her Majesty's Government of his indefatigable perseverance. On the 27th, Lord Carnarvon reiterated that expression, and proceeded to say that he had received with great satisfaction Sir Garnet Wolseley's warm commendation of Captain Glover, and of the zealous services of the officers and men who assisted him in bringing his expedition to a successful issue.

On April 28, a letter, on behalf of Lord Carnarvon, was written, as follows, to the address of Captain Glover :—

' Lord Carnarvon has much pleasure in assuring you of the high sense entertained by Her Majesty's Government of the value of the services rendered by yourself and by all under your command. Her Majesty's Government fully appreciate the signal courage, energy, and perseverance displayed in your operations against the Ashantis, carried on as they were under circumstances of extreme difficulty, and they are well aware how largely your appearance in force in the neighbourhood of Kumasi contributed to the general success of the operations, and to the ultimate signature of the terms of peace by the King of Ashanti.

' It is accordingly with much gratification that Lord Carnarvon has found himself able to announce to you that Her Majesty has been pleased on his recommendation to bestow on you and some of the officers lately under your command the marks of Her Royal favour, an intimation of which has been separately made to each person.'

On March 30, the thanks of both Houses of Parliament were conveyed in the following words :—

' That the thanks of this House be given to Commander John Hawley Glover, of the Royal Navy, for the energy, courage, and ability with which, as Her Majesty's Special Commissioner to the eastern tribes of the Gold Coast, and with the aid of other gallant officers of the Army and Navy, he led a considerable native force from the River Volta to Kumasi, thereby largely conducing to the success of the main operations of the Major-General Commanding.'

Shortly afterwards he was appointed by the Queen to be a Knight Grand Cross of the most distinguished Order of Saint Michael and Saint George.

CHAPTER X

1874—1875

AT the close of the Ashanti War, which has been
described in the preceding Chapter, Captain Glover,
with his staff of officers, returned to England.
The British public had read with interest the
doings of the native force in Africa, and when it
was known that the ship he was in was within
sight of land, a number of steamers and other
vessels went out to meet and welcome him and his
companions on their arrival. They had a most
enthusiastic reception on landing at Liverpool, and
a banquet was given them, at which Captain
Glover made a speech containing an account of
some of the events that had taken place during the
war. After this there was a special thanksgiving
service in Chester Cathedral, which he and his

staff attended in uniform, sitting in the stalls, in view of a crowded congregation. On their arrival in London there was tremendous cheering at the railway station, and they were received everywhere with ovations.

The Queen invited Captain Glover to stay at Windsor, and there recognised his services by investing him, with her own hand, with the riband and collar of the Grand Cross of the Order of St. Michael and St. George. In London he was much *fêted* and entertained. He was asked to speak at Liverpool, Manchester, Hull, and other parts of England, and many addresses were presented to him. The Colonial Office gave him a very handsome piece of plate, representing a beautifully modelled figure of a sailor and a Haussa soldier in uniform standing under an African palm tree, a crouching leopard—the emblem of Africa—half hidden by jungle grass in the background. Soon after this Sir John Glover was employed in organising a bazaar at the Duke of Wellington's riding school in aid of the Bâle Mission on the Gold Coast. In this he was assisted by Colonel Sir Francis Festing and Captain (afterwards Sir Roger) Goldsworthy.

This bazaar was a great social success, and a large sum of money was sent to Africa, but the principal part of it was furnished by Sir John himself. Just then he was asked to stand to represent Liverpool or Manchester in Parliament, and he was at this time so popular with the masses of the people that they collected at railway stations, and other public places when he travelled, to see him. He shaved off his beard, with which he returned from Ashanti, and in future wore a heavy moustache and imperial—which made him look more like a French general than an English sailor—preferring to pass unrecognised through the crowd. He had worked so hard during the war, and suffered from so much anxiety, worry, want of food, and fatigue in a pestilential climate, that on his return to England he was little more than a walking skeleton. He soon, however, recovered his health, but his medical advisers thought he required rest, and prescribed for him a course of waters on the Continent, and a few months' leave of absence.

At the close of the social season in England he proceeded to Gastein, and spent some time in the Tyrol. Then he went to Athens and Constantinople, and visited his old haunts, renewing his acquaintance with those remaining friends who remembered him there in his midshipman days. On his return home he once more felt need of active employment, and wrote to Lord Carnarvon apprising him of his arrival in England, and

offering his services for the Governorship of Fiji,
which was just then a new country, with natives
to deal with for the most part, and a considerable
future before it.   This offer was, however, not
accepted. He used to say that was the only
appointment he had ever asked the Colonial Office
for, as all other work had been brought to his hand
unsought for; but afterwards he was glad that
his request had not been granted. Having no
employment, he once more turned his steps abroad,
and visited the Rhine and Normandy. While in
France he was the guest of a charming lady and
her husband who had a house in Paris, and spent a
considerable time in each year at the Château de
Méréville. A little incident of this visit was sent
as a souvenir by Madame Mackenzie, and is given
as she wrote it : 'Lorsque j'habitais le beau
domaine de Méréville, non loin de Paris, et qui fut
construit par le Marquis de la Borde sous le règne
de Louis XVI, et dont la construction a coûté seize
millions de francs, Monsieur Mackenzie mon mari
recevait un grand nombre de connaissances et
d'amis. Parmi les derniers nous avions le plaisir
d'offrir l'hospitalité à Sir John Glover, le héro des
Ashantis, comme il fut appelé alors. La visite de
cet éminent guerrier causait une véritable joie à
tous les habitants du château. Sir John répandait
la gaieté et son aménité s'étendait à tous. Un

jour on annonçait une fête au village de Méréville ;
un cirque venant de Paris avec des chevaux magni-
fiques, des clowns, des cavaliers et surtout de très
jolies jeunes femmes devaient se faire voir et faire
tours de force, sauts à travers des cerceaux, et enfin
toutes les merveilles équestres possibles. C'était une
nouveauté pour les bons villageois ; tous les habitants
de près ou des environs demandaient des billets et
bien entendu les châtelains et leurs invités furent
les premiers à s'acheminer à l'heure indiquée vers
le cirque. Parmi les écuyers et écuyères se
trouvait une petite fille, toute rosée, blonde et
souriante. D'avance elle créait l'admiration du
public, et la voici sur un petit poney faisant ses
petites grâces équestres ; mais au moment où les
applaudissements éclataient le poney et quelques
autres chevaux faisaient des sauts insensés que le
maître écuyer ne pouvait dompter ; la petite fille
criait se tenant à la crinière du poney. On craignait
à chaque instant qu'elle ne fût écrasée. L'effroi, le
tumulte, un sauve qui peut fut épouvantable. A ce
moment terrible Sir John Glover franchit la
banquette, se jetant au milieu des chevaux, et prit
la petite fille dans ses bras. Il la porta évanouie
mais sans mal à sa mère effrayée. La bravoure, la
présence d'esprit de Sir John Glover sauva donc
l'enfant. Il recueillit les applaudissements fré-
nétiques de la foule.'

This little incident of saving the child's life was never alluded to by him. He rarely spoke of himself.

Sir John again returned to London in the spring of that year, and was still receiving despatches from the Colonial Office relating to stores and other effects that were being sold after the Ashanti War, which reduced the sum of money for which he was accountable to the Government for spending on that expedition. A considerable time after this he received from the Colonial Office a new half-crown, florin, shilling, sixpence and a threepenny bit, ' the balance due to him after all the expenses of war had been paid.' At this time he commenced writing the history of the war, which, from the causes already mentioned, was not finished by him.

In August 1875, Sir John Glover received invitations from Bishop Alexander, of Derry, and Lord Clermont to stay with them in the north of Ireland, and bring his step-sister with him. He enjoyed meeting the bishop and his charming wife and daughter, who did all they could to make the visit a pleasant one. While there he received a letter from an old lady who was a distant cousin of his family, saying that her nephew was away from home, and that therefore they were unable to ask him to stay much, as she wanted to see him once more ;

but her cousin, Mr. Scott, of Annegrove Abbey, in Queen's County, with whom she was then on a visit, expressed a hope that he and his sister would come and see her there, and stay for a night on their way to London. A letter to the same effect was received by his sister from Miss Scott, who was doing the honours of her father's house, having lost her mother in early childhood.

Sir John was anxious to see his old cousin, thinking it might be many years before he again visited Ireland, and therefore accepted the invitation, arriving, in August, at Mountrath station, and leaving on the following day, after a long ride before lunch with his hostess. In this way he made the acquaintance of Miss Scott, who impressed him so deeply that although he had foresworn matrimony after his previous disappointment, he fully made up his mind to return to Ireland at no distant date and see whether on further acquaintance with this young lady he could impart the same feelings to her that she had inspired in him. With his usual cautiousness or, possibly, from diffidence, he never wrote to her or expressed any intention of returning till the following October, when her father received a letter saying that Sir John was coming over to Ireland to shoot at Lord Sligo's with his old shipmate Lord John Browne, and that, in consequence of his sister not being included in the invitation, he would, if convenient, bring her and leave her at Annegrove Abbey, if Mr. Scott and his daughter would renew their invitation made when they were last with them, that they should offer themselves if they visited that country again.

Accordingly they came at the end of October, and, during the week that followed, Sir John fully determined to declare his feelings. Just then Mr. Scott appeared to have noticed his intentions, and told his daughter that he objected to her marrying. This made her manner cold and constrained, and Sir John, thinking that the time had not yet come for him to speak, left at once for Sligo by the night mail.

About five o'clock the following morning, the train he was in dashed into a luggage train at Westport, and he found himself crushed down amid the *débris* of the railway carriage, unable to move. The whole of the compartment was smashed and telescoped together, only the one corner that he was sitting in was not entirely destroyed and flattened. The rail above his head had been driven down and caught him across the back of the neck, and the opposite seat had been jammed forward and held his leg so tightly that it was some time before he could extricate himself. When this was achieved, finding he had no bones broken, he at once did all he could in helping the porters and the crowd that had collected to extricate the dead and wounded from the *débris*, and perceiving the engine-driver to be alive, tore up a rail, and using it as a lever helped to lift off part of the engine which was crushing out his life. It was not till the excitement and strain were over that Sir John fainted, and the doctor discovered that he was severely injured. To join the shooting party was out of the question, and he was obliged to remain in the station-master's house until he was sufficiently recovered to travel.

Mr. Scott, hearing of the accident, made his daughter write and express a hope that as soon as Sir John was able he would return to Annegrove, and wait there until he was well enough to go back to England. This he did, little thinking that during the next seven weeks he would be battling with life and death. The following is a short note written by him to his mother's sister, fearing she would be alarmed at hearing of the railway disaster : 'I got a severe shake in the railway accident the other day, but am mending ; I could not write before. Fortunately my sister was not with me. I give you an extract from the surgeon's certificate :— " Severe contusions in left thigh and leg, and severe wrench and contusions of neck." I send a rough sketch of the appearance of the carriage after the smash.   I am now staying till better at Annegrove Abbey.'

The wound in the leg had been badly managed at Westport, and erysipelas supervened.   A nurse was telegraphed for, and the local doctor, seeing the case was serious, sent to Dublin for Surgeon Butcher.   When he came he pronounced his patient to be in a very critical condition, and seeing that the invalid's sister had no idea of nursing, impressed on Miss Scott that all his orders must be carried out with the greatest care, as it was a case of life or death.   Thus she was in a great measure given the responsibility of the case, and was obliged to see that the night-nurse, and others in attendance by day, were adhering strictly to his orders.

There is no time when the helplessness of a man appeals more to the sympathy of a woman than when she is trying to win him back to life and health.   So, during the anxious days that followed, Miss Scott realised how much she cared for the man whose life was hanging on a thread.

At last the turning point came, and Dr. Butcher said all danger was past, though his nervous system had gone through such a severe shaking, it would probably shorten his life.   When conscious of returning health he expressed his hopes, and found he had won the heart of the lady he wished to make his wife. But she told him what her father had said, and expressed her fears that the difficulties of ever gaining his consent to their union would be great. They proved to be even greater than she had anticipated, and after getting a flat refusal of his consent, Sir John Glover was obliged to leave Ireland. The Queen, with thoughtful kindness, caused Lady Ely to write to him and also to Miss Scott, expressing her regret that there should be any difficulty about the engagement.

On returning to London he received the following letter from Lord Carnarvon, regarding the Governorship of Newfoundland :—

'Colonial Office, December 24, 1875.

'I am very glad to hear continued reports of your progress, and I trust you are now so far advanced in the stage of convalescence that the proposal which I am about to make may be agreeable to you.

'The Governorship of Newfoundland will be very shortly vacant, and if the offer is one which suits your views, and if you feel yourself in respect of physical strength and health completely equal to the assumption of active work, it will give me great pleasure to submit your name to the Queen. It is right that I should, after so very serious an accident as that to which you have been exposed, but from which I trust you have escaped unhurt, ask your special attention to this last point. The offer of Governor of Newfoundland is one which requires the full energies of any man, and could not be held with advantage to the public service by any one seriously out of health. I feel therefore sure that should at any time it become apparent that you have suffered from the recent railway accident more than I have every hope and reason to believe is the case, you will anticipate any suggestion which the Secretary of State would under such circumstances make with a view to a change. I have no anticipation that such will be the case; but I feel bound, in a matter of public duty, to say so much, knowing as I do the necessity of having as Governor of Newfoundland one who is possessed of full strength and vigour, and I am confident you will not misunderstand my meaning.'

This letter was soon followed by a despatch appointing Sir John Governor of Newfoundland; and the following extracts from a letter written by Sir John Cowell, Master of the Queen's Household, may be of interest :—

'I hope I need hardly assure you of the pleasure with which I have heard of your appointment, and most sincerely do I congratulate you upon this, as I hope I may upon perfect recovery from your serious accident in Ireland, which caused much upset here, I can assure you.   I have long waited for your having employment, and although the acknowledgment of your deserts in this respect has come tardily, it is none the less gratifying to your friends.[1] That this appointment may lead to others in more congenial climes I hope and expect, and I am sure you will make friends in your new home as you have done elsewhere.'

On the confirmation of his new appointment, Sir John left at once for Paris to confer with the Government on the fishery question, which he had to study, as there had been great difficulties between the French and English Governments for many years in regard to the fishing rights on the west coast of Newfoundland.   The French possess two small islands, called St. Pierre and Miquelon, on the south shore of Newfoundland, but the point of dispute is on that part of the shore where the French have concurrent rights with the Newfoundland fishermen, which, by reason of former treaties, must be respected.   They have the right to fish in certain waters, and land to dry their nets and spread their fish, but must not erect permanent landing stages and buildings on the coast.   The word foreshore

---

[1] Sir John Cowell was evidently fully aware that, on the opening of the House of Commons that year, a question was going to be asked of the Secretary of State for the Colonies, why an appointment had not been given to Sir John Glover before this time.

was introduced into one of these treaties, and much litigation thereon ensued as to the number of feet or yards from the water's edge which absolutely defines the foreshore. The matter was still unsettled, and therefore disputes arose as to whether the French encroached or remained on that portion of the shore allowed to them by law. The government of Newfoundland includes a portion of Labrador, and extends very far north to the Moravian settlements. It is bounded on the other side by Canada, and the question of the fishing rights of American and other foreign vessels in these waters is also a subject of dispute. When he had sufficiently mastered the intricacies of the subject he returned to London, with the hope that his marriage might take place before he went abroad ; but the obstacles were as yet insurmountable, and with a heavy heart he had to sail without again seeing his *fiancée*. She felt how hard the waiting was, but thought it right to try if possible to obtain her father's consent by waiting a year, and with the assurance that she would not delay their marriage after that time, he sailed, on April 7, 1876, for Halifax, there to take another steamer for St. John's, Newfoundland, as the direct line of communication was not then open on account of the ice on the coast. Upon his arrival at Halifax he was received by the Lieutenant-Governor of Nova

Scotia, and dined with the 60th Rifles, and also at
the Royal Artillery and Engineers' mess, and found
many old friends among the officers of the North
American squadron, then commanded by Sir
Cooper Key.

CHAPTER XI

1876–1881

AFTER a few days' sojourn at Halifax, his first city in the West, Sir John Glover sailed for St. John's in s.s. 'Newfoundlander,' a wooden vessel belonging to the Allan Company, constructed for carrying mails during the winter months, when the coast was so icebound that no iron vessel can venture to force its way through.   After four days' discomfort, they came in sight of St. John's harbour.   He and his staff were received with the usual honours by the judges, officials, and chief dignitaries in his new government, who were very pleased at having a sailor Governor.   In former years, when the colony was in its infancy, they had always been governed by naval men.

The following extracts from a letter written by Sir John on his first arrival in Newfoundland may be of some interest :—

'Here I am at last! We arrived late on Saturday, since which time I have been in state, and this will continue all the week. Yesterday I was sworn in; then I swore in my Council. To-morrow I hold a levée; visits; receiving endless congratulatory addresses; deputations asking me to become patron to all sorts of charitable institutions—and all this in the midst of taking over the late Governor's stock of wine, stores, horses, and carriages. Now for the description of Government House. On the ground floor, two large drawing-rooms; dining-room; and billiard room *en suite*; hall passage; my office; a smaller drawing-room, and my private secretary's office; pantry; butler's room, and an inner hall with a vestibule reaching to the top of the house; a gallery round the vestibule leading to bedrooms—in short, a large country house well furnished. Last year 1,000*l.* worth of furniture was put in. The drawing-room has a new grand piano. The whole house is lighted up by gas. Ornamental and kitchen gardens, greenhouse, good stabling, with grazing for cows on the lawn. Police orderlies are always waiting in the hall. The front of the house has an extensive view over undulating country, and, from the back, the sea and a portion of the town.'

After assuming the government, and giving a ball on the Queen's birthday, he commenced exploring the interior of the country. He was the first Governor who ever went across the island. Until then the interior was quite unknown. He was anxious to find out for himself the resources of the country, and see if minerals and coal could be found; so, taking Mr. Murray, a geologist, and several persons of importance belonging to the colony, he started off with tents and provisions for the interior. Some Mic-Mac Indians or trappers might have traversed part of it, but hitherto the wolves and deer alone made their tracks through the thick forests. It was heavy walking on account of fallen timber. Equally trying were the spongy marshes to be met with in the open country. He was accompanied on one of these tours by the Rev. Mr. Harvey, who described the journey in his book entitled, 'Across Newfoundland with the Governor.' The author remarks, among other things, that 'the poorest fisherman understands that the representative of Royalty takes an interest in his welfare, and has visited his humble homestead'; and, again, 'one of them informed me privately that "the Governor was a fine man, and that he would wade up to the neck in water for him."'

Sitting round the camp-fire at night with his companions and their Mic-Mac and Newfoundland carriers, who spent all their lives trapping, they sometimes talked of home and English sport. On one occasion the conversation turned on horses; one of these Newfoundland trappers, who had spent all his life in the woods, and who was a most silent though observant man, was noticed listening with intense interest. On being asked if he had ever seen a horse, he said, ' No.' This led to a description of that animal, as something like a cow without horns, which apparently excited his imagination, and on being asked what he would do if he saw a horse, he said, with his usual brevity of speech, ' Shoot um.' He had lived with a dog as his sole companion, and only went to the coast once a year to sell his furs. When tired of talking after a heavy day's march, they retired to beds made of fragrant fir-boughs, all placed one way so as to form a springy mattress, giving most refreshing slumber; and with the first streak of dawn the little camp was again astir, ready for another day, in which shooting, surveying, and prospecting were the chief occupations.

After two months' camping out, the Governor returned to St. John's, and there received a telegram from a friend in Kent, with whom his *fiancée* was staying, telling him to get leave, if possible, and come home. A letter followed by the next mail, explaining that the long suspense was telling on her health, and his friend saw no use in their waiting. He therefore applied for leave, which was granted, and landed in England on November 2, 1876. After making a few necessary arrangements, he was married on November 7, and sailed again for Newfoundland on the 14th, in the 'Caspian,' of the Allan line.

The life at Government House may best be illustrated by the following extracts taken from my journal, written at that time, and sent home to a near relation, who was interested in this, our oldest British colony :—

' We left Queenstown on the 14th, having paid a visit, while waiting for the steamer, to my husband's old friend Admiral Sir Harry Hillyar, who had formerly been one of his captains. After a good passage out, we arrived on Thursday morning, 23rd, at a much earlier hour than was expected. The night before the captain had sent to us to say we could be in before sunrise, but he knew the people would be disappointed if they did not receive us, as they were getting up a public reception. So it was decided that he should slow down and delay our landing till ten o'clock.

' The morning was a lovely one as we steamed quietly into the Narrows, our ship firing a salute, which was answered from the shore, and by the man-of-war in harbour. The Narrows form a most striking bit of scenery. It looks like a sudden perpendicular cut in the rocks, almost too narrow for big ships to enter, and it seems impossible for them to get in when a fog is hanging over the mouth of the harbour. The water is quite deep on both sides. Having entered, one finds oneself in a land-locked harbour surrounded by hills; the sun was shining brightly, and the harbour full of shipping and gay with colour. A strong odour of salt fish prevailed, which came from the "flakes." These were long wooden poles thatched with branches or bark to let the air through for the purpose of drying the fish in the sun. Numerous wharves with their storehouses surrounded the harbour. St. John's is situated on a slope reaching down to the water's edge on one side; on the other the hill is almost perpendicular, approached only by a long bridge at the head of the harbour; the steep rugged sides are covered by stunted fir trees, and brushwood which turns a red purplish colour in the autumn, and gives the effect of heather-clad Scotch mountains, and not unlike them in outline. The three prominent buildings on the north side of the harbour are the Roman Catholic Cathedral, built on the summit of the slope, the Church of

England Cathedral, the Athenæum, and Government House.

'As soon as we came alongside the landing-place the Government officials received us. There were crowds of people cheering and five bands playing. The police who lined the streets were well set-up men, and like the Irish constabulary. As soon as we set foot on shore another salute was fired, and the band struck up the National Anthem, when an old Irishman rushed out of the crowd and seized my foot, " to be the first to dust a foot from the Old Country." Then the cheering was quite deafening, and the horses were taken out of the carriage and we were drawn up the hill by a number of men under several triumphal arches, with messages of welcome and pretty devices. The police, though formed in line on both sides of the streets, found it very difficult to keep off the pressure of the crowd. We stood at the door of Government House, and the Governor made a little speech, which pleased the people, for they cheered again and again, and said " it was just like the Governor." Being fatigued from sea-sickness during the voyage, I went into the house, but had soon to come out, as the people *would* see us again ; so we had to stand at the door for another hour before the crowd could be got to disperse. In the evening there were fireworks at the House of

Assembly, and bonfires and torchlight processions; when we had again to show ourselves at the door, and the police had difficulty in preventing the people being hurt or being pushed into the house. To me this reception was very gratifying, as it showed how much my husband had endeared himself to the people during his sojourn among them.

'*24th.*—The next day we drove to Topsail, a pretty little watering-place, about fourteen miles from St. John's, in what was to me a novel conveyance. It was called a boat carriage, of local manufacture, which my husband had made for long excursions into the country. In the interior, when off the beaten tracks, the corduroy roads and wooden bridges are trying to the springs of an ordinary carriage. This flat-bottom boat, like a punt, was mounted on omnibus wheels, with comfortable movable seats to carry eight persons. Two or four horses could be driven in it. Moreover, it could be taken off the wheels in five minutes, and used as a punt to fish from. There were many " three cheers for the jolly-boat," as the leaders of our team gaily cantered along by the beautiful shores of Conception Bay. Even at this late season a number of fishing boats were fluttering their sails on its blue waters, and the people were hauling in nets full of silvery fishes on the beach, which they spread alive on the fields for manure.

' *Sunday, 25th.*—We went to the eleven o'clock service at the English Cathedral; a choral service and good organ, but we must try to get a surpliced choir!

'I am opening a soup kitchen this winter, as there are many poor women and children in great distress. The clergyman of each church, and of any denomination, are given so many tickets, and the people come to Government House twice a week, where I see the soup and bread distributed according to the number in each family. To-morrow the bronze and silver medals are to be given by my husband to the sailors who saved so many lives last year in the wreck of the "Water Witch."

' *January 1st*, 1877.—We asked a little dinner party, of eight only, composed of people who had no family ties to brighten up their New Year. It is the custom here, as well as on the Continent and in America, for all the gentlemen to call on their lady friends on New Year's day. So at one o'clock our reception began, and did not cease till after six. The bishop and clergy and all the officials came first. It is a pleasant custom, as this New Year call wipes off all old scores, and erases long-owed visits. It is a very tiring function, standing for so many hours, with an endless stream of people passing all the time.

' *February 4th.*—I am "at home" once a week

for a musical practice. We are getting up one of Sullivan's operettas. This is to be acted at the end of the parliamentary season, before the members return to the country. There are a number of very musical people here, and many have good voices. It is a pity to waste their talent when they are so ready to take part. These rehearsals always end in a little dance, to which others arrive at ten o'clock, after the acting is over. I find the evening "at homes" are most popular. Also once a week I have an afternoon for a drawing club class,[1] besides my "at home" day for ordinary visitors, and the result of our work is to be exhibited in the spring. My husband being so fond of music and also sketching himself is a great incentive.

'I am sending a sketch and account by this mail of two silver spoons got lately from an American ship at Labrador. They are supposed to be the last remains of Sir John Franklin, and have been handed from tribe to tribe of the Esquimaux. The last of these Esquimaux in Newfoundland was a girl, who died here of consumption. This is a fatal disease when once they are civilised and

---

[1] These drawing classes continued, and the exhibitions improved annually, and, on the second tenure of Sir John Glover's office as Governor, he and Lady Glover, in awarding prizes for designing, were pleased to see the improvement that had been made, and the number of pictures sent to the Athenæum for competition.

brought into houses to live. There are no Red Indians in the island, but a few Mic-Macs, who are trappers for furs, and act as guides and canoe men.

' The universal prevalence of the " truck " system of the payment for labour, is a cause of great discontent in Newfoundland. Whenever possible, payment for goods or payment of wages is made in kind, and not in current money. Thus the fisherman is paid for his catch of fish by an order on a merchant's store for a money equivalent—practically at the merchant's prices of stores—with which to fit out his boat for next season's fishery; or the employer of labour (who is almost invariably a storekeeper) instead of paying his labourer, say, five dollars a week as wages, allows him to have five dollars' worth of tea, flour, pork, or molasses out of the store. The amount of which commodities is equivalent to five dollars cash is necessarily fixed by the merchant. This alone creates discontent; the labourer, perhaps justly, considering that the employer has the best of the bargain; but the practical result is that almost all labourers have overdrawn their accounts, that is, they are credited in the store books with more stores supplied to them than they have earned wages. Until they can wipe out these accounts they are practically obliged to remain in their employers' service, or face starvation. Of cash these men see little; they seldom have the pleasure of handling a silver dollar —all they can hope to do is to exchange their labour for the necessities of life.

' *March* 12.—It is on this date that all the sealing steamers leave port for the great sea harvest of the Newfoundlanders—their seal fishery. In the darkness of night, as the great clock in the cathedral chimed the midnight hour, one by one the steamers slipped from their moorings, and before the last stroke of 12 o'clock had struck, they slowly glided through the Narrows out into the broad Atlantic, where for some time their lights could be seen in the clear frosty air before they turned round the point northward towards the great pack ice where the seals find their home. There was no ice in sight, and not a sound to be heard as one by one the last of the steamers passed through the Narrows and were lost to sight. But many beating hearts were left on shore who knew their all for the year depended on the success of that voyage. It is a gambling business at best. The merchants and men suffer alike if the trip is not a good one, for they never do much on the second voyage in April, as they then go out to shoot the old seals. Naturally the excitement is great when the first return " house " flag is run up to say a steamer is in sight. We went to see the men march down before going on board, and a fine sight they were, all powerfully-built, good-looking men, well clad and in long sea boots.   The life is a rough one.   The expenses are great and the work hard while it lasts.   When they come to a pan of ice covered with young seals the poor beasts are knocked over and skinned or " sculped," as it is called, which means that the skin with all the fat attached is stripped off the bones as quickly as possible.

'*April* (1877). *Squire's Hotel, Topsail.*—We have come out here for a few weeks' fresh air and change, which was necessary for my husband, and, indeed, for both of us, after the long winter.   We were obliged to keep Government House heated by hot air, which was most enervating.   The doctors say he is suffering still from the effects of blood poisoning from the bad condition of the drains.   Indeed, in such a climate, where there is snow half the year, it seems to be incredible that Government House [1] should have been built with a twelve-foot area all round for snow and wet to lodge.   There has been a Russian scare—a man-of-war, with soldiers on board talking an unknown language, has been cruising about, and this led to a council being held upon

---

[1] It was built by Sir Thomas Cochrane, and is supposed to be more or less a copy of Government House, Portsmouth, where the climate is more favourable.

the defenceless state of the Colony.   However, that is not a subject the Newfoundlanders are much excited about. One man suggested that they should put a chain across the Narrows, which would keep any ship out, as in the time of the French. Another said, when speaking of protecting the gold in the banks, "that would be easy to do, for he would just go into the bush, taking the key in his pocket." It never seemed to occur to them how easily the town could be shelled. But the result of it all was that my husband had sent the aide-de-camp up to Halifax to consult with the General about arms and ammunition in case of need, and I have spent several nights this week up to 2 o'clock A.M. doing cipher telegrams, with a mounted orderly waiting to take them in to St. John's.

'The fishery question is, of course, the burning topic here, and the French have sent out a Consul of some rank, while, hitherto, there has only been a French Consular-agent. The reason, I believe, is, that when they found that the "Golobar" of Western Africa had been sent here as Governor, having had already some experience of him at Porto Novo and the Gold Coast, the French Government thought things would probably be brought to a crisis. We like the French Consul very much, and have found all the French officers on the station quite charming. It seems to me that if the Newfoundlanders would let the affair alone it would right itself in time. There are far fewer French than formerly, and less and less come out for fishing each year. So that if this vexed question of fishery rights were allowed to rest quietly, things would die a natural death ; but no— " Newfoundland for the Newfoundlanders " is the election cry, and a bitter feeling is fostered. Moreover, there are commissions and money to be got out of it, and there is no happiness for an Englishman, or a Colonist, who has not got a grievance.

'The American fishery question is also occupying people's minds. These beautiful Yankee schooners, with their long masts of polished red pine, are beginning to be seen in our waters, buying bait from the Newfoundland fishermen. Here, again, arise the various disputes which necessitate men-of-war spending the summer months in cruising round the island to keep law and order, and also to prevent the Newfoundlanders from putting nets entirely across the rivers, and stopping the salmon from running up stream. This can never be a good agricultural country. The winters are too long and the land too poor, except on the west coast, and one or two favoured valleys where a river runs through, and there is protection to the low land from the severe winds. So, when the fishery fails, without some new enterprise it is hard for the Newfoundlander to live. New industrial developments are sadly needed, and the people should be encouraged to settle on the land in the interior, which is, in many places, fitted for small farmers. Money is wanted to enable the New-foundlander to start a homestead, which could only be done by the Government or a chartered land bank.

'*May 25th*, 1877.—The Queen's Birthday is always a gala day in all our colonies. At noon the men-of-war in St. John's harbour fired the Royal salute, and all the police force paraded on the Mall, with some sailors, in front of Government House. After the inspections the officers came in to drink the Queen's health. In the evening we had a larger official dinner party, followed by a ball, to which all were invited who had written their names in the visiting book during the past year. I had the pleasure of pinning on Mr. Murray the birthday honour of C.M.G. for his long service in the geological survey of this country.

'*June* 22, 1877.—We started for a trip to an old French town, called Placentia, on the south coast, stopping at a village called Collenette, where H.M.S. " Eclipse " was anchored outside. We dined and slept on board. Next day Captain Erskine landed us, and we proceeded in the boat carriage with four horses to Placentia. The road contractors trembled for their contracts, and said : " They were never intended to build bridges for such a ' bridge crusher ' like that which the Governor druv with his four-in-hand " ; but, as they were mostly sailors, the jolly-boat was popular besides being useful; there was room to take a groom, valet, my maid, and luggage, together with the aide-de-camp and the Premier or a member of the Government, without whom it is unconstitutional for the Governor to travel about to visit other parts of the colony. How trying this must be to a man who has always governed a Crown colony where he was free to go or come as he liked !

'At Placentia there was a warm welcome waiting us—flags, green arches, and everything done to show us hospitality and kindness. No end of boats were offered to take us out for sea trout fishing, which was just then at its best and offered exciting sport. While there we had also capital trout fishing in the river. We lighted fires on the bank to keep off mosquitos and the awful black fly, as well as to grill our fish for lunch. After dinner was the time when the men caught most of the big sea trout, while those who were tired from the heat of the day, sat on the beach to listen to the singing of one of the officers of H.M.S. " Zephyr " who was with us. It is a pity to see this charming old

French town with so little enterprise. There are many things of interest in it. We saw a parchment deed signed by Louis XIV., a bill for goods he bought in Placentia. Some old tombstones in the churchyard, dated as far back as 1609, were of French nobles. One was to a captain of a French frigate, who had been a Newfoundlander, and who was taken to France as a boy by Louis XIV. when he visited Placentia. There was also some beautiful old church plate presented by William IV., who was very much interested in this place, where he had been many times as a midshipman. The old church here had been restored by Queen Adelaide, and has a Royal coat-of-arms over the door. But some of the carved marbles (over 200 years old) are cracked and sadly neglected.

'*St. John's, July* 13, 1877.—I send you some newspaper accounts, by which you will see that there is a Sailors' Home [1] being got up. Some of the gentlemen have been most liberal, giving 300*l.* towards it, and many 150*l.*

'*August* 1877.—The Admiral, Sir Cooper Key, and his fleet arrive here this week, and we are having a gay time of it, no end of dinners and balls, cricket matches, and tennis parties ; first, a ball at

---

[1] The laying of the foundation stone of this ' Home ' was the last public act performed by my husband and me on our return to the Colony for a second term of office in June 1885 (see the description in concluding chapter).

Government House, followed by one given by the bachelors, then one by the fleet, and a farewell given by the ladies, besides private dances, the Admiral kindly lending his band. The last night one of the poor bandsmen fainted from fatigue, and I own I was nearly worn out, and am not sorry for a few days' rest. The day of the Regatta, which is *the* gala day of the year here, was a gloomy one. But still the crowd was great on both sides of the lake to see the boat races. It is a general holiday and picnic, the " Derby Day " of St. John's, and nature seems to have set the lake in an amphitheatre of hills, so that it is like a natural grand stand, whence all can see. The Government House party drove down in state with the Admiral, and I was prevailed upon to ask him to stay a day or two longer for another dance, and to allow me time to lunch on board the old H.M.S. " Argus," which I wanted to see, as she was the ship my husband and Captain Barnard (who is here now) returned from Ashanti in. So when Sir Cooper Key promised to remain, the news was received with loud cheering, as he is supposed never to change his plans of sailing under *any* persuasion.

'*August* 20*th*.—After all the recent gaiety it is nice to get away to the country again. We started this time on a trip to the northern part of the island, to visit all the new mining district ; arriving

first at Twillingate, where there was a lighthouse
to inspect, and where we were very well received
and hospitably entertained. There were three
hundred children to meet us, singing " God Save
the Queen." One little girl asked her mother if
she might make her red petticoat into a flag for
the Governor. Next day we proceeded in H.M.S.
" Zephyr " to the saw mills up the " Exploits "
river, where a good deal of lumbering is done. The
scenery was beautiful as we steamed up the river.
Each side is clothed down to the water's edge
with silver birch pines and maple, which causes the
most exquisite blending of colours. It was pretty
to watch the seals jumping out of the water after
the salmon as we passed through the numerous
islands, and to see the many coloured jelly-fish and
curious sea creatures floating lazily in the clear
water, while we sat under the awning on deck
enjoying the cool evening air after the great heat
of the day. I send a sketch I made of an old
Indian squaw sitting by her wigwam, smoking her
pipe. The people are all well to do up north, and,
rather a contrast to the south coast, much more
clean and tidy. Here we fell in with H.M.S.
" Gulnare," a surveying ship, and Captain Maxwell
took us on to Betts Cove copper mines, which are
being worked just now to a large extent. It was
rather dirty work to find oneself in a bucket being

let down eighty feet by a rope, to scramble about in a dark wet mine. All about this neighbourhood it is very rich in ore, which is, however, often only in " pockets." Just now this place is in a most flourishing condition, and well managed. Often when a new mine is discovered there is not a house for miles, when all at once a mushroom village springs up with perhaps 1,500 people in the course of a few weeks. We next visited Till Cove mines, and had a warm welcome, no end of flags, cheering, bonfires, and guns. All the school-children lined the landing place, each carrying a royal standard flag about the size of a pocket handkerchief, with the word " Welcome " in large letters. There was an old man there *perfectly* blind, and over eighty years of age, who pushed through the crowd and asked to be led up to the Governor. When he got quite close my husband took his hand, thinking he had something to say privately. The old man suddenly kissed it, and said fervently, " He could thank God now and die happy, for he had *seen* the Governor; the Queen had sent him." It is wonderful to see the loyalty in these poor people, for this is the first time that a Governor has ever gone about the country among them. I often feel a lump in my throat when I hear the way in which they speak of him, and thank the Queen for having sent them someone whom they are proud of. It seems to me that this kindly feeling is increased, and a warmer and stronger attachment to the mother country promoted, by thus allowing them to know for themselves the man who has been sent as the representative of their Sovereign. Much as they like the state and pomp, such as it is, surrounding the Governor, they still more appreciate his genial way of treating them and his personal sympathetic interest in them.

'We sometimes take long drives into the country and stop at fishermen's cottages for tea, in out of the way hamlets where we are not known, and partake of their meal with them. On one occasion an old man and his granddaughter gave us of their hospitality, tea, bread and butter, and home-made jam, made from the berries which abound in the woods. After we left, probably through our groom, they discovered who we were, and the old man came all the way next day to Government House to beg his Excellency's pardon for not knowing him. His persistence was so great that the orderly was obliged to show him into the Governor's office, where he threw himself on his knees, explaining, "But how was I to know you in them boots?" alluding to the long brown boots the Governor always wore. I suppose the old man expected to see him in full uniform.

'*September* 1877.—The September gales have

begun, and with them a large " squid," as they call it here, was blown on shore. The length of the body of this octopus was about fourteen feet, and when the long arms or feelers were spread out the whole was about twenty-eight feet. This creature was taken to New York, and there preserved in some museum, while here in our little museum we have only part of one arm of another, measuring twelve feet, which was lopped off by a fisherman with his axe while the monster was throwing it over his boat to drag it under the water. A number of girls are now being employed in tobacco, biscuit, and other factories, where they get good wages, and are therefore giving up working on the wharves—a most unfit occupation for women, which roughens and brutalises them. I was very much pleased with the hospital which we visited near St. John's this week. It is a well situated building on high ground in an open space with a garden about it. The wards were clean and tidy with plenty of air, and I was glad to find no paint, only stained wood, and the walls all panelled with white tiles. The matron's room was bright, and full of flowers and growing plants. We had a long talk with a sailor who got fearfully smashed up in a recent gale.

' *November* 14, 1877.—This is just such a day that one is glad to be alive to enjoy the sun and brightness and beauty of nature. Still winter is near, and we fear it will be a very hard one for the poor. The fishing has been bad, and we are therefore not going to give many parties, except the large official ones, and will spend all we can in helping people and enlarging my soup kitchen. The Governor is trying to induce the Government to lay in supplies, and meet the distress in time. Work is wanted—if only the dock could be begun. The mail has just come with the eagerly looked-for letters and newspapers ; for though we get a cablegram at 12 o'clock every day, it only gives us the headings in the "Times," and we have to wait for fuller particulars.

'I often think that after the active exciting life, both as soldier and sailor, that my husband has lived, with stirring events and large human interests always around him, the great change to comparative stillness here must be a severe one. He feels having his hands tied by being the Governor of a constitutional colony, yet he goes quietly about his daily duties, irksome as they are to his nature, and different in character from those he was formerly called upon to perform, while all the time he is eating his heart out for some wider field of labour. Still he is proud of helping to keep this distant portion of the Empire honest, loyal, and true, a worthy part of a powerful whole, and has, I think, learned the meaning of the

old line which teach us so much when read
aright :
<blockquote>Those also serve who only stand and wait ! '</blockquote>

Life at this time in St. John's was more or less
always the same as what has been described in the
foregoing entries in the journals. With the exception of the fishing question, and other burning
subjects of purely local interest, there was little to
occupy the attention of the outer world. People
whose duty in life it was to live there were thrown
on their own resources, and had to find or make
their own amusements. During the summer and
autumn months so much out-of-door life was
possible that this was not difficult. Thus time
went on ; and the loss of our first child caused me
to go to England for a change. During my absence
the Governor took a pretty little place, called North
Bank, on the edge of a lake, in the country, where
we could spend the summer months and be within
easy reach of Government House for all entertaining
and official purposes. This cottage was a source of
great enjoyment and rest to us, and as the Governor
had not been away from the colony for his leave
that year, we arranged to spend the following
Christmas in Canada, and visit all the towns of
interest there.

In a newspaper referring to our departure I
read : 'The Governor of Newfoundland left St.

John's last month for Canada on a visit to the Marquis of Lorne and H.R.H. the Princess Louise at Ottawa. Sir John Glover is one of the ablest and most popular Governors we have ever had. No one could have more sincerely at heart the interests of the people over whom he rules. He has done more since his arrival to promote public improvements and advance the country on the path of progress than any of his predecessors in office, and he has now won the thorough confidence of the people of all classes.'

On arriving at Halifax, we were the guests of the General then in command of the forces there, Sir Patrick and Lady MacDougall, who did everything possible to make our stay a pleasant one. Dinner parties, private theatricals, and entertainments of all kinds were given to us, besides other public ceremonies to which Sir John was invited. By the kindness of the Canadian Government a special train was put at our disposal, and we proceeded to Quebec, that lovely 'silver city' as it is called, because of its tin-covered sharply-pointed roofs and gables. They stood out clear and shining in the moonlight as we crossed the St. Lawrence. Here the old French of the eighteenth century struck the ear, and we saw the Canadians in their fur coats, belted round the waist with red sashes. Monsieur Robataille, the Governor, called, and took us for a sleigh drive to show us the most interesting places. The B. Battery, quartered at Quebec, drove us in their four-in-hand across the Plains of Abraham to the falls of Montmorency, where a large picnic was got up in our honour. After a pleasant stay here, we proceeded to Montreal, and were the guests of Sir Hugh Allan, who would not hear of our staying at the Windsor Hotel. Ravencraig is situated on the Mount Royal, from which the name of the city takes its origin. It commands a most extensive view of the town. At night, when all the street lamps were lighted and the snow lay glistening on every roof, the effect was superb, and the clear stillness of the night air was only broken by the tinkle of the sleigh-bells in the distance. It was with deep regret we said adieu to our kind friends, but time did not permit of a longer stay, as we were invited to spend Christmas and the New Year with the Governor-General at Rideau Hall. Here Lord Lorne and the Princess Louise were doing much for art, and just then were engaged in having the interior of the Houses of Parliament at Ottawa ornamented and stencilled with graceful designs, to take off the bare cold look which was such a contrast to the picturesque appearance of the exterior seen from the river. The Prime Minister, Sir John MacDonald, was included in the dinner party on Christmas Day, and his curious likeness to Disraeli struck all those who had not met him before. A huge toboggan slide was a great feature at Rideau, built by Lord Dufferin when Governor-General. Sir John, being most anxious to see Niagara, would not stay over the New Year, and, armed with a letter of introduction from Lord Lorne to the proprietor of Prospect House, a little hotel built just by the great Horseshoe Fall, and the only one open in the winter, we proceeded there on the last day of the year. The view of the Falls from the window was sublime. As we arrived the moonlight lit up the rushing water, and rested on the white spray, while the icicles which fringed its edge sparkled and shone like burnished silver. The force of the rapids and whirlpool, which we visited next day, were most impressive, and it is only after a few days' sojourn that this prodigy of Nature's handiwork can be fully realised. A visit to Toronto followed, where Colonel Zowsky, the Beverley-Robinsons, and many others, by their kind hospitality made an ineffaceable impression. This is the most English of all Canadian towns. Here the ice boats glided swiftly over the frozen surface of the great Lake Ontario, looking like white butterflies skimming along. Here schools, colleges, and universities had to be visited, and education and learning as in Boston were the chief topics. But time did not permit a longer sojourn, as a few days' visit to Mr., afterwards Sir, Adam Archibald, Governor of Nova Scotia, was promised before returning to St. John's. It was with great regret that this six weeks' visit to Canada was brought to a close. Afterwards, Sir John took his leave during the season in London, and on one of these occasions, when calling at the Colonial Office, he was asked to go out at once to the Leeward Islands, as there was some difficulty or disturbance going on there. His services were so promptly required, that he was unable to wind up his affairs in Newfoundland. He proceeded there for a few days on his way to New York, leaving me for a month in St. John's to arrange matters. I then went to Halifax, in August 1881, on a visit to the Governor and his wife, while looking for a house, where my husband was to join me in November.

The following is from a local paper referring to our departure from Newfoundland, June 21, 1881 :—

'His wise policy, and the deep interest which he has taken in the prosperity of the colony have won the confidence of our people, while his geniality and courtesy rendered him a universal favourite. During his residence, his active mind was continually devising plans for promoting public improvements of all kinds, and urging on measures calculated to promote the progress of our colony.

That he did much to increase the activity and energy which has marked our history during the last five years will be universally admitted. Though the advancement which his new appointment secures has been well merited, we cannot but part from him with deep regret, and both he and Lady Glover will carry with them the respected esteem and cordial good wishes of the people among whom they have sojourned.'

CHAPTER XII

The Government of the Leeward Islands, 1881–1883—New York—
Arrival at Antigua—Government House—Political situation—Sir
John Glover's letters — Nevis—Halifax — New York—'Nooya'
yacht—Return to the West Indies—St. Kitts—The flood—Antigua
yeomanry—Police force—Barbados—Montserrat—Lime growing
—Guadaloupe—Dominica — Roseau Valley — Leper encampment
—Layou Valley—Arrival of Commissioners from Jamaica—Return
to Antigua—Governor's illness—Sir John Commerell—Anxiety
regarding the yacht—Nurses and epidemics—Governor obtains
leave—St. Thomas—Return to England.

SIR JOHN GLOVER sailed from St. John's to New
York in July 1881, where he found the heat at this
season very trying.   He was hospitably entertained
by Mr. Colgate, in his charming villa on the left
bank of the Hudson, and in the course of a few
days proceeded to the West Indies, and landed at
Antigua on August 5, where he was received by
a guard of honour, composed of the mounted
yeomanry and police, and by the former was conducted to Government House.   On the following
morning he was sworn in as Governor at the Court
House, by the acting Chief Justice before the
Executive Council, with all the usual honours, con-

sisting of a cavalry escort, and a salute of twenty-one guns.

Before describing the life in these West Indian Islands, it may be of interest to understand the manner in which they were governed at this period. And I am indebted to Mr. Arthur Stand, a resident there, for the following short account of the various methods of government in this confederated colony. ' It must,' he writes, ' have been a novel experience for Sir John, coming from a place like Newfoundland, to administer the government of the Leeward Islands, a group of islands supposed to have been federated under one government by Sir George Berkeley's predecessor, Sir Benjamin Pine, but still carrying on anything but a uniform system of government. The Federation, as it was then and is still called, consisted of Dominica, Montserrat, Antigua—comprising the islands of Barbuda, Redonda, St. Kitts, Nevis, Anguilla, the Virgin Islands—these last being an isolated group near St. Thomas, one of the Danish West Indies, which, although boasting a President of their own, had drifted into a state of quasi-bankruptcy, and derived the greater portion of their revenue from the sale of postage stamps to dealers, who, of course, made their profit out of the transaction by retailing the stamps to collectors.   Dominica, the largest island of the Federation, with an area of 464 square miles,

and a population of 25,000 all told, was at the time
of Sir John's arrival in the colony in a very bad
financial position; but Antigua, St. Kitts, Nevis,
and Montserrat, were fairly prosperous, as at that
time the staple product of these islands, sugar,
was selling at remunerative prices, and Montserrat
had recently developed an industry in the shape
of the exportation of lime juice, which promised to
prove very lucrative. In Dominica and Antigua
the legislatures ran on very similar lines, being to
some extent representative, that is to say, half of
the members were selected by that section of the
community entitled under the existing franchise
to a vote, and the other half consisted of Government officials and nominees of the Governor, whilst
in Dominica, the President of the island, whose
appointment emanated from the Colonial Office,
and who was also, in the Governor's absence,
President of the Legislative Assembly, had a casting
vote, which naturally gave the Government element
the preponderance. In Antigua the President of
the Council was appointed direct by the Governor,
and had also a casting vote, which produced
practically the same effect. St. Kitts, Montserrat,
and Nevis were under the Crown Colony form of
government, that is to say, their councils consisted
partly of Government officials, and partly of nominees
of the Governor, who were supposed to be gentle-

men acquainted with the wants and necessities of their respective islands. In addition to these local assemblies there existed a General Federal Council, which was made up of the representatives from the various local councils together with Government officials who, most of them, were ex-officio members; and besides these bodies there was in each island, or group of islands, an Executive Council, receiving their commissions direct from Her Majesty the Queen. These Executive Councils represented the Privy Council, all their deliberations being in private, and each member being sworn to secrecy. To add to the confusion entailed by such a miscellaneous state of affairs, each Presidency had an entirely different tariff, the taxes and duties on exports and imports varying throughout this so-called federation; and it must be apparent that all these differences were not calculated to make the wheels of the Government coach run the more smoothly. Besides the difficulties to be contended with in this direction, there was among certain people a strong feeling of opposition to the introduction of any schemes of reform, and as many of the highest officials were tacitly supporting this system of opposition, from interested motives, it can readily be seen how difficult the task became for a man like Sir John, who was most anxious to remedy existing abuses and introduce measures calculated to develop the resources of the colony as a whole. Despite the obstacles he had to encounter, we find in one of the island newspapers, which had hitherto been anti· governmental in its tone, the following paragraph in the issue of August 24, 1881 : " Sir John Glover has fully met our expectations of him up to the present. He seems determined to be led by no party, to see into everything himself, and from all that is said of our new chief by those who are intimate with him, we feel satisfied that the Leeward Islands have at last got a Governor in every sense of the word." '

The harbour of Antigua was surrounded by low hills, and a fine English Cathedral was the chief building. Government House, just outside the town, was a wooden structure with a broad verandah and large reception rooms, surrounded by a garden with tennis lawn, shaded by scarlet flowering flamboyant trees and tall white blossoming cactus. The stables and quarters for the native servants were at the back, while opposite, on a hill, stood the gaol and hospital.

Life here was indeed a contrast to the North. Now, winter and summer were alike hot, and the evergreen foliage and tropical glare strange after long months of snow and ice. If it were not for the sea breeze, the heat and mosquitoes at times would have been insupportable. We had negro servants of every shade, together with coolies and Portuguese, a Canadian groom and an English valet. These latter, fearing the climate, soon left, my own Scotch maid being the only European who remained with me to the last.

The following extracts from letters written to me indicate Sir John Glover's first experience and impressions regarding his new charge :—

'Antigua : August 1881.

'Just a week to-night I have been here, and it is no use in talking about Government House now. You will find it different when you come, newly painted, and rearranged. I am superintending a clearance of fences, gates, deserted patches of gardens— looking more like places of burial than anything else - indeed, a "middy" the other day pointed it out as "the resting-place of defunct Governors." My present routine is—coffee and bread in my bedroom until I dress, and drop in, for a second time, into the marble bath. For breakfast, bread, fruit, claret and water, at ten o'clock. The Colonial Secretary comes at eleven o'clock with papers to sign, which lasts till twelve, and other people come till two. Then luncheon, and, for the first month, visitors from three to five on Tuesdays and Fridays. It is hot, and they say unusually so. The hottest time in the year is August, September,

T

and October, during which time I trust you will never be here if I can manage it.

'*September* 21*st*.—The affairs of the Leeward Islands are in a very unsatisfactory state, and I am told that at Dominica I shall find matters infinitely worse than here. I went to the Island of Nevis on Friday. My departure from the "Queen's House" was most amusing. On a truck went a pile of luggage and cooking utensils; then came the cook's boy, with a fowl in one hand and a coffee pot in the other. The valet, a very ugly old negro, with a large "gamp," was too dignified to carry anything else. The butler, another very ugly old black man, had a basket in one hand, into which he had gathered odds and ends, and a bottle in the other, which he was requested to put into the basket. Then the Governor followed, driving himself in a one horse "buggy," because the Private Secretary cannot drive. At half-past one in the day, and oh, so hot! we arrived at the place of embarkation. . . . This place is full of worry and work, and Captain Morgan and myself are feeling somewhat done up. It is now half-past four, and we have been working hard all day, with an extra clerk, and the Colonial Secretary has sent to say he is coming now. The feeling is running very high between the two parties here, and society is quite divided up by it. Nothing can be more trying

than to be sent out as a new broom to sweep up the
remains of past years in a place where everyone
is related.   Nor can anything be more unfortunate
than to begin one's term of Governorship by clearing out officials from offices which they have held
so long, and to be obliged to replace them by their
own relations.   It is a most thankless task, and
will hamper my hands on every side, by the opposition and hostile personal feeling it must produce,
and will do much to prevent me from carrying out
improvements in the colony.   I open the General
Council of the Leeward Islands on October 3, with
a dinner party of twenty-four in the evening; and
the new furniture has arrived in time for the
occasion, after having spent some weeks in travelling about the West Indies.   I told you that I
collected all the old chairs without backs, and sofas
without legs, propped up by bricks, with their
coverings torn to shreds, and had them photo-
graphed to send to the Colonial Office when asking
for new furniture.   They must have laughed when
they saw the kind of place I was going to take you
to.   So much for having a bachelor predecessor.   It
has been so hot, with such quantities of rain, that
a most abundant crop of sugar is anticipated, and
the planters are in high good humour.   I think
you will like St. Kitts—I do.   They are going to
spend a good deal of money on the house, and I

dare say will make it very nice. Nevis is only about five miles from St. Kitts, and the whole forms a lovely bay not unlike, and equal to, the Bay of Naples. It is a beautiful wreck of the past. It has the finest soil in the West Indies, though only half is under cultivation, and the poorest, idlest, and most overtaxed people. Nothing can exceed the beauty of these islands, seeing each from the other. I came here in the " Forester " gunboat, very tired, and had no sleep, being worried all night by mosquitoes. Between three and four o'clock, when I had just dozed off, a collection of fifes and fiddles struck up something like " God save the Queen," and then five bars of " Rule Britannia." I could stand it no longer, and shouted to them (they were worse than mosquitoes), when they fled.'

It may be seen from the foregoing extracts what an anxious worrying time was now in store for the Governor; but the political aspect of the situation need not be further considered, as it was of purely local interest. There was no international question, nothing that required diplomacy outside the colony, little to be done except to try and revive its flagging energies, and start new industries which became necessary from the low state of prices in sugar. But this constant friction in petty matters is of all things most trying to a man who has habitually dealt with large undertakings, and prevents the development of the country. When to this is added a certain amount of opposition, probably caused by jealousy, the worrying nature of the life may be well imagined.

Sir John Glover left the West Indies in October, to join me in Halifax, where he remained till January, and after the birth of our little daughter proceeded through Canada to New York, and stayed at the Brunswick Hotel. Mr. Edwards, the Consul, showed us much kindness, and we were so hospitably entertained that our stay was one round of gaiety.

Sir John then went to Baltimore, and there purchased the yacht 'Nooya,' which belonged to Mr. Léon Say, for the West Indies. He found it so difficult to get about from island to island, having only local steamers to travel by, and they were often uncertain in their time of sailing. He was therefore anxious that the Government should eventually possess a craft of its own to convey the Governor, judges, and officials about to the thirteen islands that comprised the colony. Having concluded the purchase of the yacht, we left for St. Kitts. The rigging of the steamer we travelled by was frozen hard, and covered with icicles when leaving New York, and after twenty-four hours at sea she fell in with a gale, and had to be battened down for a considerable time. All cattle and sheep on board were drowned, and only one other horse, besides the two fast trotters the Governor was taking down to the West Indies, survived. At last, smooth water and tropical weather were reached, and in nine days, Sombrero, Sabre, and other islands of the Danish West Indies were sighted, and soon after St. Kitts. When we arrived here the natives swarmed down to the landing place, chattering and jabbering, all eager to see the new comers.

Government House here, though comfortable, was not an imposing building. It stood in its own grounds, with a garden and tennis lawn attached. There were a few tall palm trees, and quantities of roses, hibiscus, and all tropical flowers were sent every morning from the botanical gardens, where a great dark banyan tree stretches out its branches far and near, and protects the lovely foliage and flowers from the fierce tropical sun.

St. Kitts is a garden; everything grows there, and every inch is cultivated. The soil is so friable that it requires only a hoe to till it with. There is a great volcano ridge down the centre of the island where they plant coffee, and where monkeys play about among the cocoa-nut palms. On the summit of this hill great rain clouds collect and burst with terrific violence, sweeping down in torrents into the town of Basseterre, causing loss of life and property. Once this occurred with unusual force, and the people were panic-stricken. One evening at dinner-time, when the rain was coming down as it only can do in the tropics, a frightened servant rushed into the room saying that 'the flood had come.' The scene at the back of Government House was one not easily forgotten. A torrent of water was rushing and surging past the wall. We sat there watching it rising in freshets, a foot at a time, every moment thinking the wall must give way, while the frightened people kept coming up clamouring for help. However, towards morning the flood subsided. Every effort was made to obtain sanction for building a wall to turn the force of the water past the town into another channel. The Governor undertook to do the necessary surveying and estimates himself, to save the colony expense, if only the Colonial Office would give its consent to the work being begun. After much delay, leave was granted, and the wall commenced. When it was a couple of feet high and all the stones and mortar procured, a telegram came to stop the work, and the people were left in despair.

But while this town needed protection from the violence of these sudden mountain torrents, drinking-water in some parts was much needed, and the Governor visited different places where he was anxious to make reservoirs to collect supplies.

Here the natives came in crowds pressing round the carriage, yelling and shouting, ' Water!' holding up their children to pray, implore, and beseech ' water' to be given them. The pressure became so great that it was difficult to get the horses to move on without injuring the people, who threw themselves on their knees in front of the carriage. When, for want of money, or from the difficulty of getting the home authorities to realise how much such improvements are needed, a Governor is obliged to sit quiet, and look on at the sufferings of the people, it is hard indeed to feel inaction is enforced where action is so much needed. On the first night of our arrival at St. Kitts we had the novel experience of an earthquake. The air, which at night is so full of chirping noisy insects, suddenly became still, the birds flew about in alarm, then a long low rumbling noise was heard, and a sudden trembling motion felt, which made everything vibrate and rattle. Government House being built of wood escaped, but its foundations, which were of brick, were cracked right through. Here the people are most hospitable, and quantities of fruit and flowers were sent by those who did not entertain.

We had a cheery little race meeting, and one of the American trotters, which survived the bad passage from New York, distinguished himself.

However, this poor animal never got accustomed to the change of country, and the rustling of the canes when shivering in the breeze frightened him to such an extent that he was useless for ordinary work. The race-course near Basseterre is prettily surrounded by low hills, but racing is not as popular here as in some of the other West Indian islands. The people cannot afford to keep horses for that purpose, and everyone is too busy sugar making.

It seemed incredible that this group of islands, forming one colony, should have each a different form of government. At Nevis, which is only a few miles from St. Kitts, ships had to clear and pay Custom dues when leaving or entering port just as if going to a foreign country. There was much delay and difficulty before Sir John could have this change effected. The wheels of office move slowly, and Downing Street is a long way off.

The importation of Chinese labourers into Antigua did not promise well, for soon after the arrival of three hundred of them from Hong Kong, they murdered one of the overseers in a barbarous manner. A black woman was witness of the crime, which led to their conviction, and death sentence was passed on two of them. On the day of execution hundreds of negroes swarmed all round the gaol, but no hangman could be found among them. A Chinaman at last volunteered to execute his brothers.

This did not apparently increase the popularity of the race among the Creoles.

The natives have a curious way of transplanting, so to speak, their wooden houses. If the distance were long, and the move could not be effected in one day, we might meet a house on the roadside waiting till dawn, when again the men would begin their sing-song chant as they all pulled in unison. Thus the wooden structure would be moved slowly along on rollers.

The deep clay soil in Antigua had to be tilled by steam ploughs, and great heavy teams of white oxen were used to haul the carts with cane loads to the sugar mills. The manager's house on most estates was built on the highest bit of ground, where a huge windmill stretched out its arms, as it were, to mark the spot and protect it. These windmills were prominent features in the landscape. The native houses were clustered round them, and the cattle, mules, and horses form picturesque groups standing about or lying on the cane locally called 'magasse.' Everything is of use in this plant; even the refuse cane after the juice is extracted makes fuel to feed the boilers, and the little negro children suck the cane as they bask in the sun and grow fat and shiny. The tree oyster, which hangs in bunches on the branches of the mangrove trees in the swamps by the sea, is gathered at low tide, and brought into market by the natives. These curious crustacea are not bivalves, three shells covering every two oysters. Crayfish and eels abound, and wild duck and teal are sometimes plentiful, otherwise sport is not to be had. Quails and plover may sometimes be shot, and rabbits, in the island of Barbuda, which is entirely devoted to raising cattle, horses, and guinea-fowl, all running more or less wild, the place being only inhabited by natives and the one Englishman who rents it.

In Montserrat the groves of limes, oranges, and lemons fill the air with fragrance, and where nature is allowed to have her way the parasites and foliage form tangled masses of deep dark green, great garlands of orchids and creeping plants intermingling with the starlike flowers of the Vanilla and Granadilla, a kind of passion-flower, which also bears a delicious fruit. The manager of the lime juice company and his wife entertained us most hospitably, and showed the Governor all over the works. Here the women, in white cambric frocks and bright coloured turbans, ' rime ' the limes, to extract the essence or essential oil by turning the fruit swiftly round with their hands in little copper dishes which prick the skin of the limes. The fruit is afterwards boiled down in vats to a black pitch-like mass, and then shipped to England for dyeing purposes. Sugar is hardly cultivated here. The island is too dry and hilly, and good as are the roads, they are too steep for very heavy traffic. There is no Government House in this island, so the Governor's visits are consequently short; but it was an easy sail across in the ' Nooya.' This being a well-to-do island, there was contentment and little official work to be done.

The most beautiful of all the islands in this colony is Dominica. The volcanic ranges of hills are packed one behind the other down the entire centre of the island. These hills are four or five thousand feet in height. Here the rains are violent, and sometimes the ravines are torn out by wild torrents of water. The air is soft and damp, with a clear blue sky. A rainbow generally hangs in an arch over the island, which is set like a gem in surroundings of water having even a deeper azure hue than in the other parts of the Caribbean Sea. The forests which clothe the mountains are of the loveliest green. Roseau lies nestled in the trees; tall palms raise their graceful heads over banyan and bread-fruit trees. Tamarinds and acacias shade the crotons, and begonias and variegated plants fill the botanical garden, which forms a terrace overhanging the sea. Masses of bougainvillia, stephanotis, and yellow alamanda mingle in wild profusion over the houses. The air is heavy with the scent of the tuberoses and gardenias, intermingled with that peculiar odour which hangs over every native village. The town of Roseau is beautifully situated by the sea-shore at the base of the mountains. Long terraces of houses face the landing place. To the right is a fort, now used as a police barrack. The roads leading out of the town and the streets themselves had been carefully paved, but the grass is growing between the stones, and the houses are generally in a dilapidated condition. The old French Catholic Cathedral and Anglican Church can be seen at a little distance. White native villages gleam among the palms along the shore, where the negroes are busily employed fishing, but the cool of the early morn is the time to see the people. The market girls come into town to sell their vegetables and fruit, each of them carrying heavy baskets of over eighty pounds on her head, and stepping along lightly with her burden. The road up the Roseau valley lies for a short way through an old part of the town where the rarest gold and silver fronded ferns peep out of every wall and crevice, shaded by nutmeg, clove, allspice and cinnamon trees. On leaving the town the ride is under groves of limes, oranges and citrons, their branches meeting over head and forming a protection against the noonday sun. Soon the white starlike flowers of the Liberian coffee trees are to be seen, under their canopy of dark green leaves, and plantations of young cocoa trees, sheltering under a few older ones, show their heavy orange pods beside the unripe green ones.

The road leading to the 'Soufre,' or sulphur springs, lies on the edge of the river. As the ascent gets steeper it passes under large forest timber trees, covered with festoons of parasites and flowering orchids. High on the mountain ridge, where the branches meet overhead, the air is cool on the hottest day. There, little vistas show glimpses of the sea, and the winding river below, fringed by bamboos, and overhanging spice trees. As one turns, for a moment, to rest and wonder at the still solemn silence of this dark primeval forest, the clear flute-like note of the little brown mountain bird may be heard. This rare and solitary creature is only to be found in the highest places. Even the great purple-breasted imperial parrot, once a lover of these lonely woods, has disappeared, and no living thing, save a startled lizard, breaks the deathlike silence.

This may account for the quiet manners of the Caribs with their yellow-brown, expressionless faces, who live in the unfrequented parts of the island. Their blue lips, and long straight hair, denote their descent from the Red Indian. At one time, these Caribs populated all the islands in the Caribbean Sea. Now only about eighty of them are left in Dominica, and these people are the principal road makers. They follow the peaceful occupation of fishing and basket-making, never mixing with the negroes, and talking their own language. A part of the island is known as the Carib quarter, and is set apart for them by the Government.

From the result of the great facility of growing their own produce, and from the poverty of the white residents, who cannot afford to give good wages, the negroes live a lazy life. They speak a French patois, and are more French than English in their ideas. They believe in ' Obeah,' and have quaint superstitions and beliefs in ' jumbies ' and wood spirits. The jumbie tree, that grows in the high mountains, bears a bright red seed, the size of a small hazel-nut, and these are supposed to be the home of the spirits. There is also a climbing ' jumbie ' plant with long pods containing vermilion-coloured hard round seeds. These the natives make into necklaces, and various articles of sale for protection against evil. ' Duppies,' or ghosts, they frequently profess to see, and the African ' Obeah ' still has a powerful hold over their minds. But when people were suffering illness from ' Obeah,' the real cause was looked upon with the gravest suspicion, because the natives understood medicine and secret poisons made from vegetable matter, the traces of which cannot be discovered even by a post-mortem examination. The curious, childlike simplicity combined with craft and cunning —remnants of barbarism—in the negro character, forms an interesting study. Their low gentle voices and soft brown eyes, and lithe movements, all make one forget the stronger, fiercer elements that are lying hidden in the background, ready at any moment to burst forth. Many of them are faithful unto death to their masters, especially the pure African negro. It is universally found that the mixture of white blood leads to discontent, jealousy, and many vices never known to the negroes of full blood, and they themselves have a great contempt for the half-castes. A few negroes born in Africa are living in this island quite apart from the natives. These people were the last of the slaves, taken from a slave ship and set free in Dominica. As soon as they learned that the new Governor was the 'Golobar' of their people in Africa, they came to see him, beating their drums or 'tum-tums' in welcome. He found the 'Aku' marks, and could speak to them in their own language ; but most of the younger people had forgotten it, and spoke only patois French.

Our road homeward lay through the 'Morne,' the old barracks, a lovely spot, situated on a grass-covered plateau on a high cliff overhanging the sea, where the setting sun, in all its golden glory, was fading into yellow and purple, before sinking below the horizon into the violet water. From this sunlit sea we turned to look at the dwellings around us. The barracks were now a 'leper encampment,' where all the most loathsome forms of human suffering were congregated together in every stage of disease. Nothing could be done for them except to try and make their few remaining days less miserable. In Dominica there is an even worse illness than leprosy, and of a more malignant character, called 'Yaws' by the natives, and unknown in the other islands.

As we approached the town, Government House stood out grey in the dusk against its background of palm, mangoes, and banyan trees. It is a stone building, with a trellis on either side of the door, covered with stephanotis, which hung in festoons over the entrance. A hedge of roses and gardenias bordered the drive, and a fountain, in a bower of oleanders, played in the garden. After sundown the air was alive with beetles, singing frogs, and the buzz of every imaginable insect. Great fire-flies darted about like shining meteors through the trees and flowers. 'La belle,' as the natives called them, insufficiently described their beauty. The deep croak of the bull frog or 'crapaud' in the distance betrayed his vicinity to his captors. They were in great request, being a delicacy of food, as was also the land crab, and the cabbage palm served as a vegetable, each dish costing the life of a tree. 'Calaoo' soup, made from the edible Caladium, was also peculiar to this island. Occasionally 'agutees' and 'manacues' could be obtained. These were small animals found in the woods, and rather good eating. The fish was excellent, and turtle, flying-fish, and others of brilliant hue with local names, were always for sale in the market. Beef was rarely seen ; mutton, possibly twice a week, was procurable. Fowls, and generally pork, could be obtained, and fruit of every kind in profusion, with yams and a variety of vegetables.

The view from Government House was entrancing. Both colour, form, and atmosphere were by nature used to make this island the fairest jewel in the Caribbean Sea. From here we could see the mountain gorge, its slopes covered with forest, one bold crag of the topmost range standing out brown and bare, half buried in the mist. Acacias, hibiscus, flamboyant trees in full flower added little splashes of vivid colour to soft backgrounds of varied green, while the air was perfumed with orange blossoms. There was nothing to break the silence, save the tinkling of the bells at morn and eve in the convent at the back of Government

House.   Here the French nuns taught the native children, and did good work among the people. Little streams ran through the town of Roseau to the sea, where the clear blue water rippled through the brown wooden stakes of the landing-stage, revealing the orange and black striped pilot-fish, darting about in search of food, if not occupied in attendance on a shark.

At this time there was not enough money collected by the Treasury even to pay the low salaries of the officials.   To enable this to be done the Governor put a small tax on goods landed on the wharf.   He was anxious to make a road to enable the produce being carried down from the interior for embarkation, and to open up the Layou valley at the other end of the island. The following despatch, written by him, will show those who are interested in Dominica what was done at that time: 'You are aware that for some time past preparations have been made in the above-named district, by the erections of Agoupas for the purpose of affording shelter, and by cutlassing a path across the country, for facilitating the progress of an exploring party whose object would be to ascertain the value of Crown lands, and what facility there may be for settlement, and for the development of the natural resources of the district generally.   I have considered that some portion of the Crown lands fund might legitimately be employed in meeting the expenses of this expedition. One of the principal objects of the expedition is to determine the practicability of building a tramway from sea to sea, and to lay down the levels of the proposed road.'

Dominica threw its spell of fascination over the Governor, possibly from being more like Africa in climate and foliage than any other of the islands. He determined to try and get it out of its bankrupt condition. Seeing that sugar was no longer a produce fit for this island, he gave a great impetus to the growing of cocoa, coffee, limes, and spices, and bought a property of some two or three hundred acres to show by example what could be done by cultivation, bringing down his Portuguese gardener from Antigua to take charge of the place. This man, having come from Madeira, understood the possibility of bringing this very neglected estate into a high state of perfection. Dr. Nichol, an English gentleman, who had been for some time practising in the island, had already begun to cultivate the soil upon scientific principles on his property of some twenty or thirty acres. Here he was manufacturing citric acid from the limes, essences for perfumes, and growing Liberian coffee and cocoa with great success. He invited us to stay for a change of air at his place, which is situated on a plateau of high land, over which cool breezes were wafted from the deep gorge in the Roseau valley, and our visit to his house, with its beautiful surroundings, was among the pleasantest memories of our stay in Dominica.

One day an old negro butler came and asked leave to go to a party that night at the judge's house. Permission being given, he still lingered about in a hesitating manner, and at last summoned up courage to make a little speech which he had evidently prepared. 'I respectfully request that your ladyship will lend me your " Shakespeare " for this occasion, for seeing that we consider a party to be frivolous, and leads to idle talking and gossiping, which is not good, we have decided that our entertainment shall be for the improvement of our minds. I therefore am taking the part of Brutus, and the judge's butler that of Cassius, and thus spend our time in a way that is profitable unto us. I therefore take the liberty of respectfully begging of you to grant me this favour.' I never inquired how the party went off; but the effect must have been comical, as the men who were to personate these heroes were about the most miserable and ugly specimens of negro humanity to be met with; they were entirely unfit for out-of-door work, and utterly unlike most of the fine field labourers to be seen working in the cane fields. These people work in gangs, the strongest man and best worker leading, the others being obliged to keep up to them.

At the end of three months' visit to Dominica, the Governor was obliged to return in the 'Nooya' to attend to business in Antigua. A few days after his departure I received a telegram from him, asking me to return there at once. The mail steamer was expected that evening. After a hasty packing up of linen, wine, and effects, sending the horses to be shipped, and a staff of servants to be ready, my maid and child accompanied me on board the steamer, where I was received by the captain, and told that the Commissioners from Jamaica were on board, and were proceeding to Antigua to be our guests. As all this had been arranged by telegram, I was unaware of it. The captain then introduced General (afterwards Sir William) Crossman, Mr. (afterwards Sir George) Baden-Powell, and their secretary, Mr. Harris from the Colonial Office; and I learned, while sitting on deck enjoying the cool evening breeze, that Jamaica was not ready for the Commissioners, and therefore they came on to Antigua some time before they had intended. On arriving next day in the harbour of St. John, Mr. Bennett, a merchant there, and also a member of the Legislative Council, came on board to meet me, saying our carriage with the aide-de-camp was waiting for the Commissioners, and that he had come to bring me on shore, and drive me up to Government House in his buggy. When we got near the house he explained to me, in the kindest manner, the reason he had come was that the Governor was unable to do so as he had fallen over an iron bar on board the yacht, and had hurt his leg so badly he could not walk nor leave his room. It was some time before he was able to be about again as usual, and he could not see much of the Commissioners while they were staying with us. When better he went to St. Kitts, and there was able to entertain them.

In December, Admiral Sir John Commerell was expected in the 'Bellerophon,' and several ships were to accompany him. This was to be a very gay time at Antigua. Besides dinner parties, we were giving a fancy dress ball at Government House. The morning of the day the fleet arrived the Governor felt ill, and thought a few hours' rest might enable him to be well enough to receive the Admiral; but by the time he and the other officers called to pay their official visit, Sir John was in a high state of fever, and remained for days in a most critical condition. He wished, however, all the official entertainments to take place as had been previously arranged. On the day of the ball he was so much worse, that I was compelled to speak to the Admiral and doctor on the advisability of having it postponed. When I suggested this to the Governor, the idea of altering arrangements on account of his illness excited him to such an extent that I was obliged to abandon the idea, and though tired out by anxiety and fatigue, sitting up with him at night, and entertaining all day, I was obliged to receive my guests as usual, and try and look as if I, too, were enjoying the gay scene. At last the crisis came, and though weakened from the severity of the attack, the Governor recovered, and went to St. Kitts in the yacht. When returning he telegraphed to me saying that he would arrive at Antigua that evening in time for dinner, and asked me to invite some officials to dine. Dinner hour arrived, and no yacht was in sight. Next day she was not heard of. A telegram came from the Governor of an adjacent colony, which I opened. It contained the startling news that the new engineer on board the ' Nooya ' had forged certificates, was not an engineer, and had escaped from prison. This alarmed me the more, but I dared not tell anyone, as the people were in the gravest anxiety already about their various relatives who were on board the yacht with the Governor. It was difficult to keep up their spirits by giving any hope. After days of watching and sending ships out to search, and vainly telegraphing to the Admiral and Governors of other colonies, just as all hope of ever seeing the little craft again was well nigh over, she was sighted by the mail steamer off Montserrat, which brought the intelligence to St. John's that the ' Nooya ' was sailing in the direction of that port. The excitement was great when the Governor's flag was once more run up, and crowds came to offer their congratulations, and hear what had happened. It appeared, while the Governor and his friends were at lunch, soon after leaving St. Kitts, a black stoker rushed terrified and naked into the saloon gasping out, ' Oh, Governor, quick ! quick ! we are sinking.' Sir John went to the engine room, and found there a desperate state of things. The engineer had turned on some wrong valves, and the place was full of water nearly up to the fires. The two black stokers had been working up to their waists in water, vainly trying to get it under, and every moment fearing an explosion. One of them broke away from the engineer, who was trying to detain him, and rushed to the Governor for help, and thus saved the lives of the whole party. The fires had to be immediately put out, and in the condition the vessel was then in, there was nothing to be done except to run her ashore at the nearest place to keep her from sinking. It was some days before she was pumped dry again, and could be got off, and then she could only sail to Antigua, as the engineer was under arrest, and the stokers too frightened to light the fires. Montserrat was unfortunately the only island with which there was no telegraphic communication.

In the spring of 1883 the Governor had another attack of fever, when his life was despaired of. On Easter Sunday the doctor came before the morning service, having already been at dawn, and told me he could not live till 3 o'clock. I asked if he would try ice to allay the fever, but this the doctor said would kill him. However, as soon as he left, thinking, if it was only a matter of a few hours, something must be done, I sent to my kind friend, Mr. Bennett, and asked him to have the town ice-house opened and send me a supply at once. This I placed on the head and spine, and got two black women to waft the cool air over him with large fans. Worn out from anxiety and long nights of watching, I sat down to see the result. Soon I found the pulse beat slower, and when the doctor came his patient was in a quiet sleep. He told me afterwards when he found the house so still he felt he should hear the worst, and added that the Governor had been prayed for that day in all the churches.

The constant nursing I had to do while in the

West Indies brought strongly before me the necessity for a trained band of nurses, in case of an
outbreak of yellow fever or any other epidemic.
There was no one in the islands to send for, and
from the suddenness of some of these illnesses
they require careful and experienced watching.
But I found it very hard to get the doctors to see
any necessity for a change or improvement in this
matter, as many of them were quite content with the
services of the uneducated negro women who were
the only nurses in the hospital.

After this second very severe attack of malarial
fever it was thought advisable that the Governor
should go on leave of absence for a change to
England. He had found the work very worrying,
and the strong opposition to progress most heartbreaking and trying to his nature. He decided, if
possible, never to return. This, however, he did
not mention in Antigua. When he was leaving, on
June 1, large crowds came down to the wharf to
say good-bye, and wish us ' God speed ' and a ' safe
return.' Just as we were pushing off in the boat
the band struck up ' Can auld acquaintance be
forgot,' and I fairly broke down, knowing I should
never see the place again nor many of our kind
friends whom we had left behind us. We found,
both here and at St. Kitts, which we passed on our
way to St. Thomas's, that our cabin had been filled

with flowers and choicest fruits sent us as parting gifts.   As the steamer carried us swiftly away, leaving a long dark wreath of smoke on the still evening air, and we saw for the last time those verdant green islands bathed in the golden light of the setting sun, we felt that strong bond of sympathy with those from whom we had parted, that can only be experienced by people who have worked, and toiled, and suffered together in foreign climes.

CHAPTER XIII

1883–1884

Fishery Commission—Return from the West Indies—Landing at Plymouth—Visit to Germany—Prince of Wales at Homburg —Visits in England and Ireland—Summons to Windsor—Deputation to Paris regarding the Fishery Commission—Reappointment to Governorship of Newfoundland—Life in Paris and Compiègne—Return to England—Departure for Newfoundland— Arrival in St. John's—Last year, 1884–1885—The Queen's birthday ball—Return of Mr. Greely—Life at Government House—Departure of Mr. Ford and Mr. Pennell—Railway to Harbour Grace— Opening of Sailors' Home—The new graving dock—Arrival of French man-of-war—Cariboo shooting—Illness of the Governor —Drive to Topsail—Applying for leave—Return to England— Homburg—Death of Sir Harry Ord—Return to London—Illness and death of Sir John Glover—Kensal Green.

On the journey home from the West Indies nothing occurred of particular interest. After fourteen monotonous days we hailed with joy the cool grey English atmosphere at Plymouth, a relief after the burning tropical sky and the never changing foliage, which soon wearies the eye.

Although the journey home did somewhat to restore Sir John a little in health, he was still far from having recovered from the effects of the malarial fever contracted in Antigua. He was advised by Dr. Broadbent to go to Homburg at once, to try the healing qualities of the waters there. Without much delay, therefore, we left London, and went slowly up the Rhine, visiting Bonn, to him so full of by-gone memories, and other places he knew in days of yore. There was much just then in Germany to interest him. We paid frequent visits to the opera at Frankfort, after dining at the palm-gardens, and saw the Crown Prince review the troops when he and the Emperor William were staying at the Schloss at Homburg. Here the Prince of Wales, when taking his morning walk ' under the Lindens,' gratified my husband much by an act of characteristic thoughtfulness in showing him a telegram he had just received from the young Princes, who the day previously had landed in St. John's, saying : ' I thought it would please you to hear of the hearty reception my sons have received in your old colony.' Later, the great autumn manœuvres, which took place in September of that year, brought Sir John once more into touch with the improvements that had been made in all that pertained to the art of war, and he again mixed with soldiers and diplomatists.

After this we proceeded to Ireland, to stay with my father, and spent some little time in visiting friends both there and in England. In December we received a summons to go to Windsor, where the Queen invited him to dine and stay. On this occasion Her Majesty expressed to me her pleasure

at hearing that he was recovering from the effects
of the West Indian climate, and asked me many
questions about the Colonies.

On our return to London Sir John found that
a new post was about to be made in the South
Pacific, where there would be a good deal of sea
work—in fact, that something like a new colony was
to be formed. In former years this work would have
been his delight, but now, with a wife and child, this
roving life in a bad climate was not desirable. Thus
a colony in South Africa seemed to be a more hopeful
field of labour. Before this new appointment was
fully arranged, a telegram came announcing the sad
news of the death of Sir Henry Maxse, the Governor
of Newfoundland. Just then Mr. (afterwards Sir)
Clare Ford, and Mr. Burke Pennell were about to
proceed to Paris, where the French Fishery Commissioners were to meet. The Colonial Office did
not at first like to ask Sir John to return to his
former governorship, as they were about to give him
a better one ; but seeing the necessity of having a
man who understood the fishery question to represent the colony, they asked him to return to Newfoundland for a year, and in the meantime proceed
to Paris on behalf of Newfoundland till the Fishery
Commission was finished. This he accordingly
did.

On arriving in Paris, we took up our residence

in the Champs Elysées. Lord Lyons was then the ambassador. He gave us a warm welcome at the Embassy, where he entertained with all the hospitable charm for which he was renowned. Renewing acquaintance with him was among the many pleasant memories of our sojourn there. Here too, again, Monsieur and Madame Mackenzie welcomed us to their *salon*. This stay in Paris was the only real holiday that Sir John had enjoyed for many years, for though he had to visit the Embassy a good deal to confer with the Commissioners, and had also to go frequently to London to see Sir Julian Pauncefote on questions concerning the fishery treaty, he still had time to enjoy the brightness of life in Paris. Picture galleries and studios we much frequented, and made the acquaintance of some of the most charming and gifted artists, Carolus Duran and Henner, among others. The excitement about General Gordon was great just then. The French talked about subscribing to get up an expedition to send to relieve him at Khartoum. Being a personal friend of General Gordon, Sir John had gone to Brussels a little time before to see him on his way through Europe, on that fateful occasion. Both seemed to feel it was a last good-bye.

The Comte du Lesseps was at this time living in Paris, and was to be seen taking his daily ride past the hotel in the Champs Elysées to the Bois de Boulogne. This white-haired, gallant old gentleman was always followed by his large family of beautiful children, the older ones first, and the little ones on tiny ponies, with their long brown hair streaming in the wind. If the children fell off they were obliged to mount as best they could, for their father never waited.

It is needless here to follow all the details of the fishery questions. They are of no material interest to the general public, and must be confusing because of the frequent discussions, arbitrations, and treaties. It is sufficient, therefore, to say that, in May 1884, when the Commissioners' work was completed in Paris, Sir John Glover returned to England, and we stayed for a few days in Suffolk with Sir Harry Ord, formerly a Governor of the Straits Settlements. His son, Captain St. John Ord, in the Royal Artillery, was to accompany my husband as private secretary to Newfoundland, but our visit was cut short by an urgent request from the Administrator, Sir Frederic Carter, who was then acting there as Governor, that Sir John should come out at once, as judicial trials were going on about the shooting of some men who had taken part in the processions of the Orange Society and the Irish Society, both having chosen the same day for marching ; with the result that when they met, the lives of several were sacrificed. The feeling in the colony was running so high, that conviction of murder seemed pretty certain, and the Administrator, being the Chief Justice, could not act in the double capacity. Accordingly, after a hurried preparation, Sir John sailed from Liverpool on June 4, once more bound for the North, Mr. Clare Ford and Mr. Pennell accompanying him.

On board the mail steamer were several old Newfoundland friends. Lord Strathallan was bound for St. John's. He was going out to shoot, and to join his cousin Captain Drummond, who commanded H.M.S. 'Tenedos'; this ship had to be kept there for a year before the feelings of the excited people could be allayed.

The voyage was an uneventful one, and when the Governor once more landed in St. John's he was very heartily received by his old friends, who were pleased again to welcome their sailor Governor. Thus twice in his colonial career did he return to his former government, and on each occasion it was at the express desire and to the gratification of the colony.

On the return of the Governor to St. John's, he wished, late though it was, to give 'The Queen's Birthday Ball.' This event was the occasion of meeting again most of his former friends in this colony. There was little time to send out invitations, therefore it was decided to put a notice into the ' Royal Gazette ' to the effect, ' That all who had previously been on the Government House visiting list were expected.' They therefore came for the double purpose of celebrating Her Majesty's birthday and of welcoming her representative on his return among them. This gave rise to a number of small dances, got up in an informal manner.

Just then, Mr. Greely was brought back by the relief party, which had been sent to his rescue from New York, and the Governor went on board to see him, and offer what hospitality or assistance he could to the remnant of this North Pole expedition. Little could be done for them after their great privation and starvation, except to supply them with fresh eggs and milk, as stronger food was forbidden by the doctors in their then weakened condition. Few who witnessed the sufferings of the men and dogs that survived would care to see any friends undertake a like mission—scurvy, starvation, madness, and nameless horrors being the only result. The description given by the survivors of what they and their dead companions had suffered was truly awful—nothing had been achieved, and nothing seen except endless icefields. The year before a vessel had been sent, as far as she could go north, with supplies, which were left in a cairn. These Mr. Greely had found, together with some newspapers. One of the latest date contained an account of Sir John Glover's leaving Newfoundland on his appointment to the Leeward Islands. He was therefore surprised to meet the Governor again on his return from his long exile.

The life at Government House was much the same as it had been in former years. A good many friends from England came out to stay for shooting, and except a fancy dress children's dance and other social duties, no event of any importance took place. Mr. Clare Ford and Mr. Pennell did not stay more than six weeks, during which time they were daily conferring with the Newfoundland Government about the fishery question, which had been discussed in Paris between the English and French Governments.

The railway from St. John's to Harbour Grace had been finished, and was in working order, also the graving dock, which was to be opened by one of the men-of-war before its departure from Newfoundland for the winter.

The ' Sailors' Home,' which was first set on foot during Sir John's former term of office, was about to be built, as the money was now collected for that purpose. When the day was fixed for laying the foundation stone, a large number of people came to witness the ceremony, which was one of great interest to a sea-faring people. I was asked to lay the first stone, and a pretty little trowel was manufactured for that purpose in St. John's, and presented to me on this occasion. I have this little silver trowel lying before me as I write, and I well remember the day when it was handed to me to lay the foundation stone of the 'Sailors' Home,' and my feelings as I heard my husband's words, ' This occasion will be for Lady Glover one of her pleasantest memories of Newfoundland.' It was, indeed, most gratifying that we should both be associated with the founding of an institution so greatly needed in this seagoing colony; but I felt, as he spoke, that strange unaccountable sensation— a warning of coming trouble. It seemed to foreshadow that the laying of the foundation stone of this sailors' home would be his last act in trying to promote the comfort, cleanliness, and happiness of others, before he himself entered on his long and well-earned rest. It came, alas! before another year had closed. This was the last occasion on which he addressed a crowded audience out of doors.

Later in the year he opened the graving dock in St. John's Harbour, another of his pet projects, which was carried out during his lifetime, and for which he had worked so hard during his former term in Newfoundland. This occasion was one of great rejoicing and public demonstration. The Government House party lunched on board H.M.S.

'Tenedos,' after which Captain Drummond weighed
anchor, with all his flags flying and his band playing.
We slowly steamed up the harbour to be the first
ship to enter the dock. Thousands of people came
to watch the ceremony, and every ship in the
harbour was crowded with bunting. The weather
was all that could be desired. Owing to some
trivial matter going wrong, the caisson did not
swing back to its full extent, and Captain
Drummond, fearing it might touch the sides of his
ship, would not enter the dock completely, so it had
to be declared 'open' from the deck of the 'Tenedos'
before she was really in. However, this was not
a serious matter, and the dock remains one of the
greatest permanent improvements—if not the
greatest of all—that has ever been effected in
St. John's, bringing in money and trade so sorely
needed in these latter years when, from fire and
other causes, the colony was drifting into a bankrupt
condition.

Soon after this, Captain Raymond Parr and his
brother-in-law, Mr. Chambre Ponsonby, came out to
stay with us, and Lord Strathallan and the private
secretary, Captain Ord, were all to go up country with
the Governor for deer-stalking. Sir John had not
been feeling quite in his usual health ever since he
left the West Indies, and thought when once more
he got into the woods and smelt the fragrance of

the fir trees, and camped out again in his old haunts, he would forget for a time all the worries of civilised life, and return, as of yore, a different man. Just then a French man-of-war came into harbour. The officers had to be entertained, so the shooting party started without him. He followed a fortnight later, when the weather was breaking up, and the snow and wind made his quarters damp and uncomfortable. He returned with only one cariboo head, having contracted a severe chill, and in no way better for the change.

Those who knew his active mind and vigorous nature saw that he was failing in health that winter. On March 2, 1885, after a long day at office work, when he had no time for lunch, and an interview with the Prime Minister had lasted so late that dinner had to be put off till nine o'clock, he suddenly felt nature give way, but with his usual courage said nothing. Lord John Scott and some other officers staying in the house were dining with him at the time and did not notice anything wrong. From that moment until the end his sufferings were great. When the doctor came he said the Governor was suffering from an over-strained heart, and sent him to Topsail for rest and quiet. This seaside place is about fourteen miles from St. John's. He drove himself out in the boat carriage. When near the end of the drive a buggy with a fast trotting horse excited the animals he was driving. There was a steep hill down to the sea, and a precipice on one side. The old fire of emulation must have been strong in his breast, for even then he would not be beaten. Putting his horses at their best he so carefully drove them that they passed the light buggy with its American trotter at a terrific pace down the hill and up the slope to the Hermitage. Those who were in the carriage held their breath. One false turn of the wrist would have sent them all over the precipice before being hurled into the sea.

When they arrived at their destination Sir John was gasping for breath, and this difficulty in breathing continued to the end. The rest at Topsail was of little avail, so he applied for leave, and sailed for England in order to have better London advice. An officer who travelled home in the same steamer, though unaware at the time of the sad circumstances in which he was returning to England, writes to me that he was particularly struck as they left the harbour by seeing Sir John Glover sitting by the rail of the ship looking towards the shore 'with a far-away look in his eyes, like one who was leaving something most near to his heart and looking on it for the last time. During the voyage,' he continues, 'I sat opposite Sir John at the same table, and was struck by the extraordinary cheerfulness he displayed, and the interest he took in all that went on about him, even telling anecdotes and listening with amusement to those of others.'   On his arrival, in June, he was ordered to Homburg.   So his old friend, Sir Harry Ord, with whom he was again staying in Suffolk, decided that he and his family should go there also.

In his enfeebled health the journey over was very terrible for him, and most trying for those who were watching his sufferings.   After resting a few days at Homburg, with some difficulty he went for a drive with Sir Harry Ord, a courier attending them.   These two friends had much to say about by-gone days, when they were both serving under the British flag in foreign climes, and after the drive sat and talked together by the window for the last time in the cool of the evening of that hot August day.   As it drew near dinner time Sir Harry rose to leave, and a few minutes afterwards died quite suddenly.   In the state my husband was then in I dared not tell him.   At dinner I said Sir Harry was ill, and by degrees broke the truth as gently as possible.   He was greatly affected by the loss of his friend, and would insist, unable to walk as he was, in driving to the railway station, where he could see the remains of his friend being borne away.

The next day the doctor said that unless Sir

John was taken back to England at once he could not be moved later. It was easy now to persuade him to leave. Therefore, with the kind help of Captain Charrington, who offered to accompany him, we made preparations to start. The journey home was effected with the greatest difficulty. We stayed on our return at Harley Street, to be near the best medical aid, but though the most skilful physicians were employed, their treatment was of no avail.

Little more need be said. It is better to draw a veil over the sufferings of a man whose mental vigour, power of will and muscular strength made his struggle for life all the harder. He was unable to go to bed or lie down for more than three months, and the necessity of sitting in an upright position day and night added much to his bodily fatigue, yet no murmur escaped his lips. When the difficulty in breathing became very laboured he occasionally talked of the sea, and longed to see it once more. His difficulty in speaking from this cause increased daily, and though his mind was painfully clear and acute to the last moment, this gasping for breath prevented him from being able to impart any final wishes or directions.

Thus passed away, in Harley Street, on September 30, 1885, a man whose works follow him, and whose influence is still felt by those who knew him. He was in the fifty-sixth year of his age, forty-five of which had been spent in the service of his country.

Many friends followed him to his last resting-place in Kensal Green, and the white wreaths and flowers that covered his coffin mingled with the first falling leaves of autumn on that bright October morning. As the mourners were taking their last look, an old servant, who had been a personal attendant in former years in one of the colonies, was seen taking a handful of earth from the grave, to keep, he said, 'In memory of the best master a man ever served.'

CHAPTER XIV

IN MEMORIAM

Public Memorials in Kensal Green and St. Paul's—Subscription to
erect a memorial in Lagos—Sir John Glover and the Haussas—
His farewell speech and gift of his sword—The Hauseas at the
Diamond Jubilee: testimony of Captain Houston—Sir John
Glover's influence on the West Coast—The Hinterland in 1896—
The future of the Leeward Islands—Testimony of the 'Times'
and of a Newfoundland newspaper.

THE desire to commemorate the services of so
strenuous a public servant, and so loyal a colleague,
was soon manifested in a variety of ways, and no
time was lost by some of John Glover's brother
officers and friends in setting on foot a public
subscription for the purpose of erecting a fitting
monument to his memory in Kensal Green, and
also a tablet, with a life-size marble bust, in St.
Paul's Cathedral. This bust was executed from
photographs by an Italian artist, in Rome, and was
placed in the crypt of St. Paul's, next to that of
Nelson. A replica of this monument was sent out
to St. John's, to be placed in the Cathedral there ;
this building, it may be added, was a work of Sir

Gilbert Scott's, and was just finished at the time of Sir John's death.

Great was the sorrow in Lagos when they heard that 'Golobar' was no more. And the people at once set on foot a subscription to put up a memorial to keep his name ever fresh in the memories of the inhabitants of that colony. They raised a public subscription with the object of finishing a work which he had begun when he was their Governor, that of building a town hall, public library and reading room, and endowing a school for native children. The following letter was addressed to the people by Sir Alfred Moloney, then Governor of Lagos :—

'Government House: February 11, 1886.

'A scheme, which promises to be of great utility and productive of much good, is being rapidly developed in our midst in the direction of raising a fund sufficient to supply to this capital a town hall, public library, and reading room.

'It will be a landmark of importance in our history. At the same time, I may here fittingly remind you of the fact that the death of Sir John Glover, late Governor of Newfoundland, and one of our early Governors, whose name even now is not only a household word in the Yoruba country, but has been and is still very generally applied to his successors, whose life has been doubtless shortened by his earnest efforts to promote the well-being of the people over whom he was placed, aroused here feelings of such sincere sympathy as may well seek suitable expression by the erection in our midst of such a public work as I have mentioned.

' Were proof of the form such expression should take required, or testimony needed as to what would have been most pleasing to Sir John Glover, had he before his death anticipated such a general wish to record by a memorial the respect and esteem which have been so generally felt for him, we may recall the fact that during his administration of this Government he started a fund for a Lagos library, and that the amount collected at the time— 192*l*. 13*s*. 3*d*.—is now in the trust of this Government.'

A good sum of money was soon collected, and it was the wish of the people to erect a large statue in front of the town hall or library. Sir Edgar Boehm undertook to execute it in bronze, ' for love,' that is, asking only to be paid what it cost him in material for making it. He was engaged upon finishing this work at the time of his death, and the statue was afterwards sent in terra-cotta to the Naval Exhibition, by the kind permission of his executors.

The authorities at the Colonial Office, appreciating the feelings and efforts of the people of

Lagos, granted them some land with buildings already erected, so that they could begin the library and endow their school at once.

Sir John Glover's relations with the force of Haussas, the creation of which was not the least signal of his services to the Empire, had long since won for him the title of their 'Father.' Before leaving Africa he had called them together and bade them farewell in a parable, such as they could understand: 'Remember,' he said, 'that you are a small tree which I have planted, but you will grow big and stretch forth far, with wide-spreading branches, and you will take deep root in the ground; you must never let this tree wither, but water it day by day, till it grows and flourishes, and spreads all over West Africa. Only a few of you now serve the Great White Queen, but the day will come when many of you will serve her, and then you will eat of the fruit of the tree, which will provide for you and your children, who will enter her service to fight for her.' He then gave them the sword with which he had fought in Ashanti, to be handed down in their tribe to the head man for the time being. This sword is now held by one of the men who enlisted in 1873, and has also fought during the recent war, under Sir Francis Scott. For his signal good conduct, and his courage in the field, he has been given a commission, and Lieutenant

Donbarow's tall soldierly figure was conspicuous as, with 'Golobar's' sword in hand, he led his men at the Diamond Jubilee Procession. This sword is looked upon as a talisman by the natives on the Gold Coast, while the Lagos men cherish Captain Glover's naval sword which I presented after his death to the Haussas on that part of the coast.

Here it may not be amiss to quote a few words from an interesting letter, written to me in July 1897, by Captain Houston : 'As for the Haussas, I think you know almost as much about them as I do; but I think you may like to hear what a splendid account they have given of themselves during the Jubilee. A most eloquent testimony to your husband's forethought in raising the corps and his work among them and faith in them is the fact that for seven weeks we had twenty-nine natives from the Gold Coast—Haussas—with at times as much as 8*l.* or 10*l.* in their pockets, and open to all the temptations—and great they were to colonials, especially to the native troops—of London, and yet in all that time we never had a single man absent from duty or parade a single day, from illness or any other cause, nor had we a single complaint against any one of them; that is, I think, a truly *splendid record*, and one which I personally am exceedingly proud of, as you will admit.'

Even after the lapse of more than twenty years the name of Captain Glover still holds a powerful sway over the minds of the people on the West Coast of Africa, and has been handed down by them to their children. The late popular Governor, Sir Gilbert Carter, bears testimony to this, for in a letter he wrote me, enclosing a cutting from a Lagos newspaper, he said, that the highest compliment that had ever been paid him was by that newspaper saying he was the best Governor they had had since ' Golobar,' and ' long might he walk in his footsteps.' Also, in a letter of recent date, ' that he was now trying to carry out all his (Glover's) policy, and he was proud that it had been left for him to do.' I may add that as the pages of this volume are passing through the press, I hear that it has been decided that the form which the permanent Jubilee Memorial at Lagos is to take is the completion of the Hall which bears the name of Sir John Glover.

Before finishing the last Chapter of this Book, which, from various reasons, has not been written for so long after the death of the man whose Memoirs are recorded, it is of interest to note that in Africa, where he laboured for many years, and had the interest of the colony so close to his heart, many schemes, in the execution of which he was once opposed, have since, one and all, been carried out, or are now on the road to be achieved in the near future.   His interest in this colony never flagged; but he had a theory that it is unwise for a governor to keep up communication with the people of the colony he has worked in after his tenure of office is over, as it might lead to jealousy between the people and their new chief.   This often caused him much pain, as he was constantly receiving letters from the Haussas and natives.   He did not write in return, and feared that they would not understand his motive in being thus silent.   In a letter written by a friend, who some years after Captain Glover left Lagos had received an appointment in that colony, we find that he asked him to put this right, and explain the reason of his apparent apathy towards the people.

In an article in the 'Morning Post,' dated February 14, 1896, it is stated that the Yorubas are still a powerful people, and have 800 cavalry. There is a new iron bridge being made connecting the island of Lagos with the mainland.   The railway work in the colony is progressing, and the first section has been commenced.   The ultimate destination of this line is Ibadan, and the progress of such work will do much to restore order in the Hinterland, which has constantly been in a state of friction during recent years.   The line will in all probability go to Ibadan *via* Abeokuta, the chief town of the Egbas ; and they have at last expressed their willingness that it should go through their country.

The French are again giving trouble in Porto Novo, and are already in force at Boussa. The fertile Niger country once more threatens to become a scene of warfare and strife. Thus the policy of allowing things to *drift* during recent years has borne fruit.

Massaba, the king, who has been mentioned in these pages, has long since been dead; he was a powerful chief and a great ally in raising the Haussas, who are now a force of over 4,000 strong, and their numbers are to be still further increased. The present Emir of Ilorin is very hostile to the British. In the following extract from the 'Eagle,' we find : 'Lagos is now a flourishing colony, and the name of "Golobar" is still a household word among the people and widely known among the natives here and in the Hinterland.'

The Leeward Islands have fared during the last ten years much in the old way, but it would appear that the home Government are now considering that they must continue the improvements that were first suggested during Sir John Glover's term of office. Dominica he saw would sink into an utterly bankrupt condition unless new enterprise and money were introduced. It is needless here to dwell on the state into which it lapsed after he left the colony. Suffice it to say that, in July 1895, Mr. Templer, an official who had considerable practical experience in Ceylon, was appointed administrator; and, in the following December, Mr. Davies, a landed proprietor in Dominica, came to England at the request of the colonials to represent to the home authorities that a sum of 300,000*l.* had been taken from the funds of the colony in the latter part of last century, by the home Government, and that they now wanted some compensation in the way of a loan to enable the colony to construct either roads or light railways to develop the resources of the island. Up to the time of these pages going to press nothing definite has been done, though the West India Royal Commission, which visited these islands early in 1897, has reported in favour of grants to Dominica from the Imperial Exchequer to construct roads and to enable the settlement of the labouring population on the land to be carried out. Failing the realisation of this proposal perhaps some English capitalists may be induced to visit the beautiful and fertile Layou valley, and to build the road that was surveyed in 1882.

Newfoundland being the last colony over which Sir John Glover ruled, a few words must be said with regard to its progress. From one cause or another the island has been in a sad condition of late years. Fire raged in the town of St. John's, and swept

away the principal part of the houses ; political disturbances of local interest and want of commercial
credit have combined to mar its prosperity. The
London 'Times,' of Saturday, January 23, 1886,
writes, 'Sir John Glover was as discreet and judicious on his constitutional vice-throne as, in West
Africa, he had been courageously strong-handed.
So long as he kept his health he held the reins even,
none could charge him with bias and prejudice.
On his lamented death the island waited patiently
for the successor.'

Finally, I may bring this record to a close with
the following tribute from a Newfoundland newspaper : 'His name will long be remembered with
gratitude and warm esteem by the people. He
enjoyed their entire confidence, and was deservedly
the most popular Governor ever appointed to the
charge of this colony. During his *régime* here he
had the satisfaction of seeing the country obtain a
degree of prosperity which it had never reached
previously, and many important public works
initiated which gave a new impulse to trade and
enterprise. Personally Sir John Glover was
highly esteemed, his kindness and unfailing
courtesy, his genial hearty manner, his accessi-
bility to everyone, his consideration for the poor,
were qualities which marked his character and won
him warm regard in return. We shall not soon
look upon his like again.'

INDEX OF PROPER NAMES

9 783337 332792